DEAD ON
ARRIVAL

CH

Also by Kiki Swinson

The Playing Dirty Series: *Playing Dirty* and *Notorious*
The Candy Shop
A Sticky Situation
The Wifey Series: *Wifey, I'm Still Wifey, Life After Wifey,
Still Wifey Material*
Wife Extraordinaire Series: *Wife Extraordinaire* and *Wife
Extraordinaire Returns*
Cheaper to Keep Her Series: *Books 1-5*
The Score Series: *The Score* and *The Mark*
Dead on Arrival
The Black Market

Anthologies
Sleeping with the Enemy (with Wahida Clark)
Heist and *Heist 2* (with De'nesha Diamond)
Lifestyles of the Rich and *Shameless* (with Noire)
A Gangster and a Gentleman (with De'nesha Diamond)
Most Wanted (with Nikki Turner)
Still Candy Shopping (with Amaleka McCall)
Fistful of Benjamins (with De'nesha Diamond)
Schemes and *Dirty Tricks* (with Saundra)
Bad Behavior (with Noire)

Published by Kensington Publishing Corp.

DEAD ON ARRIVAL

Kiki Swinson

Kensington Publishing Corp.

www.kensingtonbooks.com

DAFINA BOOKS are published by

Kensington Publishing Corp.
119 West 40th Street
New York, NY 10018

All Kensington titles, imprints, and distributed lines are available at special quantity discounts for bulk purchases for sales promotion, premiums, fund-raising, and educational or institutional use.

Special book excerpts or customized printings can also be created to fit specific needs. For details, write or phone the office of the Kensington Sales Manager: Kensington Publishing Corp., 119 West 40th Street, New York, NY 10018. Attn. Sales Department. Phone: 1-800-221-2647.

Library of Congress Card Catalogue Number: 2017955333

Dafina and the Dafina logo Reg. U.S. Pat. & TM Off.

First Kensington Hardcover Edition: May 2018

ISBN-13: 978-1-4967-1277-6
ISBN-10: 1-4967-1277-3
First Kensington Trade Paperback Printing: March 2019

ISBN-13: 978-1-4967-1279-0 (ebook)
ISBN-10: 1-4967-1279-X   (ebook)
First Kensington Electronic Edition: May 2018

10 9 8 7 6 5 4 3 2 1

Printed in the United States of America

DEAD ON
ARRIVAL

PROLOGUE

DAWN

Where the fuck was he?

I looked at the clock and noticed that I'd been sleeping for a couple of hours. I'd dozed off waiting for Reese to come home so we could talk about where we were going when we left town. He told me he was leaving his grandmother's house and was gonna make a quick stop at NIT. Then he was coming straight here. So, where the fuck was he?

Before I could grab my cell phone and dial his number, my phone started ringing. I picked it up from the nightstand next to my bed and looked down at the caller ID. I let out a sigh of relief when I saw that it was Reese calling me.

"Hello," I said.

"Did I wake you up?" he asked. He sounded kind of weird.

"Reese, where are you?" I asked, ignoring his question.

"I'm about to pull up to the house, so put on something and meet me outside," he instructed.

"Meet you outside for what? *Do you know what time it is?*" I screeched. He was making me angrier by the second because he was displaying some very odd behavior.

"Please don't ask me any questions. Just do what I said," he replied calmly.

"Bye," I said, and then I disconnected our call.

I was furious at the thought that I had to get out of my bed and meet him outside. What kind of fucking game was he trying to play?

I grabbed a sweatshirt and a pair of sweatpants from my dresser drawer and a pair of sneakers from my closet and got dressed. After I grabbed a jacket from the hall closet by my bedroom, I headed toward the front door. My adrenaline was pumping. I was already thinking of what I was going to say to him if he was making me come outside for nothing. He was going to feel my wrath.

Blinded by the headlights of Reese's car parked in our driveway, I blinked my eyes a few times and held up my left arm to shield my eyes. I saw the silhouette of Reese's body sitting in the driver seat, so I closed the front door behind me and walked over to his car. I was heading toward the driver side, until he rolled his window down halfway and told me to get into the car from the passenger side.

I obeyed his instructions and got into the car with him. As soon as I closed the door, I turned around and looked at him. "What the fuck is so important that I had to come outside and get into the car?" I asked him.

Reese wouldn't open his mouth to respond.

"What's wrong with you?" I questioned him.

A voice from behind me said, "He's dead!"

I turned my face slightly to the left and saw an Asian man with a gun and a silencer pointed directly at me. My heart dropped into the pit of my stomach. Anxiety and fear crippled me as I slowly moved my eyes away from the Asian man, back to my husband's face. At that moment, that's when I noticed the blood seeping from the hole in his head. I instantly froze. I knew then that this man was about to take my life too.

1

REESE

I knew Dawn was going to jump down my throat when I walked through the front door of our home. Not only did I not come straight home from work, I didn't answer my cell phone when she called me over a dozen times, and I didn't have the $800 I promised her I would have. Shit hasn't been going right for us these last six months, so she'd been breathing down my neck because of it. To be more candid, we'd been having some financial problems for the last couple of years. Our car payments were past due, our credit cards were maxed out, our light bills had more than tripled, and our home was in fucking foreclosure. Taking a boatload of flat-screen smart televisions, laptop computers, and fur coats here and there helped me pay a few of our bills. It also helped me get into a few poker games at my homeboy Edward Cuffy's spot, which was exactly where I was when Dawn called me earlier. Edward was one of the senior operators at the Norfolk International Terminal. So far, he's got twenty-four years under his belt. In other words, he had seniority, so nothing got by him. If anything was stolen out of the shipping containers and sold for a handsome profit, Ed definitely got his cut. No ifs, ands, or buts about it.

Edward was like a big brother to me. He wasn't a big guy, but he made up for it in height and walked around like he owned the world. He was like Samuel L. Jackson. Sixty-five percent of the longshoremen on the pier liked Edward, but the other thirty-five percent hated him. My wife, Dawn, was one of them. "Did you just come from Ed's house?" she didn't hesitate to ask as she walked toward me. I knew she had just come from the kitchen because I smelled the aroma of tomato sauce, she wore a cooking apron, and she held a plastic mixing spoon in her left hand.

"Why are you asking me that?" I instantly became defensive after I locked the front door.

"Because I called you over a dozen times and you kept sending me to your voicemail," she spat as she stood before me. Dawn and I got married two years ago. We dated for a year before I popped the question. When I first met her, she was gorgeous. She resembled the actress Toni Braxton. She was sexy too. Plus, she wasn't this fucking nagging. I remember when she used to walk around our house almost naked, on a daily basis. Now I can't get her to take off her terry-cloth robe. She went from looking like a Playboy bunny to a Catholic nun. She assumed on several occasions that I was cheating on her because I complained about her appearance, but my guilty pleasure was gambling.

"I was at the pier. This new guy named Nate needed some help with a few containers, so I stuck around and helped him," I lied as I passed her and strolled into the kitchen. She knew I was lying, so she followed me.

"So, if I call down to the office and ask Porsha' to check your time sheet, it's gonna show that you were still at work?"

I gave her a head nod and then I turned my attention toward the pot of boiling water. When I looked closer and saw spaghetti noodles, I knew I was having spaghetti for dinner.

I changed the subject. "When will the food be done?" Dawn knew that I wasn't confrontational. I'd do anything to stay away from an argument, especially with her. She was famous for backing me into a corner, and I hated it.

"As soon as you hand over the eight hundred dollars you promised to bring home to me," she answered as she stood two feet away from me.

Hearing her ask me for the money hit me like a ton of bricks. Anxiety consumed me. I literally felt like a fucking little kid who just got caught stealing money from my mother's wallet. I tried to think of a good excuse as to why I didn't have the money, but my mind went totally blank.

"Reese, where is the money?"

"I don't have it yet." I dreaded my own words.

"What the fuck you mean you don't have it yet?" she roared. I could tell that she was at her wit's end.

"Listen, Dawn, I've been working on a few things, so as soon as it comes through, I'll get the money," I tried to explain.

"You're still stealing from those shipping containers, huh?"

"Why are you concerning yourself with that?"

"Because I don't want you going to jail," she said. "Do you know that the port police are doing a lot more patrolling than usual?"

"Stop being so paranoid. I know what I'm doing," I assured her.

"So, how much longer am I gonna have to wait for the money?"

"Give me until tomorrow. I'll definitely have it by then," I told her, even though I wasn't sure. I needed to say something to get her off my back, at least for now.

"Reese, I'm telling you right now that if you don't have the money tomorrow, I'm taking your fucking Rolex watch down to the pawn shop and pawning it," she threatened, and then she turned around and walked to the stove.

I didn't comment one way or another because if she knew that I had already pawned my Rolex, she'd really be breathing down my neck. It was important to her to get this money from me because for one, she lent the $800 to me a couple weeks ago and two, she needed it for a fertility treatment. Having a baby was the most important thing to her. I had children from a previous relationship, but I didn't have any children with Dawn.

I've told her time and time again that if she and I don't ever have kids that I won't love her any less. But she doesn't believe it. She thinks that having a child with me will bring us closer together. I don't believe that. I think things are good the way they are. We don't need another mouth to feed. Shit! I bring home around $85,000 a year and Dawn about $50,000. But we're still in fucking debt. She pays the little things like the light bills, gas bills, and her $750 BMW car note. I pay most of the bills, like our $2,500 mortgage payment, $700 a month in child support for my other kids, my $1,300 truck payment, and then I gamble up the rest. So, tell me how bringing home another mouth to feed is going to bring us closer together? It won't.

I headed to the bathroom and took a quick shower. After I was done, I slipped on a pair of shorts, a white T-shirt, and then I headed back to the kitchen. Dawn had my plate of spaghetti on the kitchen table waiting for my return. She was already sitting down and eating when I walked in. "Looks good," I mentioned as I took a seat in the chair across from her.

Instead of thanking me for the compliment, she rolled her eyes and continued to eat. We sat there in an awkward silence for at least five minutes. I started to get up a few times and take my plate in the living room so I could watch a little TV, but I knew that would send her up the wall, so I decided against it. Thankfully, the doorbell rang.

I pushed my chair back to get up, but Dawn insisted that she answer the door while she got to her feet. So I scooted my chair back toward the table and continued to eat.

I heard Dawn as she walked across the hardwood floors to the front door. And when she yelled through the door and asked the person on the other side to announce themselves, I listened for their answer. "It's me, Alexia," I heard the lady say, and then I heard Dawn unlock the front door and open it. "What brings you by?" I heard Dawn ask Alexia.

"I was in the neighborhood," she replied.

Alexia was Dawn's older sister. She was five years older, to be exact. She closely resembled Gabrielle Union. She had this overly confident personality. When she walked in a room, she always commanded the attention of everyone there. I personally didn't like her because she always had something negative to say about Dawn's and my marriage. And to keep from cursing her ass out, I did my very best to avoid her.

"Wait, I smell food," she continued, and then I heard two sets of footsteps walking in my direction. I knew that at any moment I was going to come face-to-face with Alexia, so I needed to keep my composure. She knew how to ruffle my feathers, but I wasn't going to let her get to me today. I had too much other shit going on in my personal life, so I refused to let her add anything to it.

"Look at what we have here," she commented after turning the corner to enter the kitchen. She gave me this cunning look.

"What's up?" I said, and then I buried my face back into my plate.

"Nah, what's up with you? I see you got my sister slaving over the hot stove again," she replied sarcastically, as she sat down in an empty chair at the table.

"Isn't that what a wife is supposed to do when she has a family?" I told her.

"Speaking of family, Dad's been complaining about how he's been giving you guys money so you can make ends meet around here," Alexia said while she gave me the evil eye.

I got defensive immediately. "I don't know why you're looking at me. I don't owe your daddy shit!" I roared, firmly gripping my fork.

"Alexia, Reese didn't go to Dad to get the money, I did," Dawn chimed in.

"He might as well have gotten the money from Daddy, because if he was handling his business with the money he made from the terminal, then you wouldn't be in this situation."

"Bitch, why don't you just mind your fucking business!"

"You're the bitch! Got my sister around here running to my parents for money so y'all won't lose your house and cars. You aren't a real man. Real men take care of their family and make sure there's nothing lacking in the household. Not you. You rather throw your money away gambling while your wife does what she can with the money she makes and the money she gets from my parents."

"Alexia, you promised that you wouldn't say anything else!" Dawn yelled.

"He started it with me."

"Fuck her! She out of line, coming in my house talking all that fly shit out of her mouth."

"Nah, nigga, fuck you!"

"Reese, please stop. You too, Alexia. Y'all are about to give me an anxiety attack!" Dawn yelled once more.

"So, it's okay for her lonely ass to walk in here and start talking her shit to me?" I hissed.

"Stand up and be a man, and then I wouldn't talk shit to you," Alexia spat.

Dawn walked over toward Alexia and grabbed her by the arm. "Come with me, please." She led Alexia out of the kitchen. I realized that Dawn had taken Alexia outside after I heard the front door open and close. I heard bits and pieces of their conversation, with Alexia talking louder than Dawn, of course. Their spat only lasted a couple of minutes and then they came back in the house. This time when Alexia entered the kitchen, she focused on carrying on a conversation with Dawn, instead of me.

Alexia started talking about some bullshit-ass nigga she just started dating who wanted to have kids with her already. "We've only been dating for a month and a half and the nigga wants me to have a baby. I told him he was crazy."

"I thought you couldn't have any kids," I blurted out. I swear I couldn't let her slide by with that bullshit-ass statement, especially since she started running her mouth at me as soon as she walked into my kitchen. In my eyes, this was the perfect time to put her ass back in check.

"Don't worry about me. Worry about the fact that you haven't gotten my sister pregnant." Alexia hurled her words at me. I swear, I wanted to ignore her and not feed into her bullshit, but she started hitting nerves I didn't know I had.

Dawn jumped to my defense. "Come on now, Alexia, that's hitting below the belt. And besides, it's not his fault that I haven't gotten pregnant."

"Well, who's fault is it, my sister? He's a fucking loser." Alexia pressed the issue.

My blood was boiling. I wanted so badly to stand up and slap the shit out of her no-job, meddling ass. But I knew that putting my hands on her would be a huge mistake, so I got her where I knew it would hurt, and that was her personal life. All the niggas she fucked and continued to fuck.

"You got a fucking nerve coming in my house and disrespecting me. If you weren't Dawn's sister I would drag you by your hair and haul your ass out of here," I told her.

"Do it, nigga! Do it!" She stepped closer to me.

Dawn stepped between us. "You're a lucky-ass bitch!" I said.

"Nah, nigga. You're the lucky one because if I had it my way, I would file the divorce papers for my sister myself."

"Well, thank God you're not. Now mind your business before I call the cops and have your ass thrown out of here," I replied while clenching my teeth. I had so much other shit I wanted to tell her. For starters, she was a fucking unemployed high school dropout and a whore. Everyone down at Norfolk International Terminal had fucked her. Talking about Dawn not being able to get pregnant, she can't get pregnant either. So for her to come in my damn house and start stirring up drama between my wife and me is unacceptable. This bitch needs to know who's really in charge.

"I swear I can't believe that you married this nigga! You would've done so much better if you'd married that nigga Blake," Alexia continued.

"Well, she didn't, so deal with it," I snapped.

"I don't have to deal with that shit."

"Well, I'll tell you what, deal with the fact that you had to have over a dozen abortions because you were fucking two and three niggas at one time and you had no idea who the father was." I hissed like I had venom spewing from my mouth.

"Nigga, you don't know shit about me!" Alexia shouted.

"Reese, are you fucking kidding me right now?" Dawn said as she stood between us.

"I know you're a fucking ho! And I know every nigga you slept with. I mean, hell, every nigga at NIT know who you slept with," I continued. I was digging deep in my bag of information so I could humiliate the hell out of her. Judging from her facial expression, my tactic was working, but I could also tell that my words were hurting Dawn.

"Reese, stop it right now! I fucking mean it!" Dawn yelled at me.

I stood on my feet. "Tell *her* to stop it! She started this whole fucking thing!"

"Fuck him, Dawn! He's a fucking loser anyway!"

"Bitch, you're the fucking loser! That's why you can't keep a man! Nobody wants you," I roared.

"Oh, but you wanted me," Alexia said. She and I were standing at opposite sides of the kitchen table.

"Bitch, I never wanted you!" I protested, but she was right. About one month before I met Dawn, I met Alexia at the nightclub Upscale in Chesapeake. I was with one of my friends, who pointed out that he knew Alexia and that she was easy to get into bed. So, being the adventurous man that I was, I bought her a few drinks and then I tried to talk her into coming back to my apartment so I could fuck her. Now the only reason it didn't happen was because she was with two of her homegirls, and she drove. So she gave me her number that night. I can't tell you why I never called her, it just didn't happen.

"I want both of y'all to shut the fuck up right now!" Dawn roared as she stood between us.

"I'm not doing shit! This is my fucking house. Just send that bitch on her merry way."

"I ain't gotta go nowhere! This is my sister's house too," Alexia griped as she stood her ground.

"Dawn, get that ho out of my house right now! I'm not gonna say it anymore," I warned her.

Without saying another word, Dawn grabbed Alexia's hand and tried to pull her in the direction of the front door. "Come on, Alexia," she said.

But Alexia snatched her arm away from Dawn. "Are you scared of this nigga or something?" she blurted out.

"Nah, she ain't scared of me. She ain't got a reason to be," I told her as I took a step toward her.

"So, whatcha about to do?" Alexia asked me while Dawn grabbed her arm once again and started pulling her.

"I'm not about to do anything."

"So, why you walking toward me like you're about to do something?"

"Bitch, just get out of my fucking house! You're not wanted here," I concluded, and then I walked around her and Dawn. I started walking down the hallway toward my bedroom so I didn't have to hear Alexia's mouth anymore. I swear, if she were my woman, talking to me like that, I would've choked all the breath out of her body and gladly taken the thirty-year prison sentence to go with it.

I closed the door after I entered my bedroom. I heard Alexia utter a few more words to Dawn and then I didn't hear her voice anymore. I didn't hear Dawn's voice either. I figured she must've walked outside with Alexia, or even left for that matter. Either way, silence was something I needed to unwind. With the drama surrounding my relationship with Dawn, the bills we had and the gambling debt I couldn't get rid of, I needed this time to think. I needed to figure out how I was going to get things back on track. I needed a plan and I needed it right now. I just hoped that whatever I came up with eliminated my problems completely. If it didn't, then it would be a waste of my time.

2

DAWN

That argument between my sister Alexia and Reese was way out of line. Now I understood why my sister jumped to my defense, but I'm a grown woman so I can handle my affairs concerning Reese. The last thing I wanted to happen was for Reese and Alexia to get into an argument. I loved them both, so I didn't want to pick sides. I wanted things between them to be civilized and nothing more.

"You do know you were wrong for picking that fight with Reese," I pointed out as we sat in her car, which was parked in our driveway.

"Fuck him! He's a big boy. He'll be all right," Alexia said.

"You know he's not gonna want you coming over here anytime soon."

"But this ain't his house. Daddy helped y'all with the down payment that his trifling ass hasn't paid back yet. So he shouldn't have a say whatsoever about who comes and goes from this house."

"Alexia, you're starting to give me a headache right now. Let it go so we can talk about something else."

"I don't wanna let it go, Dawn. You're too good for

him. Have you ever thought about why his baby mama moved out of the state? She moved way down South because she didn't want her kids around that evil-ass nigga every day. Now they only see him maybe twice a year, if that. And have you ever thought that the reason why God hasn't allowed you to get pregnant is because Reese Spencer isn't the man you're supposed to be with? I mean, look at him. He doesn't care about anyone but himself. He a narcissist. He's frugal as hell. He's immature and he's ignorant. Plus he doesn't pay y'all's bills on time because he's gambling it away at the gambling spot. When he does give you money for the bills, it's never enough, which is why you always gotta go and borrow money from Dad. I say cut your losses and leave that nigga now."

"It's not all his fault that we're behind on bills. You know I use the bulk of my paychecks on the fertility treatments. Those visits are very expensive," I told her.

"See, that's the thing, you wouldn't have to pay for your fertility treatments if Reese was handling his business like he's supposed to."

"You've got a point there," I agreed. She was right. If Reese was holding me down and taking care of our household properly, then we wouldn't have all of these financial issues. I think it's time to give him an ultimatum.

"So, whatcha gonna do?"

"I don't know. But I'll figure it out," I assured Alexia, and then I changed the subject. "Has Mom figured out what she's going to do for Dad's birthday?"

"She said something about taking him on a seven-day cruise to Cozumel, Mexico, and the Cayman Islands. So that's probably where they're gonna end up," Alexia replied.

"That sounds nice."

"If your husband didn't owe everyone, he'd probably be able to take you to places like that too," Alexia blurted out.

I gave her the evil eye. "Let me get out of this car before I say something I may regret later," I warned Alexia, and then I opened the passenger-side door and stepped out of the car.

"Don't be mad! You know I love you!" Alexia yelled as I pulled the door closed.

"Yeah, right! Sure you do," I replied, and walked away from her car. I waved Alexia off as she backed out of my driveway. As she started driving away, I turned my back and stepped back into my house. Immediately after I closed and locked the front door, I went into the kitchen to clean things up. I heard the television in the bedroom, so I knew Reese was probably lying in bed watching it—or maybe replaying the argument he'd had with Alexia, over and over in his head. With Reese, anything was possible. I just hoped that whatever he was doing, it wouldn't fester and linger into tomorrow. I swear, I couldn't take another day of drama with Reese. It was mentally draining, and I didn't have another ounce of strength to put into that nonsense.

After I cleaned up the kitchen, I grabbed a blanket from the hallway linen closet and lay down on the living room sofa. I powered on the television so I could take my mind off everything that had unfolded earlier. I wanted a peaceful life, and I was going to do everything within my power to get just that.

3

REESE

I couldn't believe that I had a good night's sleep, especially after everything that happened last night. The argument that Alexia and I had was pretty heated, but for some reason I was all right today. All that bullshit she was talking I let roll off my back. But I would let Dawn know that Alexia was not allowed in my house anymore. And I meant it.

After I got out of bed and went into the bathroom to take a piss, I walked back into my bedroom to get dressed for work. Once I got dressed, I put on a pair of socks and my work boots, and then I headed into the kitchen to get a bowl of cereal. When I passed Dawn and saw that she was lying on the living room sofa with her back to me, I strolled by her like she wasn't there.

In the kitchen, I took a bowl from the cabinet over the stove and then I grabbed the container of milk from the refrigerator and a spoon from the silverware drawer. I had been craving a bowl of cereal for the last two days, so I was in food heaven.

Three minutes into my breakfast, my cell phone started ring, so I raced to the bedroom to retrieve my phone. I answered the call while I headed back down the hallway toward the kitchen. "Hello," I said.

"Yo, dude, we got something really big coming our way," my homeboy Todd said. Todd Dale and I were very close. We both got hired to work at NIT around the same time. He and I were both around the same age, but Todd was a daredevil. It was nothing for him to do something outlandish. He was known for taking risks without thinking twice about the consequences. So when he called me this morning, I knew he was going to ask me to go along with something I might regret later.

"What's up?" I finally answered him as I went back into the kitchen.

"I've got a solution to your financial problems," he said.

Hearing the word *solution*, I was overjoyed. Excitement engulfed me. "What is it?" I asked while I stood in the middle of the kitchen floor.

"Something big is coming down the pipeline in a few days, so I want you to get ready because the payoff is going to be fucking huge."

"How much are we talking?"

"I'm talking like fifteen grand each," Todd said.

"Fifteen grand?" I replied, wanting some reassurance. "You got to be pulling my leg, right?"

"Nope."

"What is it? Exotic cars? A ton of drugs?"

"Nah, man. It ain't none of that. But I'll explain it to you when you come to work. So look for me as soon as you get here."

"Will do," I assured him, and then I disconnected the call.

Curious about what Todd had in store for me, I decided not to eat my usual bowl of cereal. Instead I grabbed a bottle of Ensure from the refrigerator, snatched my car keys and wallet up from the countertop, and headed toward the front door. Before I was able to grab ahold of the doorknob, I heard Dawn say, "So your homeboys on the pier got another heist they want you to get in on?"

I stopped in my tracks and slightly turned my head around to face Dawn, who by this time was looking straight at me, with the blanket tucked underneath her chin. "What are you talking about?" I asked her, even though I knew where this conversation was going.

"You know what I'm talking about. So don't play mind games with me."

"Dawn, are you really trying to start an argument right now? It is too early in the morning for that bullshit!"

"I'm trying to keep your dumb ass out of jail."

"Who said I was going to jail?"

"If you keep fucking with those containers, jail is where you gonna end up."

"Don't worry about me. I know what I'm doing." I opened the door and left.

I heard her mumbling something before I closed the front door, but I ignored it and continued on my journey.

On my way to the terminal I was eager to find out a little more about the job Todd called me about, so I grabbed my cell phone from the cup holder and called Ed.

"Hey, brother, what's up?" Edward greeted me.

"Nothing much, are you down at the pier yet?"

"Just got here a minute ago. Is everything all right?"

"It wasn't, until I got a call from Todd not too long ago."

"So, you're down?"

"What kind of question is that? Of course I am. The quicker I can get Dawn off my back about the bills that keep piling up in the mailbox, the better my life will be."

"I hear you."

"So, what we gotta do?"

"Come on now, Reese, you know we don't discuss things like that over the phone."

"Yeah, I know. But Todd said we're doing something different, so I thought—"

"Stop thinking so much and get your ass down to the pier and we'll talk then," Ed interjected.

"A'ight, I'll see you in a few minutes," I told him.

"Yeah, a'ight."

After I got off the call with Edward, my cell phone started ringing while I was putting it back in the cup holder. I looked at the caller ID and noticed that it was my grandmother, Mrs. Mary, calling. She is a very special lady because she raised me from when I was three years old. After my mother went to prison to serve a life sentence for killing her boyfriend, my grandmother took me in and raised me all on her own with no man in the house. My mother wasn't the only child my grandmother had, but it seemed like it. My uncle Ernest went away and joined the military. I remember he used to come and visit once or twice a year and everybody would say how proud they were of him. My grandmother used to have parties for him. But after serving ten years, he was discharged be-cause of some mental health issues. When he tried to apply for jobs, no one would hire him, so he started using drugs and OD'd on a bad batch of heroin. That shit sent my grandmother into a bad emotional state. She lost both of her kids. I couldn't tell you how, but she snapped out of it and did everything she could to raise me in the best way she knew how. But still, I was a product of my mother and my uncle. I couldn't tell you how my father was because I never met him. But if he was anything like my mother's crazy, alcoholic ass, then the apple didn't fall too far from the tree.

"Hey, Grandma, how you doing?" I asked her. My grandmother was seventy-two years old. She'd been living in the same house for forty-five years. She couldn't drive herself around because she was blind in one eye, but she still knew how to tell me what to do.

"I'm doing fine. Now when am I going to see you? You promised to stop by here this past weekend, but I didn't see your butt."

"I know, Grandma. I've been working a lot of long hours, so when I finally clock out for the day, all I wanna do is go home."

"Boy, I don't wanna hear that mess. I am your grandmother. And I want to see you. So you better bring your behind over here tomorrow. You hear me?"

"Yes, ma'am."

"And before you come, stop by that seafood place I like and bring me some of the fried croakers they sell. Make sure it's hot too."

"Okay, Grandma. I got it."

"All right, baby. Well, I'll see you then."

4

DAWN

I hated the idea of Reese stealing things from the shipping containers on the pier, but things had gotten extremely hard in our household, so turning a blind eye here and there so he could make a few extra dollars wasn't going to hurt nobody. But when he got greedy and wanted to break into a container every night to see what he could walk off with, that's when I had a problem with him. Reese didn't understand when enough is enough. I told him all the time that if something happened to him, my job could very well be in jeopardy. But he didn't listen and that irritated the hell out of me.

Thankfully, I was off work today. Running into Reese on the pier wasn't something I wanted to do today, especially after the argument we had last night. I also wasn't in the mood to face my supervisor, Mrs. Leslie Powell. She was like a mother figure to me, so she knew my mood swings like the back of her hand. Like my parents, Mrs. Powell also disliked Reese. She reminded me as often as she could that he didn't deserve to have me in his life. She warned me not to marry him too. But I loved Reese and I wasn't going to allow anyone to make me walk away from him. Looking back, I could now see what everyone was talking about. But what's done is done. I took the vow, *for better or for worse*, so I was going to make this marriage work.

I planned to run a few errands and stop by my parents' house while I was off today. My parents would love to see me since I hadn't been by their place in over a week. They only lived ten miles away, so I'd normally stop by there at least three times a week. But with everything going on with Reese and me, I wasn't up for hanging around my family. They tended to offer their opinions on how I should handle issues in my marriage whenever they saw fit, and frankly, I'd grown tired of it. I figured the less I talked to them, the less I would hear the bashing.

I finally got up, showered, and got dressed. I slipped on a lavender-and-white, floral-print Adidas sweat suit with a pair of lavender Fenty flip-flops by Rihanna.

After I took one last look at my sandy-brown curls in the mirror, and realized that everything about me was intact, I smiled and headed out the front door.

When I pulled up curbside to my parents' house, I saw my mother on her knees, leaning over in her flowerbed, planting new flowers. Making sure her house had curb appeal was one of my mother's favorite pastimes.

I got out of my car and walked up the sidewalk that led to her house. "Hey, Mrs. Joe Bryant," I said.

"You better address me as Mommy before I lay your butt across my knees and give you a good spanking," my mother threatened while she laid the hand trowel down and stood. She stumbled a bit, but she managed not to fall.

"Mommy, you gotta be careful getting up like that. You know Daddy would lose his mind if you fall down and hurt yourself."

"Oh, your father will be all right," she started off. "So, why aren't you at work?"

"I took one of my vacation days so I could run a few errands," I replied while I continued to walk up the sidewalk. As soon as I got within arm's reach of my mother, I leaned toward her short, small frame and gave her a hug and a kiss on the cheek. Everyone in the neighborhood called her Ms. Cicely Tyson because she looked and acted just like her.

"Well, I'm glad you stopped by. Your dad's been extremely worried about you," my mother said as she removed her gardening gloves.

"Why is he worried about me? I'm fine."

"He's been hearing some things and he's not happy about it."

"Trust me, whatever Dad is hearing is all lies," I tried to assure her.

"Listen, honey, I'm not calling you a liar, but it seems as though everybody is saying the same thing."

"Who is everybody?"

"Some of the guys that used to work with your father," she said.

"Where is Dad now?" I asked.

"He's in the den reading his newspaper."

"Okay, well, I'm going in there and straightening this thing out right now," I said and walked away from my mother. I entered the house and walked down the long hallway that led to the den at the back of my parents' house. I saw my father sitting in his favorite recliner, buried in the morning newspaper. He looked shocked to see me. I smiled as I walked toward him. "Hey, Daddy," I said, and kissed him on the cheek.

"And hi to you," he replied, while I took a seat in my mother's recliner, right beside his. He looked at me from head to toe. "Why aren't you at work?"

"I took the day off so I could run some errands."

"What brings you by here?"

I continued smiling like a little kid in a candy store. "I stopped by because I missed you and Mommy."

"Your sister must've told you that your mother and I have been missing you."

"Yes, she told me, but that's not why I stopped by," I lied. He was right, I was trying to avoid seeing my father and mother as long as I could, so they couldn't pick my brain with a bunch of questions about my relationship with Reese. I knew my husband wasn't handling his business like he should be, but that was not their problem, it was mine.

"So then tell me why you stopped by."

I chuckled a bit. "Dad, why are you looking at me so suspicious?" He was making me feel like he could see through me.

"You think so?"

I chuckled a little more while I covered my mouth with my hand. After I removed my hand, I said, "Daddy, look, I came by here to see you and Mommy because I missed y'all. That's it."

"So, you're not here to borrow more money?"

"No, Daddy, I'm not. Reese has been picking up more hours on the pier, so things are looking better for us," I lied once again. I think my dad knew it too because of the way he looked at me for a second or two. I wasn't going to change my story just because there might be some doubt in his mind. That was my story and I was sticking to it.

"How is he picking up extra hours when NIT has a ban on overtime now?"

"Dad, I know that. But he's picking up hours from a few of the guys in the union who haven't been able to work because of personal issues," I explained.

"I heard he's still gambling."

"Come on, Daddy, this is not why I came over here. Can we please talk about something else?" I was getting sick and tired of him asking me questions about Reese. "Leave Reese alone."

"Okay. Okay. I'll drop it for now. But if I keep hearing

about him throwing his money away at the poker table and stealing televisions from those containers, I'm gonna have another man-to-man talk with him. And he's not going to like my approach the next time we have that talk," my father warned.

I sucked my teeth. "All right, Dad. All right!" I huffed.

"What's on the agenda for you today?"

Before I could answer my father's question, Alexia walked into the den. Her eyes lit up when she saw me sitting in the recliner next to our father. She smiled and said, "Hubby let you come out the dungeon, huh?"

I rolled my eyes and sucked my teeth. "You sure love being messy, don't you?" I commented. I had just got my father to stop talking about Reese, now here came Alexia, adding fuel to the fire I'd just put out.

"Oh hush! You know I'm just playing with you." Alexia smirked and took a seat on the couch across from my father and me.

"You know you can't play around Daddy, especially if it has something to do with Reese," I reminded her.

"Where is his sensitive tail anyway?" Alexia wanted to know.

"He's on the pier. Where else would he be?"

"At the gambling spot. Or hanging out with some side chick," Alexia said sarcastically, and then she looked at our father, who gave us a snide look.

"There you go again, being messy!" I was starting to lose my patience with Alexia and I let her know it. "I don't know what you're trying to do right now, so I'm asking you to stop it or I am going to leave."

"Stop whining. I'm just teasing you," she said. But it was a lie. I knew what she was doing and so did she.

"All right, Alexia, cut it out. I've heard enough," my father interjected, and I was glad he did.

My father changed the subject and we started talking about his birthday, which wasn't too far away. He was turning sixty-five years old. And the beautiful thing about it was that he looked like he was fifteen years younger. "So, Dad, tell me—what do you want for your birthday?" I asked him.

"I don't want anything from you girls. The fact that you're spending time with me right now is the best present I could ever have."

"Dad, why do you have to be so sentimental? I'm trying to buy you a birthday gift and you're talking about quality time."

"That's because time with you girls is so much more precious than any gift you could ever give me," he explained.

"Have you and Mommy figured out where you guys are going?" I wanted to know.

"Yeah, Dad, where are you and Mom going this year?" Alexia asked.

"He doesn't know. I'm planning everything myself," my mother said as she walked around the wall that led her right into the den with us.

Alexia chuckled. "Mom, don't let me find out you were standing around the corner eavesdropping on our conversation with Dad," she joked.

"I don't have to eavesdrop in my own house. I'll leave that for you two girls to do," my mother replied in a feisty manner as she sat down on the couch next to Alexia. "So, what else were y'all talking about?"

I spoke first. "Nothing really." The last thing I wanted to do was breathe life back into that dead conversation about Reese. I have made it clear that anything concerning him is off limits.

"So, are you hungry? Want me to whip you up some breakfast?" my mother asked me.

"No, I'm good, Mommy. I'm gonna get something while I'm out running errands."

"You're too good to eat your mama's cooking?" my dad blurted out.

I turned my attention to him. "Of course not, Dad."

"Then why won't you let her cook you something?" he asked.

"Because I've got to be somewhere in the next thirty minutes," I lied.

"Where do you have to be?" my mother interjected.

"Probably to the fertility clinic," Alexia blurted out.

I gave Alexia the nastiest look I could muster up. "Did they ask you?" I hissed. Alexia was aggravating me all over again.

"You're still giving those doctors all that money so they can put a baby inside of you?" my mother said.

"Yes, that's what you gotta do when conventional efforts don't work," I clarified.

My father said, "Has it ever crossed your mind that maybe God doesn't want you to have a baby with that man? I mean, come on, Dawn, you're a very smart girl. Look at how he treats his other kids."

"What do you mean, how he treats his other kids? They live in another state," I snapped.

My father kept questioning me. "That's my point. They live in another state. When was the last time those kids stopped by the house and spent time with their father?"

"I don't keep up with stuff like that."

"Just answer the question."

"I can't say. But it's been a while."

"And why is that?" he continued.

"Because their mother is silly and she's being vindictive because he moved on to be with me."

"That's not the real reason. That woman suffered years of him cheating on her and gambling," my father said.

Heated by the fact that I was starting to feel like I was being tag teamed, I looked at my dad and said, "What is it, gang-up-on-Dawn day? It seems like the only person that cares about my marriage and me having a baby is Reese's grandmother. She's so supportive." My blood was boiling right now.

"That's because she's senile," my father blurted.

"Dad, that was not right," I spat.

"We're not ganging up on you, sweetheart! Your dad and I just want you to explore the fact that maybe God has another plan for you. That's all," my mother said, trying to defuse the situation.

My father said, "That's not all. You're giving that doctor too much money. Money you don't even have. I say that if you can't have a baby naturally, then that means that it's not meant for you to have one."

At that moment, I knew it was time for me to go. I wasn't going to continue to sit there and allow my family to ridicule me about my personal life, so I said, "Let me get out of here," and then I stood up from the recliner.

"Don't leave, honey," my mother begged.

"Mommy, I gotta go. I told y'all I've gotta be somewhere in thirty minutes," I replied as I walked by her. She and Alexia followed me down the hallway and out the front door.

"I'm sorry if your dad upset you," my mother apologized as we stepped onto the front porch.

"It's okay. I'm good," I lied. I was irritated by everyone there, and I wanted nothing else but to get in my car and leave.

"When are you coming by again?" my mother asked.

"I'll probably stop by tomorrow after I get off work," I fibbed once again. I had no desire to come back to my parents' house for at least another week. If they'd stop bashing my husband to my face, I wouldn't mind spending more time with them. I've told them more than a handful of times, but they don't listen.

"Mommy, trust me, she's not coming over here for a while," Alexia exclaimed.

I lightly punched Alexia in her left arm. "Oh, be quiet. You don't know when to stop talking, do you?"

"Owwww, that hurts!" she said, and started massaging the area of her arm that I hit.

"Oh, toughen up. And get a job while you're at it," I suggested sarcastically, and then I leaned over and kissed my mother on her cheek. "I love you, Mommy! And I'll call you later." Then I walked off the porch.

She stood there and watched me walk toward my car. "What about your father?" she yelled.

"Tell him I love him too," I screamed back.

5

REESE

I drove into the Norfolk International Terminal through the Baker Street entrance. A long line of trucks waited to get their loads and head back out of the terminal. After I went through the checkpoint, I headed over to NIT North. I was solely focused on finding Ed and Todd so they could fill me in on what kind of job we were getting ready to take on.

It took me about five minutes to find them both. I wasted no time getting them to give me the details. They were standing in a huddle with two more of our accomplices, near a stack of new containers that had just arrived overnight. The other two guys that worked with us were Gene Harris and Brian Butler. They were both around the same age as Edward, with salt-and-pepper hair, mustaches, and beards. They were also considered OGs. They looked like two ordinary blue collar guys like the rest of us, except Gene Harris was a very short guy and Brian Butler was the tallest of all of us.

"What's going on, fellas?" I asked the moment they all looked in my direction.

Edward spoke first. "We're talking about this new job we're about to do."

"I'm all ears," I replied right after I closed the circle of their huddle. I became anxious as I stood there, giving Edward my undivided attention.

"We're about to hit the mother lode with this next job," Edward started off. "I just had a meeting with this Chinese guy named Que Ming, and that guy got money coming out of his ass. He owns like five Chinese restaurants, that big-ass Asian grocery store in Virginia Beach, and he owns all of the Chinese buses that travel to and from Virginia Beach to New York. He's also a connected man. He knows a lot of people. I guess when you're wealthy like him, you can buy a friend." Edward chuckled.

"What was the meeting about?" I asked. I wanted Edward to cut out the preliminaries and get on with the fucking story.

"He wants us to grab two containers from the ship that's coming to this port tomorrow night, and he's gonna pay us fifteen thousand dollars each."

"What the fuck is in those containers? Nuclear bombs?" I blurted out, and chuckled because no one has ever paid us that much to confiscate containers once they hit the pier.

"No, there's gonna be people in them," Edward said.

Shocked by his answer, my mouth dropped wide-open. "People?" I repeated. I needed some clarity.

"Yes, people. There's going to be thirty Asian immigrants in each container. So, as soon as they hit the pier, we have to remove the containers from the ship and put them on the railroad cars on the second and third row, and the Asian guy will take it from there."

"Where are they coming from?" I asked, hoping I wasn't giving away my disgust at being included in this mess.

"They're coming from somewhere in Asia. See, the containers were supposed to be dropped off at the port in Baltimore, Maryland, but someone dropped the ball and now they're coming here, since this is the last stop for the East Coast."

"You mean to tell me that those Asians been on that boat for at least thirty days?" I wondered aloud. I couldn't believe I was having a conversation about people being transported like products.

"Yep," Ed answered, while Todd, Gene, and Brian nodded their heads.

"How the fuck have they been able to survive? Those containers are hot as fuck inside, and there's little or no air in them," I pointed out.

"That's not our problem. We're being paid to take the containers off the ships and hide them. Anything outside of that falls on the Asian guy," Edward clarified.

"Okay, so let me ask you one more time."

"Sure, go ahead."

"So, you're telling us that there's a rich-ass Chinese guy that's gonna pay us fifteen thousand dollars each to hide two shipping containers with people in them so they can be snuck off the terminal?"

"Yep," Ed answered.

I paused and took a deep breath. These people were already on their way here. I wasn't part of getting them in those containers, so was it so bad making sure they got out of them? Damn, this was shitty, but, "When are we getting paid?" I asked.

"Well, today you're all getting five grand," Ed replied as he reached into his jacket pocket and pulled out stacks of one-hundred-dollar bills with $5,000 money sleeves wrapped around them. "And after the job is completed, we get the rest," he continued as he handed everyone their portion of the money.

"Get the fuck out of here! Is this a joke?" I replied in disbelief.

"Nope. This is real big-boy shit. It's so real that after we take this money, there's no going back. We're locked in," Edward added.

Everyone, including myself, held the money in our hands and had a look of excitement. Brian and Gene vocalized their reaction.

"Do you know what I can do with this?" Gene started off.

"I know what I'm going to do with it," Brian said.

I curved my lips in what I hoped looked like a smile and said, "Ed, you don't know how happy you just made me."

"Good, I'm glad everybody is happy. But we can't fuck this up. Mr. Ming said that if we do good tomorrow night, he'll pay us more the next time around," Edward announced.

"You should've told 'em that he had the best crew on the pier," Gene boasted.

"I second that," Brian agreed.

While I was pushing the $5,000 down into my front pants pocket, I thought about how happy as hell Dawn was going to be, knowing I could give her the money she needed to take care of her business. Having money was a good feeling to have, especially when you had pressing things that needed to be taken care of, like the car payments and the mortgage. I couldn't forget about the fertility treatments that she'd been putting on the back burner because of our financial problems. Now we could move on. And hopefully I could bow out on being included in more people smuggling.

"I guess all of us got bills to pay," Edward joined in.

"Well, after we handle this job, we're gonna all be in a much better place," I announced. Everyone standing in the huddle nodded their heads in agreement. After Edward said a few more words, we broke up the huddle and headed into our designated areas to start our work day.

6

DAWN

I ended up going to the grocery store to pick up a few things after I left my parents' house. What really pissed me off was how my sister, Alexia, kept throwing me under the bus. Shit, I thought she was on my side. She had never ratted me out in front of my parents before. I guess she felt the need to do it because of how Reese had treated her when she was at our apartment last night. I knew one thing, she better not throw me under the bus anymore in front of them. If she did, then I was going to cut her ass off, permanently.

On my way to the checkout counter, my cell phone started ringing. I pulled it from my handbag, looked at the caller ID, and saw that it was Reese calling me. My first thought was to ignore his call, but then my heart overpowered my thoughts, so I answered it. "Hello," I said nonchalantly. I wanted to project that I was still upset with him from last night.

"Are you still mad at me?" he asked. I could tell he was trying to poke and pry to see what kind of mood I was in. He was famous for that.

"I haven't thought about it," I told him, even though I

was still a little ticked off with him. And it didn't help that I had just come from my parents' house, where they pulled the Band-Aid off the wound that I had gotten from the drama that had ensued while Alexia was at my house the night before. Was I not supposed to still be upset?

"Well, if you're still upset with me, I'm gonna give you some news that will put a smile on your face," Reese insisted.

I let out a long sigh. "What is it?"

"I got a fifteen-thousand-dollar payday coming, and it's gonna take care of all our problems."

"Oh Lord, I'm scared to ask you what it is," I commented.

"Baby, listen, I know you don't like when I do my side hustles. But you're gonna be okay with this because it's not gonna require me to do a lot of work and I don't have to sell anything," he explained.

"Wait, I'm confused," I began. "If you're not gonna sell anything, then how are you going to make fifteen thousand dollars?"

"I'll explain that part to you when I get home later."

I let out another sigh. "Okay. Well, I guess I'll see you later."

"A'ight. I love you!"

"I love you," I said, and then I disconnected our call.

I paid for my items and left the store. I headed over to Party City so I could pick up a few party favors for a surprise birthday celebration in Mrs. Powell's honor. No one knew how old she would be tomorrow, since she'd never divulged her age to anyone in the office, so we were just gonna wish her a happy birthday by surprising her with a couple of balloons, a blinged-out birthday crown, and a dozen tasty cupcakes that I planned to pick up on my way to work in the morning.

Pacing down the aisles of Party City got me to thinking about the conversation Reese and I had while I was at the grocery store. Was he fucking serious when he said he's about to get a fifteen-thousand-dollar payday? And if so, what in the hell does he have to do to get it? While I love the idea of us getting out from underneath all the debt we've accrued, I don't want him doing something stupid that he won't be able to get out of. I just hope that whatever he was talking about, we won't regret it somewhere down the line.

Reese made it back home from work around six fifteen in the evening. And when he walked into the house, he made a beeline for the kitchen because he heard me moving things around in there. He seemed extremely happy the moment he laid eyes on me. "Baby, things are about to start looking up for us," he said as he grabbed me and pulled me into his arms. He held me tight and kissed me on the lips.

I wanted to be happy for him, but something about this new hustle of his just didn't feel right to me. So I went into question mode. "Tell me what's going on."

"Before you say anything, hear me out first, okay?" Reese said, and then he released his embrace and took a couple steps back. He took a seat on one of the bar stools placed alongside our marble-top island.

I folded my arms and gave him a head nod.

"Okay, check it out. A rich Asian guy went to Edward and told him that he'll give him and four other guys fifteen thousand dollars each if we grab two containers and hide them, so his people can come and pick them up."

I burst into laughter listening to his idiotic story. I mean, who shelled out that much money for two freaking containers? No one I knew.

"Oh, so you think it's funny?" Reese asked me as he reached into his pants pocket and pulled out a stack of one-hundred-dollar bills.

"Okay, wait a minute, what's going on?" I asked him with a puzzled expression on my face.

"I'm trying to tell you, but you're acting like you want me to play games with you," he replied as he tapped the bundle of bills against his palm.

"That's fifteen grand in your hands?"

"No, it's five grand. I get the other ten grand tomorrow night," he told me.

"Have you checked that money out to see if it's counterfeit?" Even though the money looked real, I wasn't completely sold on the idea that some Asian guy wanted to pay him and his other work buddies fifteen thousand dollars each to pull two metal containers down from the merchant-seamen vessels and hide them until they could pick them up.

"Dawn, the money is real. Here, look at it," he instructed as he handed me the stack of bills.

I examined it closely for a few seconds. I felt the texture of the bills. I held one of them up to the light to look at the watermarks and to see if the metal strip was intact. I even looked at the serial numbers to see if they were aligned correctly. After I covered all those areas, I was convinced that these bills were real. "So, what happens now?" I asked, while I continued to hold on to the money.

"I pitch in to help Edward and the rest of the guys do the job and then we get the rest of the money that's owed to us."

Still skeptical about the story that Reese was telling me, I probed him a little more because something wasn't adding up to me. I mean, who gives someone fifteen grand to take two metal containers from the merchant-seamen vessels? There's something he's not saying. "Tell me what's in the containers," I demanded.

He froze up for a moment like he wasn't sure if it would be a good idea to tell me. And that's when I knew I had his back against the wall. I could've backed him against the wall even further, but I didn't. I figured the best way to get him to talk to me would be to act like I wasn't going to get mad, no matter what he told me. "It's okay. I won't get mad or give you the side eye," I assured him.

"You promise?" he replied, searching my face for the answer.

"Yes, I promise."

Reese hesitated for another second and then he said, "There's gonna be people inside them."

"People!" I repeated, not knowing if I heard him correctly.

"Yes, people."

"What kind of people?"

"What do you mean, what kind of people? Humans like me and you. But these people are coming from third-world countries like the Philippines and North Korea."

"Are you out of your damn mind?" I spat. I was losing my cool at the speed of lightning.

"See, this is exactly why I didn't want to tell you," Reese expressed as he stood up from the bar stool.

"Reese, I'm sorry for yelling, but this new hustle of yours is not going to work."

"Why do you have to shoot down everything I do? You always got something negative to say."

I walked over to where Reese was standing, grabbed both of his hands, and looked him straight in the eyes. "I'm sorry if you think I'm being negative right now. But what you are getting into is called human trafficking. And if you ever get caught, that charge carries a lot of prison time."

Reese snatched his hands away from me. "But I'm not gonna get caught. The guys and I got a nice plan in motion, so everything is going to run smoothly. And after we hide the containers, the Asian guy is going to pay us our money."

"Yeah, and that's what a couple of longshoremen said about ten years ago when they got caught doing the same thing. Human trafficking didn't just start a couple of days ago. This has been going on for a long time. Speaking of which, who is this Asian guy? And where did he come from?"

"I haven't met him. Edward met up with him earlier today at one of his Chinese restaurants."

"Which Chinese restaurant?"

"He didn't tell me all of that. All he did was tell us what needed to be done and then he gave us the five grand," Reese replied, as if my continuous questions were irritating him.

"Reese, I don't know about this one, baby. The last time a few longshoremen did that, they got busted by US Customs and got twenty years in a federal prison."

"Well, that ain't happening to me. Edward and Todd got this shit planned out to a tee. So, we're gonna be all right."

I let out a long sigh. "All right! All right! I'm done with this conversation. Do what you want to do," I said, then I turned around and walked back over to the stove. "Your food will be ready in about ten minutes," I continued as I turned my focus back to the food I was cooking.

"A'ight, well, I'm gonna go and hop in the shower, so put the money away and I'll be back when I'm done," he said as he exited the kitchen.

I couldn't get my mind off the fact that he was about to involve himself in human trafficking. Was he freaking crazy? Human trafficking is a serious charge and it carries a lot of time. But no, he didn't want to listen. He thought I was talking out the side of my neck and didn't know what I was talking about. I'd been working at NIT for a very long time, so I was there when another crew of longshoremen got arrested for being involved with human trafficking. I knew one thing, if Reese decided to go through with it, he better hit it then quit it.

7

REESE

After having that pow-wow with Dawn, I tossed and turned all night, thinking about what the chances were that the boys and I would get caught hiding the containers with Asian immigrants inside of them. Edward promised us that his plan was failure proof, so I was holding on to the hope that he was right. The thought of getting busted by US Customs and the port police and bringing shame to Dawn didn't sit well with me, considering how her family believed that I didn't deserve a woman of her caliber. Her parents were against me marrying her from the beginning, so getting caught wasn't an option, which meant that I had to make sure that the guys and I dotted all our *i*'s and crossed all our *t*'s.

After watching the clock on the DVR from 3:00 a.m. to 6:00 a.m., I decided to crawl out of bed, since I wasn't going to get at least six hours of sleep. Dawn must've heard me in the kitchen fixing myself a bowl of cereal because she joined me immediately after I took a seat at the kitchen table. "What time do you have to be at work?" she asked while I was pouring milk in my bowl of Fruity Pebbles.

"Not until twelve o'clock," I told her.

"If you don't go to work until six hours from now, then why are you up this early?"

"Because I couldn't sleep," I replied between chews.

"Is it because of our argument last night?" she asked as she took a seat in the chair on the opposite side of the table.

"That's part of it," I said while I continued eating my food.

"Reese, I may come off as a nag sometimes, but I love you and I don't want to see you fall. So, when I got mad last night about that job you're going to do tonight, it was coming from a place of concern. This is not the first time that a couple of longshoremen got paid under the table in exchange for allowing containers filled with immigrants to be smuggled into the country. So, please be careful."

I took one long look at her and said, "I really appreciate you for coming to me so we could iron this situation out."

"No problem, baby. Just know that when you win, I win too."

I smiled at her. "Come here," I instructed.

She smiled back but hesitated to walk toward me. "What do you want?" she asked jokingly.

I stood up from the bar stool and walked toward her. I reached out and grabbed her face in my hands and brought it close to me. Instinctively, she and I closed our eyes while I placed my lips on hers and we began kissing passionately. Her lips tasted so good. I could feel my dick as it hardened and grew in size as I ground it against her pelvis, so I moved in closer. "Baby, I love you so much!" she whispered softly to me as we continued kissing. Next I put my hand on her breast and squeezed it gently. She let out a short gasp while my hands massaged different places of her body. "You make me feel so good," she whispered while she kissed me around my neck and my earlobes.

"You make me feel good too," I told her while I thought about how I was going to fuck her. I knew I was going to bury my dick deep down inside her, but thinking about the position was critical.

"Oh, baby! I can't take it anymore. Fuck me now!" she begged softly as she ground her hips and pelvis against me, trying to press her clit on my rock-hard dick. I wanted to feel the inside of her just as bad as she wanted it. So without saying another word, I lifted up her pajama shirt and loosened her bra. A couple seconds later, the bra collapsed on the floor. Her C-cup breasts popped out and I put my mouth around a nipple. "Ohhh," she moaned as she moved her head from side to side. Each time she moved, I sucked on her breasts harder and harder. I couldn't control myself. "You got me so wet! I want you inside of me now!" she screamed out. So that was my cue right there to go in for the kill. I lifted her up and placed her on the countertop. I quickly pulled down my boxer shorts and then I snatched her panties off. I spread her legs open so I could get a good look at her creamy pussy.

"Mmmm, baby, your pussy looks so good!" I complimented her and then I reached down and put my index finger in her pussy. I fingered it while Dawn watched me. This shit turned me on even more.

"Baby, you're making me feel so good," she moaned once again as she grabbed my dick. "C'mon . . . give it to me," she told me. So I pulled her to the edge of the countertop and hoisted her up against me. "Put your legs up around my waist and straddle me," I instructed her. After she did it she held on to my neck while I guided my dick inside of her pussy.

"Owww!" she screamed when I pushed my thick, solid dick into her. After I got the rhythm of my strokes, I started thrusting harder and harder. "Baby, your dick feels so good inside of me. Please don't stop," she begged me.

"Damn, baby! This shit feels so good!" I growled. I felt like I was about to explode any minute now, so I stopped stroking her.

"What are you doing?" she asked me, sounding puzzled.

"I wanna hit your pussy from the back." I helped her down from the countertop. Just like I instructed, Dawn slid down, and then she turned around and bent over. I rubbed my dick against her ass and then I rubbed it between her ass checks. A couple seconds later, I guided my dick to her pussy and pushed my dick back inside of her. The sight of my dick penetrating her wet pussy made my dick harder and made it throb. "Awww fuck!" I moaned and then I slapped her ass cheeks.

"Fuck me harder!" she begged me as she threw her pussy back at me. The rhythm of my gyrating and the movement of her hips and ass mesmerized me. I don't know if I was just horny or it was the fact that we were having makeup sex, but it sent me to cloud nine. A few moments later, I was about to cum. I wanted to slow my movement down so I could penetrate Dawn just a little bit longer, but the intoxicating feeling of her pussy wouldn't allow me to stop. So I continued to pound her with each stroke. I stroked her a handful of times and then I exploded. "Agggghhhh!" I bucked and screamed. A thousand feelings erupted inside of me while I pumped my cum inside of Dawn.

When I had emptied out all of my cum juices, I pulled my dick out of Dawn and stuffed it back inside my boxer shorts. Dawn stood back up, turned around, and smiled at me. "You did good," she told me, and then she rubbed her hand across my dick.

I leaned toward her and gave her a kiss on the lips. "You did good too," I replied. I turned around and grabbed my bowl of cereal up from the kitchen table. It had become soggy so I walked over to the sink, dumped it down the disposal, and then I placed the bowl and spoon into the sink.

"What are you about to do now?" Dawn wanted to know as she watched me.

"I'm going to lie back down until about eleven thirty and then I'm gonna take a shower and go to work."

"Well, I'm about to get ready and go to work. So please be careful," she warned me.

"I will," I assured her, and then I left her standing in the kitchen.

I promised my grandmother that I'd stop by the house to see her and bring her some fresh, fried tilapia from her favorite seafood shop. I let myself in her house with a house key that she gave me over twenty years ago. "Reese, sweetie, is that you?" she yelled from her bedroom.

"Yeah, Grandma, it's me," I yelled back while I was locking the door behind me.

"I'm in my bedroom, darling," she yelled once again.

I peered around the corner of her bedroom with the biggest smile I could muster up. She smiled back at me while she sat in her lounge chair, watching TV in her bedroom. She extended her arms to hug me when I got within arm's reach. I kissed her forehead while she hugged me. "Is that mine?" she asked, still smiling.

"You already know," I replied and handed her the white plastic bag with a white Styrofoam container in it.

"It smells good," my grandmother said, and took the bag from my hands and set it down on her lap.

I took a seat on the edge of her bed. "The people that sold it to me said they just took it out of the grease."

"Thank you, darling. So, how is everything?" she asked after she looked at me from head to toe.

"Everything is good," I told her even though my life was spiraling out of control. I really wanted to tell her I was in debt up to my neck. And I couldn't get it together to save my life. "I sense that you're lying to me," she said, pressing the issue. I don't know how my grandmother does it, but she always knows when something is wrong with me and when I'm lying to her about it.

"Okay, well, I'm not fine. But the stuff I've got on my plate is manageable," I told her, hoping she'd believe me.

"You're not having any money issues, are you?" She looked straight into my eyes. It was almost like she could see through me. The shit was unreal.

"Who isn't?" I commented.

"How much you need?" she pressed.

"Grandma, keep your money. I can handle it." I tried reassuring her. But on some real shit, I wanted her to be like, *Look, boy, take this twenty thousand dollars and pay off all your bills*. Wishful thinking on my part.

"How are things going with Dawn? Has she been able to get pregnant yet?"

"No, and she's stressing me out about it too."

"That's only because she wants to be a mother."

"She can play mother with my kids."

"That's not the same, Reese. It's a beautiful thing when a woman has a child that she carried in her stomach for nine months. It's that connection we feel with the baby. It's like we're one body and one soul."

"Yeah, all of that is cute. But it gets really expensive after that soul comes out of you," I commented sarcastically. I didn't come over here to talk about Dawn. I just wanted to drop the food off and head to work.

"Yes, it does. But try to see it from her perspective, Reese. They say happy wife, happy life," my grandmother said and cracked a smile.

I played along and chuckled a bit and then I stood up from her bed. "I gotta get out of here and head to work."

"You're leaving so soon?" she said, obviously disappointed. I could tell that she wanted me to stay longer, but I couldn't. I was fixed on getting to work so I could get this job under way that Edward had given us.

"I'll tell you what, I'll come see you the day after tomorrow. That's two days from now."

"Why in two days? You got somewhere to be?"

"Yeah, I'm working double shifts today and tomorrow. So I'll see you after that," I lied once again. Truth was I wasn't in the mood to come around here and do a lot of smiling when I knew my life was fucked up. I just wanted to get my paper from this job so I could pull my head out from under some of this debt. After that, I could walk around with a smile.

I gave my grandmother a kiss and reassured her that she'd see me in two days. After that, I made my exit.

When I got back into my truck I sat there for a moment and thought about all the countless shit I'd done to fuck up my life. It seemed like no matter what avenues I took to make my life go in the right direction, something bad happened. Was I ever going to catch a break? Would I ever be the loving, caring, and responsible husband that Dawn wanted me to be? Would I ever get caught up on my bills or help her get pregnant? I didn't have the answers now, but hopefully after this payday tonight, things would look up for the both of us.

8

DAWN

Having a smile on my face when I walked into the north business office at NIT made my supervisor, Mrs. Powell, take notice.

"So, what do we have here?" she said loud enough for everyone in the office to hear.

Our business office wasn't that big. Seven others also reported to Mrs. Powell, but their cubicles were on the opposite side of the floor.

I blushed as I approached her with the balloons, the birthday crown, and a dozen vanilla cupcakes. "What I have are cupcakes for you so everybody in here can help wish you a happy birthday," I told her as I set the cupcakes down on her desk.

"Now you know you didn't have to do that," she said.

"I know I didn't. But guess what? I did. Now hold still so I can put this birthday crown on your head," I instructed her while I set the crown on top of her head. "Now, look at you. You look so pretty!"

"Why, thank you, dear," she replied as she inspected the cupcakes. "They look mighty good in that container."

"I know. That's what I said when I picked them up from

the bakery this morning." I opened the plastic container. "Hmmm, they smell good too."

"I hope you don't think I'm going to eat one of those cupcakes right now. Shucks, I just had a large cup of coffee."

"Okay, well, can we at least sing happy birthday to you?" I asked.

"Right now?" She looked around the room at the employees sitting in their cubicles.

"Yes, now," I told her. I turned around and faced the other employees. "Can y'all come over here for a minute so we can sing happy birthday to Mrs. Powell?" I yelled.

Mrs. Powell gave me a look of uncertainty. "Don't you think we need to do this later? What if Mr. Donovan walks in here from the other business office and sees us standing around like we have nothing to do?" Mrs. Powell seemed nervous.

"Don't worry about him, Mrs. Powell. But if he does come over to our office, then tell him to take the stick out of his butt." I burst into laughter. She laughed too. By this time everyone had greeted us. Most of the employees here were white. We did have a Hispanic woman working in this office too, but she was very quiet and mild mannered. I hardly ever heard her talk.

After everyone gathered in a circle we started singing happy birthday to Mrs. Powell. We skipped the *how old are you?* part and Mrs. Powell was okay with it. Before everyone headed back to their seat, they took a cupcake with them.

"Thank you for the balloons and cupcakes for my birthday."

"You're welcome, Mrs. Powell," I said. Mrs. Powell was a sweet lady. She was like mother figure to me and I cherished her. Too bad she was not fond of Reese. I remembered some time ago when she told me that she was going to pray Reese out of my life. Now I wasn't sure if she actually prayed that prayer, but I was sure that if she ever got on her knees and asked God to get rid of Reese, it would happen.

I texted Reese around ten thirty and instructed him to text me as soon as he got through the gate of the pier. So, when I got his text at eleven thirty, I took my lunch break so I could see him before he clocked in for his shift.

I got in my car and raced to the west side of the terminal. When I pulled up to the area where he was assigned to work, I parked my car and slid out of the driver seat. I walked like a couple hundred feet, and out popped Reese. He smiled as he approached me, and I smiled back. He started up the conversation. "What brings you over this side?"

"Well, first of all I wanted to thank you for fucking me real good earlier, and two, I wanted to tell you that I love you."

Reese's smile widened and then he pulled me into his arms. "I appreciate you saying that."

"I'm glad to hear that," I told him. My smile got bigger. "What time do you get off tonight?"

"Probably ten or eleven o'clock. Maybe later. It all depends on the loads that're coming in tonight."

"Speaking of loads, baby, please be careful," I pleaded with him as he held me tight in his arms.

He looked down at me and kissed me on my forehead. "Trust me, I will."

I let out a long sigh. "Thank you."

Reese and I talked for a total of ten minutes before he gave me the cue that he had to clock in for his shift. "If you cook tonight, put my food in the microwave, okay?"

"Yeah, okay," I said while I watched him head in the direction of the cranes.

I stood there and watched him as he disappeared around a stack of containers. I had a bad feeling about this. We needed the money, but this was all wrong. I felt like we were being used as part of someone's bigger, evil scheme. My only hope now was that everything worked out for him and he brought home that $15,000. With all the bills and things we had on our plates, an extra $10,000 on top of the $5,000 that Reese brought home would help tremendously. Stopping him from gambling would also do the trick. I would never understand this addiction that made people like my husband like to give their money away. I guess all I could do now was stand by him and hope that he didn't get caught in the process.

9

REESE

For the life of me I couldn't figure out how the hours in this particular day raced by so fast. The sun had just set, so this was the perfect time to do all the dirty deeds your heart desired. I tried to pretend like I wasn't nervous in front of Edward and Todd, but I was scared shitless. I was so afraid of getting caught with the containers that I was very close to calling the whole thing off. I watched as Todd and Edward sat inside the cabs of their cranes, moving containers from the ship. Brian and Gene stood alongside me. The ship had been docked for a few hours now, so Todd and Edward were working very quickly to get both of the containers down from the ship. "How many more containers do Todd and Ed have to move before they get to ours?" I asked Gene.

"Ed just pulled one down," Brian answered.

"Where is it?" I asked.

Brian pointed. "Todd stacked it on the blue container in the fifth row beside the orange Maersk container."

I saw the container he was referring to, and turned my focus back on Edward and Todd in their cranes. "How many more containers we gotta pull down to get to the other one?"

Gene answered this time. "I think like ten."

"Has the guys from Customs come by yet?"

"I saw them when they boarded the ship twenty minutes ago," Brian interjected.

"Well, let's get to work," I said, and walked off. I headed to the straddle carrier so I could take both containers and put them on railroad cars. It didn't take me long to crawl into the straddle carrier and wheel it over to where the first container was. I'd never been scared of stealing shit from the metal containers, but for some reason, I was scared shitless. I thought about so many different scenarios pertaining to us getting caught. Hearing Dawn tell me about the other niggas that got busted doing this job some years back kind of spooked me. I dared not admit it, though. She would've scolded my ass for sure. I just hoped that everything went right because I had a lot of things to take care of after we got paid. So, fucking up this job wasn't an option.

Using the lift gauge on the straddle carrier, I secured a hold on all four sides of the first container and carried it over to the railroad cars. Once I had the container positioned right, I set it down on the third-to-the-last railroad car. It looked perfectly right, but then again something about it was off, so I turned off the machine so I could think clearly. The moment I powered off the machine I heard a faint cry and I immediately went into panic mode. I sat there in the seat of the straddle carrier, trying to figure out what to do.

"Fuck!" I said, barely audible. I grabbed the door handle to open the door, but then I decided against it. I couldn't unsee what was in that container. "What the fuck am I doing?"

That's when it hit me that I should call Edward. I pulled my cell phone from my pants pocket and called him. "Yo, Ed, I just dropped off the first can on the tracks and I heard somebody crying," I explained as soon as Ed answered his cell.

"Are you sure?"

"Yeah, I'm sure. Do you hear my machine running?" I asked sarcastically. It irritated me that he asked me that question. I knew what crying sounded like.

"Is it loud?"

"No. But I can still hear it," I told him.

"Look, Reese, that's not our concern. Turn the machine back on and come back over here and wait for me to pull the other container down from the ship."

"A'ight," I said, and I ended the call. I sat there quietly for a second before I heard the faint cry again. I felt guilty as hell, but I couldn't do anything about what had already happened to the people in that container. Edward made it perfectly clear that we couldn't fuck this mission up. Therefore, I had to stuff my feelings in my pockets and keep moving.

"Let's go, Reese, all you gotta do is move one more container," I said to myself. I put the gears in drive and sped off back in the direction of the vessel. Timing could not have been better, because as soon as I pulled back into my spot on the pier, Ed was ready to hand over the last container. Anxious to get this job over and done with, I grabbed the container immediately after Ed placed it on the ground, and headed back over to the railroad cars.

I knew that there was a strong possibility I was going to hear that person crying again. And if I heard it long enough I'd probably do something about it. So I started prepping myself, en route to the cars, to tune out anything I heard that would cause me to fuck up this mission. "Reese, you can't let that shit interfere with this operation. That shit that's going on inside of that container does not concern you. Under no circumstances are you supposed to let anything come before that ten thousand dollars that you're owed. So, do your job and then you're home free."

After my final pep talk, I carried the last container to the railroad cars and dropped it off on the designated car. I turned the straddle carrier around and then I drove out of there as fast as I could.

Edward saw me rolling back toward the pier and texted me: Good job. I smiled at the text and then I texted him back: We're in this shit together! He sent me a thumbs-up emoji and that concluded our texting back and forth.

The rest of the night everything ran smooth. I continued to work until my shift was over, and after I clocked out, Edward, myself, and the rest of the guys huddled near Todd's car and planned to meet the following day so we could break bread with one another.

"I'm picking the money up from the Asian guy around noon, so I'll hit you guys up as soon as I get it in my hands," Edward told us.

I said, "Damn, I can't wait until I get the rest of the money." And be done with this, I thought.

"Me too. I gotta get my car serviced ASAP," Todd said.

"I've got a lot of shit to do with my portion of the money too," Gene chimed in.

"Well, it looks like all of us got things we need to do with that money. We're gonna all be ten thousand dollars richer tomorrow, so have your cell phones near you because I'm gonna be calling you," Edward said.

"Oh, don't worry, I'm gonna have my cell phone in my pocket the whole time," Todd said.

"I'm gonna have mine in my hands right after I hop out the bed," Gene added.

"All right, cool. I'll get with y'all tomorrow." Ed gave all of us handshakes. Immediately after that, our circle broke and we got into our vehicles. While I drove away from the terminal, all I thought about was what I was going to do with the additional $10,000 I was going to have in my possession in less than twenty-four hours. I knew Dawn thought I was going to hand over the entire amount to her after I got it in my hands, but she would be sadly mistaken. I'd give her $5,000 so she could handle the past-due bills we got, but that was it. I could hear her yelling throughout the house, saying that the $5,000 wasn't enough to catch up on our bills, but she was just going to have to deal with it. I had bookies that I owed money to, and if I didn't satisfy my debts, I could get beat up really bad. But I couldn't tell her that because she'd freak out about it.

When I got home, I went into the bedroom and noticed that Dawn was in bed asleep. Since her back was to me, I elected not to bother her and decided to head back out of the room. But before I could cross the threshold, she opened her mouth and spoke.

"So, did everything go as planned?" Her voice was low.

Somewhat caught off guard, I turned around slightly and said, "I thought you were asleep."

"I was until I heard you walk into the house. So how did everything go?"

"Everything went smooth. Ed said we should have the rest of our money before we go to work tomorrow."

"Where are you going now?"

"I'm going to the living room to watch a little bit of TV."

"All right," she said and then silence filled the air.

Without saying another word, I turned back around and headed toward the living room. After I sat down on the sofa, I kicked off my work boots and stretched my entire body out across the cotton cushions. I grabbed the remote control and powered on the television, even though I had no plans to watch it. I eventually turned my back to it, closed my eyes, and went into deep thought about what I was going to do with the $10,000 payoff I had coming to me in a few hours. I even thought about the financial situation Dawn and I were in before I landed the this job. Her sister was right, if I was handling my business Dawn wouldn't have ever had to go to her parents and ask for loans so she could help with our household bills. Hearing Alexia attack my manhood didn't sit well with me. You can't come in a man's house and disrespect him in front of his wife because he ain't carrying his weight with the bills. That kind of talk wounds a man's ego, and I wasn't having that. There had been a few times when Alexia made her remarks to me that I wanted to punch her in her damn mouth. I swear, when that bitch started running her mouth, she didn't know how to stop. I knew one thing: If I was her man and she talked to me like that, she would've lost her teeth a long time ago.

10

DAWN

I was a nervous wreck until I heard Reese walk through our front door. I knew he thought he was doing what he needed to do to get us out of this hole he was in, but there had still got to be some boundaries. I couldn't have my husband getting involved in that kind of illegal activity, regardless of how our bank accounts looked. I needed him on the streets with me. Not some federal prison with limited visitation rights.

I don't know how I fell back asleep after talking to Reese when he came home in the middle of the night. I must've been really tired because all I could think about was that he was home safe and that very soon Ed would be giving him the balance of the money that was owed to Reese.

I got up to greet the sunlight that was coming through the blinds covering my bedroom windows. I immediately noticed that Reese hadn't gotten in the bed with me after he returned home.

I crawled out of the bed and did my usual bathroom routine. Normally after I exit the bathroom I always go to the kitchen and boil hot water so I can fix myself a hot cup of tea. On my way there, I walked through the living room and noticed that Reese was already awake with a cup of hot tea in his hand, his full attention on the television directly in front of him.

"Finally up?" he said after he looked at me briefly.

"Yeah, but I'm surprised to see you up though," I commented as I continued on toward the kitchen.

"I tried going to sleep a few times last night, but I couldn't, for some reason," I heard him say while I grabbed a coffee mug from the tray next to the stove.

"Is that why you didn't come to bed last night?" I asked with my back to him. I wanted to be very careful while pouring the hot water from the pot that Reese had already set on the stove. Immediately thereafter I grabbed a pack of tea from the pullout drawer in front of me and dropped it into my mug.

"Yeah, I guess it was."

"Have you talked to Ed this morning?" I asked while I walked toward him, holding my cup of tea as carefully as I could.

"Nah, not yet."

"Have you thought about who we're gonna pay first? Because I think we should get the car notes and the mortgage first, since that's the bulk of our bills. The car insurance should be next because if the policy lapses, we could get hit with a five-hundred-dollar uninsured-motorist fee, and we can't afford to let that happen. And I think we should take care of the gas bill too. We're behind like three months on that bill and we're not gonna get another extension." I took a seat next to him on the sofa.

"You got it all planned out, huh?" he commented in a cynical fashion.

"Aren't I supposed to? If I don't do it, then who's gonna do it, you?" I responded sarcastically, while I gritted my teeth at him.

"Yeah, I guess. But I've got shit I need to do with some of that money too, so somebody ain't gonna get paid right now."

"What do you mean, somebody ain't gonna get paid? Do you know how much debt we're in, Reese? Do you know how embarrassed I feel when I've got to call and make payment arrangements with our creditors because I've already asked my parents to loan me money for the other bills we have?"

Reese tried downplaying our situation. "I don't know why you're embarrassed. Everybody I know is behind on their bills. Shit is rough out here. So stop whining and deal with it."

"My parents aren't going through financial problems. As a matter of fact, their house is paid off and their cars are paid off too." I swear, I wanted to throw my whole cup of hot tea in his fucking face. He was getting under my skin with all his fucking excuses about why we're struggling to pay our bills.

"They don't even count. When they bought their house, it was only thirty-five thousand dollars back then. And besides, they've been saving their money since they started working in the nineteen sixties. Name someone our age that's not struggling to pay their bills like us," Reese protested.

"I'm not playing the name game with you. Just tell me how much money you're giving me to pay our bills," I insisted.

"I'm gonna give you another five grand. I think ten thousand will be enough to cover the most important bills. And whatever else we got left will be dealt with as soon as more money comes through."

I swear, my blood started boiling rapidly. I knew that if I didn't get up and leave this nigga sitting on this couch, I was going to say something to him that I wouldn't be able to take back. "You're so fucking pathetic, it's a shame!" I roared, and then I stood up on my feet. I was losing patience with Reese and his reasoning for our financial problems. He was literally refusing to take the blame for it.

"You always run away when I'm right," he taunted.

"I'm running away from you to keep from cussing your ass out!" I gritted my teeth once again as I stormed down the hallway toward our bedroom.

"You'll get over it!" he yelled out.

As badly as I wanted to turn around and hurl my cup of hot tea at him, I held my composure and continued on to the bedroom. I needed to get ready for work, so that's what I did.

11

REESE

I sat on the sofa and continued watching TV like nothing had just happened. Whether Dawn knew it or not, I wasn't about to let her ruin my day with all the bill talk. Shit, I had other things to do. She needed to be grateful that I was giving her two-thirds of the $15,000. I knew plenty of niggas that lived with their girlfriends and wives and they didn't pay for half of the bills Dawn's got me paying.

While I continued to watch television and drink my tea, Dawn made it her business to open and slam every door in the house while she got ready for work. I almost said something to her after I heard her slam the door for the sixth time, but I didn't bother. I knew she was trying to get a reaction out of me, so I decided to leave the whole thing alone.

Thankfully, all of her shenanigans ended forty minutes later when she walked out of the front door. She didn't speak to me on her way out and I didn't speak to her either.

Not long after Dawn left, I decided to hop in the shower and get dressed so I could be ready to leave when Ed called. It didn't take me long to get myself together. I was out of the shower and dressed in a matter of thirty minutes. I crashed back on the sofa and waited patiently for Edward to call me with the time that he wanted to meet up with me, but he did me one better. Around ten thirty, Edward called me and asked me if I was dressed.

"Yeah, I'm dressed. What's up?" I asked.

"Our Asian connection wants to meet everyone in our crew this morning."

"Whatcha mean, everyone?" I asked, trying to get clarity.

"I'm talking about all of us. You, me, Gene, Todd, and Brian."

I didn't want to get into more of this than I had to. But I couldn't think of a quick excuse, so I said, "Where?"

"At one of his restaurants."

"What time?"

"At eleven o'clock, so leave your house now."

"A'ight. I'm leaving out right now." I got up from the couch. I grabbed my car keys from the table in the foyer and proceeded toward the front door. "What's the name of the restaurant?"

"The one we're meeting him at is in the shopping center off Virginia Beach Boulevard, right behind the T-Mobile store."

"Oh, you're talking about that big, all-you-can-eat Chinese buffet spot in the same shopping center with FedEx and the Jamaican restaurant?"

"Yeah, that's the one," Edward said.

"Are you there yet?" I asked.

"No, I'm en route now. Todd, Gene, and Brian should already be there because they're all in Todd's truck."

"A'ight, well, I'll see you in a few minutes."

"See you then," Ed said, then we disconnected our call.

The ride to that Asian buffet spot in Norfolk didn't take long at all. I arrived at the location a couple minutes before eleven. Before I got out of my truck, I looked around the parking lot and saw Todd's SUV two rows over from where I was.

I drove over and parked in the space next to him. He lowered his driver-side window. "Ready to meet the big man?" he asked me, giving me the biggest smile he could muster up.

No. "Yeah, I guess. But whatcha think about him wanting to see us?"

"I think he might be trying to put us on his payroll," Brian yelled over Todd's head.

"Do you think he may not have the rest of our money?" Gene asked from the back seat of Todd's SUV.

"Nah, I doubt that. If he didn't have our money, he wouldn't have invited us to meet with him," I reasoned. I couldn't believe I was in this situation. If I didn't need that money so bad . . .

"Yeah, that sounds about right," Todd chimed in.

The guys and I kept throwing questions back and forth at one another until Edward showed up. "Boss man is here," Todd said, and we all turned in the direction Todd was looking.

Edward parked his vehicle a couple spots away from us. He stepped outside of it a couple seconds later. We followed suit. "Y'all negroes ready to take our business affairs to the next level?" Edward asked as we approached him.

Brian spoke first. "If he has anything to do with making more money, then you know I'm all for it."

"As long as I'm not risking my life, then you know I'm down too," Gene chimed in.

I could see this train was leaving the station, so I had to agree. "You know I need the money no matter what," I interjected, while Todd only nodded his head. We all knew what that meant. He was down for the cause too.

The moment we were within arm's distance of Ed, we

took turns giving him the proper handshake. "You guys hungry?" he asked us.

"I'm always hungry," I replied.

"Shit, me too," Gene added as we all turned and started walking toward the front door of the restaurant.

A young Asian woman opened the door and greeted us. "Will you gentlemen follow me, please?" she said, and led the way to a table in the back of the restaurant, behind a privacy screen. We all took our seats. "Will you be eating from the buffet?" she asked.

We all nodded our heads.

"Can I get your choice of beverages?" she continued.

I spoke first. "I'll take water."

"Yeah, I'll have that too," Gene said.

"Bring me sweet tea if you have it," Brian chimed in.

"I need something strong, so bring me a Sprite," Edward told the lady.

"Yeah, me too." Todd said.

"Okay, I'll be right back," she said, and walked off.

We all got up from the table and headed toward the buffet line. "This food looks good as hell!" I pointed out as I checked out the varieties of food on display.

"Yeah, this shit does look good," Brian agreed as he piled his plate with food.

Gene, Edward, and Todd followed suit. We filled our plates and headed back to our table. We started eating immediately after we sat down. A few minutes later, the woman came back with our drinks and set them down on the table in front of us. She told us that Mr. Que Ming would be with us shortly. After Edward thanked her, she left.

While we were stuffing our faces like hungry dogs, Que Ming appeared before us. He greeted us and walked around the table and shook everyone's hand. Que Ming was a very modest-looking Asian guy. I couldn't say how old he was, but I could say that he looked like he was in his late forties. He was about five foot eleven and it looked like he weighed about one forty. He wasn't stylish at all, sporting a pair of blue jeans, a plain black belt, and a beige factory-worker's shirt with a pocket stitched on the left side of his chest. I was from the streets and I could tell you right now that this geeky-looking dude wouldn't be able to hang out in my hood.

He took a seat in a chair next to Edward and started the conversation. "I wanna thank all you guys for a job well done."

I gave this guy my undivided attention because for one he spoke perfectly good English and two, he congratulated us on a job well done. Everyone thanked him one by one.

"Here's the money I owe you guys," he said as he pulled a manila envelope from the inside jacket pocket and handed it to Edward.

"Thank you, Mr. Ming. We really appreciate this," Edward told him as he stuffed the envelope in his jacket pocket.

Mr. Ming smiled. "You're welcome. Now, since you guys did such a great job, I would love it if you could help me out with another shipment that will be coming our way two days from now."

"Will it be the same number of containers?" Ed asked.

"Yes," Mr. Ming replied.

"What time will the vessel arrive at the pier?" Ed continued.

"The same time."

"Will the pay be the same?"

"Yes."

"Well, then, let's do it," Edward said without giving any of us eye contact. I mean, it wasn't like we would've turned down the offer, but getting our say-so would've shown me that our input mattered. It was apparent that Edward didn't see things the way I did. I guess he figured that he knew what was best for us. I didn't agree with him committing us to this new job, but the money we were making agreed with me, so I kept my mouth shut.

"Before you guys leave, stop by the register and the young lady who escorted you to the table will give you the deposit for the new job."

"Got it." Edward said.

"All right, well, I'm gonna let you gentlemen finish eating your food. It's on the house, so eat as much as you want," Mr. Ming said as he stood up from the chair.

As he pushed the chair back toward the table, I blurted out, "Do you know that I heard someone crying in one of those containers when I was transporting it to the railroad cars?" Everyone at the table looked at me with pure shock on their faces, including Ed. We all knew there were people in those containers, so I wasn't sure why they were so shocked by my question.

"What do you mean, crying?" Mr. Ming asked me as he gave me a stern look.

I didn't know if I was supposed to elaborate more or shut my mouth altogether. So I chose the former and answered him. "I heard somebody crying from inside the container, so I called Ed and asked him what to do about it, but he basically told me not to be concerned with it and do my job. So, I'm asking you, what should I do if I hear somebody else crying?"

Mr. Ming stood before the entire table and said, "We're transporting very expensive artifacts from Asia, so I'm sure what you heard wasn't a person crying. We could get into a lot of trouble if people were inside those containers."

I watched Mr. Ming deliver this lie with ease. I also felt heat coming at me from the seat Edward was sitting in. And I saw his expression in my peripheral vision.

"Yeah, I told him the same thing," Edward interjected.

I immediately took my attention off Mr. Ming and turned to Ed, who was by this time looking like he could kill me. I knew then that I was talking too much and decided to change my tune. "You know what? You're probably right," I responded to Mr. Ming, and then I looked back down to my food and started eating again.

"All right, gentlemen, I want to thank you again for your assistance. And please enjoy your food," Mr. Ming concluded. He turned around and walked away from the table.

"What the fuck just happened? And why did you say that to him?" Edward snapped in a low voice.

I looked back up from my plate. "Shit! I didn't know I couldn't say that to him. I thought he knew that we knew what was inside the containers," I explained.

"Never mind if he thought we knew what was really in the containers. We can't discuss that type of shit in an open environment. One of us could've been recording him. So, do you think he's going to admit to that shit?" Edward was heated with me. He was so mad that he must have lost his appetite because he pushed his plate forward and just sat there and shook his head in disbelief.

"So, what's gonna happen now?" I wondered aloud.

"We're gonna stop by the register, get the money, and then we're gonna walk our asses out of this restaurant and get ready to go to work," Edward told us.

"Damn, nigga, you done fucked up the whole meeting," Brian commented.

"Yeah, what made you say that shit to the man?" Todd wanted to know.

Gene didn't say a word. He sat there in complete silence.

"What the fuck do y'all want me to say? It was a fucking mistake. Get over it." I wasn't going to let these niggas dictate how I was supposed to act. Okay, yeah, I screwed up and opened my mouth when I wasn't supposed to. Big fucking deal!

"I'll tell you what, if that dude ever wants to meet up with all of us again, please make sure you keep your mouth closed the entire time. You got it?" Edward said.

"Yeah, I got it," I replied, and then I continued to eat my food.

While the rest of us ate, Edward pulled out the manila envelope and handed us the rest of the money that was owed to us. He counted out $10,000 each and placed the stack of money next to our plates. I swear it felt so good to finally have the rest of that money in my hands. But what felt even better was that the Asian cat was giving us another opportunity to make another $15,000, and we were taking part of that money home today as well. I could honestly say that I was having a great day, despite the argument I had with Dawn earlier. I guess now I could give her the other $5,000 she wanted to pay the bills. It was gonna feel good to finally get her worrisome ass off my back. Things were starting to look up for me now.

12

DAWN

I sat at my desk all morning thinking about that bullshit-ass argument Reese and I had. Was he fucking serious when he said that he was only giving me another five grand? And to add insult to injury, hearing him basically say that he was doing me a favor by paying most of the bills in our household because other niggas weren't doing it for their women. I swear, this nigga must be on drugs or something, because nothing he said made any sense. I knew one thing: If he didn't come through with a total of $10,000, his ass was going straight in the doghouse.

For some reason, today was going pretty fast and my lunch break was here before I knew it. I didn't bring anything from home to eat, so I went to the vending machine on the main hallway and got a bag of pretzels and a bottle of grape juice, since those were the only appealing items to choose from. After I had my items in hand I decided to hang out in the lounge area of the building and play a game of solitaire on my cell phone.

But as soon as I started walking in that direction, I noticed Reese walking down the hallway toward me. Seeing him set off a load of mixed feelings. I didn't know whether to smile and run into his arms or tell him to kiss my ass and turn my back on him. And before I could make that decision, he smiled at me and said, "Got some good news for you."

Good news! I thought to myself. What kind of good news could he have for me? The only thing I wanted to talk about was getting the rest of the money he had so I could pay *all* our bills, not *some*.

"What do you want, Reese?"

"I came here to bring you a gift." His smile had gotten bigger.

I stopped in my tracks because I really didn't want to deal with him or his games right now. And before I could really tell him how I was feeling, he reached down into his front pants pocket, pulled out a huge wad of money, and extended his arm in my direction.

"What is that?" I asked him.

"It's the other ten grand you wanted. It means that now you got the whole fifteen grand." He continued toward me, holding out the money in his hand.

Hearing him tell me that he was giving me the money he earned on this last job made me feel so happy inside. I couldn't believe that I was really getting that money.

"Don't play with me, Reese," I warned him with a half smile.

"I'm not playing, baby. See, look." When he got within arm's reach of me, he put all the money in my hands. I examined it and then I looked back at Reese.

"This is the ten grand, for real?"

"Yes, baby, it is."

"What made you change your mind?"

"Because I thought about what you said."

"Reese, stop playing with me and be honest for once in your life," I begged him.

"Okay, all right. Me and the rest of the guys met up

with that Asian dude, and after he gave us our money, he told us he wanted us to do another job for him and he will pay us another fifteen thousand."

"Wait, hold up. You met who? And you're gonna do *what*?" I asked him. I needed to give him a chance to back-track and rethink this nonsense.

"Edward took me and the other guys to meet that Asian dude so he could thank us and pay us the money he owed us," he clarified.

"Okay, I got that part, but what's up with this other job he wants y'all to do? I thought this was a one-time thing." I wasn't happy about the news I was getting from Reese right now.

"Calm down, baby, everything is going to go smoothly just like the job we did last night."

"What if it doesn't?"

"Stop being so negative. Everything is going to work out fine. Just trust me."

"You may need to give me another word that would re-assure me, because the word *trust* doesn't mean anything to me," I said sarcastically.

"Are you going to take it easy or what?"

"Just tell me when you gotta do that job?"

"The day after tomorrow."

"Baby, I don't know about that. It's too soon, don't you think?"

"Look, do me a favor."

"And what is that?"

"Go back to your office and ask your supervisor if you could take an extended lunch break so I can take you out to eat."

"Where are we going?"

"Don't worry about all of that. Just go do like I told you and put that money away before somebody robs you," he said, and then he turned me around and ushered me off in the direction of Mrs. Powell's office.

"Don't rush me," I protested half-heartedly.

Instead of saying something else, Reese smacked me across my butt, pushing me forward. I looked back at him and noticed that he was staring at me.

"What are you looking at?" I asked him from three feet away.

"I'm looking at that big ole bootie you got!" He smiled.

"Don't smile at me like everything is all good. You still got more explaining to do," I warned him.

"Yeah, okay," he replied, as if he was taking my words lightly.

After taking a few more steps, I turned into the next hallway and made my way into my office. Before I walked over to my supervisor's desk, I put the money away. I tried to think of a good excuse for me to get off for the rest of the day. Once I had the lie forged in my head, I headed over to Mrs. Powell's desk.

13

REESE

I was so glad that I had the idea to take Dawn out for lunch. After filling up her belly and giving her the money, it felt like I was home free. She tried to talk me out of doing the second job for Mr. Ming, but I told her that wasn't going to happen. We needed the money, so therefore the job would get done.

On the drive back to her office, she became inquisitive about the meeting with Mr. Ming, but I kept it simple and sweet.

"How does he look?" she asked.

"He looks Asian."

"Is he tall or short?"

"He's tall."

"Is he old or young?"

"He looks kind of young. Maybe late thirties or early forties."

"Does he look mean?"

"Nah, as a matter of fact, he doesn't. He looks like one of the drivers who delivers takeout from a Chinese restaurant around here. But the difference between him and that driver is that he's got plenty of money and the driver doesn't."

"Do you think he's gonna ask y'all to do another job after this one?"

"Baby, I don't know," I replied, and let out a long sigh. I really wasn't trying to touch that subject. Not now anyway. I wanted to tell her to ask me that question after I completed this job the day after tomorrow. But I left it alone.

"Well, answer this."

"What?" I replied, dreading what she was about to say.

"Did that guy pay y'all another five grand up front?"

"Yeah, why?"

"Because I just wanted to know."

"You're not trying to take that money from me too, are you?" I asked her, taking my eyes off the cars in front of me for a second before turning my focus back to what was going on in front of me.

"No, I'm not. I just want you to be smart about where you're gonna spend it. We have a little bit of a cushion right now, and blowing it up on fruitless things is going to put us right back in debt all over again."

"Well, I'm not going to blow it up on fruitless things, and to prove that to you, I want you to hold it for me," I said, and handed her the wad of cash I had in my front pants pocket. She looked at me really weird as she took the money from my hands.

"Are you turning over a new leaf?" she asked me as she tucked the money away in her handbag.

"Look, just put it away for me." I gave her a half smile and then I turned up the volume on the radio.

In return, she gave me a facial expression like she was impressed with me. I didn't want to spoil the mood by asking her about it, so I left well enough alone and enjoyed the ride back to her job in peace.

"Make sure you have a good day," I said after I pulled up in front of the office building.

"And you do the same." She smiled and then she leaned over and kissed me on the lips.

I couldn't believe how time flew by so quickly. It seemed like it was just yesterday that the guys and I met Mr. Ming and he gave us our dough. But it wasn't. Today was the day that Ed, myself, and the rest of the guys had to make sure that Mr. Ming's property, whether it was people or artifacts, was placed on the railroad cars. There were no ifs, ands, or buts about it. The job had to be executed and we were the guys that were being paid to do it.

I was amped up this morning when I got up. I thought it was because I was going to have another ten grand in my pocket in less than twenty-four hours after the job was done. I was going to have a field day with that money. I was going to pay back the bookies I owed and I was going to put some money away just in case my hands started to itch. When my hands start to itch, it means that money is coming my way. And in the business I dabbled in, that meant that I needed to run to the nearest poker table. Boy, was I going to have me some fun after I got the rest of my money. It was gonna feel like Christmas.

Like the first time, Edward, myself, and the rest of the guys formed a huddle near the ship and mapped out our plans for this shipment. Right after we got our assignments from Ed, we headed to our positions.

Tonight felt like a good night. Besides the timekeepers and the union managers roaming around the pier, everything else was easy breezy.

I crawled into my straddle carrier, buckled myself in my seat, and headed over to the ship we were retrieving the containers from. I texted Edward after I got in position. He texted me back with the thumbs-up emoji.

I sat there for about twenty minutes before he handed me off the first container. And after I had it within my grasp, I took it and headed over to the railroad cars as quickly as I could without attracting any attention. Thankfully the drive wasn't long. I was over by the railroad cars in less than three minutes. I positioned the straddle carrier carefully and used the lift gauge to place the container on the railcar. But for some reason, the fucking container looked off.

"Shit!" I huffed loudly because I knew I was gonna have to get out of the carrier to make sure the container was secured.

I powered off the machine and hopped out of it. I had to walk across a million fucking rocks to get on the other side of the railroad car. I almost busted my ass when I crossed the track. Lucky for me, I kept my balance and kept it moving.

Aside from that, it was chilly outside and it was kind of dark too, which is why I carried my flashlight at all times. When I turned on the flashlight and pointed it toward the container, I heard someone banging on the container from the inside.

"Hello," I said in a low whisper. "Who's there?" I continued in the same tone, trying to prevent anyone at the terminal from hearing me. And that's when I heard a faint cry. Then the cry turned into words. But I didn't understand the language.

"Artifacts, my ass!" I muttered, not knowing what to do. But then it quickly dawned on me that this was not my fight. I had nothing to do with what was inside of that container. Mr. Ming confirmed that notion when I spoke out about this shit the first time I heard it. And then what did he do? He looked at me like I was fucking crazy for even bringing that shit to his attention. Everybody at the table eating with me gave me that same look. Since I wasn't trying to relive that, after I made sure the container was secured, I turned my ass back around and traveled across all the fucking rocks I had just walked over.

As soon as I crawled back into the straddle carrier, I turned it around and drove back toward the ship to get the second container. On my way back, I couldn't get that person's voice and cry out of my head. But what was disturbing about this ordeal was that this was the second time I heard someone crying from inside a container that belonged to Mr. Ming. Were these people crying out for help? Or were they crying out because they were hurt? I figured whatever the reason was, those people did not want to be in there.

My heartbeat quickened as I steered the machine back to the pickup location. The thought of the port police or US Customs agents finding the containers put a load of fear upon me and I couldn't shake it. "Come on, Reese, stay calm and remain focused so we can get through this job," I said softly so only I could hear my voice. "You can do this. Keep yourself levelheaded. You don't wanna bring any attention to yourself. You've got too much to lose. You also gotta prove to Dawn that you can pull this job off with no problems. You especially can't go to jail behind this shit." I had a two-minute conversation with myself. But it did nothing to allay the fear I felt in my heart, because I was a nervous fucking wreck.

I parked the straddle carrier a few yards from Edward and Todd, and sat there with the machine idling as I waited for Edward to hand the second container to me. While I watched Edward secure the container, my attention was diverted to three US Customs agents examining the twenty-digit ID tags on a set of containers on the right side of the ship. Then I saw two more US Customs agents snooping around a dozen metal containers that Todd had just unloaded from the ship. To add more anxiety to this picture, the port police were rolling deep tonight. Normally they'd do their rounds every thirty minutes. But for some reason, they'd been strolling through here like every ten to fifteen minutes. I was starting to believe that someone had tipped them off. I wanted to get Ed back on the phone to tell me what was going on down there, but I decided against it. For one, I was paranoid. And two, I could be overreacting. Edward did tell me to stay focused, so that's what I intended to do.

After I'd been waiting for nearly eight minutes, Edward pulled down the second container and placed it on the ground so I could grab it. Knowing that a couple of US Customs agents were a few feet from the container, I wasted no time in securing it and lifting it up in the air. As soon as I had it locked and loaded, I turned the straddle carrier around and drove out of there.

Once again, I was on the journey to the railroad, and I figured the quicker I got there the quicker I could off-load this fucking container and get the hell out of there before the port police got the urge to come snooping around. Shit, we couldn't afford to let this job fall by the wayside. Getting that other ten grand was necessary, especially with Dawn nagging me about the bills we've got.

The ride back to the railroad cars took me less time than before. What a feeling of relief that was. So, as I positioned the container to be placed on the other railroad car, I also had to position the headlights on the straddle machine so I could make sure I set the container down on all four points of the train car. I harnessed the container directly over the railcar and let it down easy. As I began to lower the container, two people ran by the train car and it scared the hell out of me. A wave of fear and anxiety engulfed me and I immediately lost sight of what I was doing. With the container leveled midway in the air, I tried to gather my thoughts. But then another little person ran by the train car. And I got a better look at this one. And when I realized that this last person was a barefoot Asian, I almost pissed in my pants. My heart nearly leaped out of my chest.

"Fuck! Fuck! Fuck!" I roared. I couldn't leave the container in midair without someone noticing it, so I took a deep breath and continued to off-load the container onto the railcar.

After two tries, I managed to set the container down without any hiccups. I had to find those people running around the pier before someone other than Edward and the boys saw them.

I powered the machine off and hopped out of it with my heart rate running at sixty-five miles per hour. I knew I couldn't do this alone, so I got Edward back on the phone and started to follow the people who had escaped the container. He answered on the first ring. "What's up?" he said.

"Three people got out of the container," I replied with urgency.

"How'd they get out?"

"I don't know. When I was in the machine off-loading the second container, they popped out of nowhere and started running in the opposite direction of the train."

"Where they at?"

"I don't know. I'm looking for them now," I said, and right after I answered his question, I noticed that I had another caller trying to get through on my other line. I pulled the phone away from my ear and looked down at the caller ID. "Fuck!" I said.

"What's wrong now?" Edward said.

"Dawn is calling me on the other end."

"You're gonna have to call her back. Because we've got more important things to do on this end first," Edward told me.

"Yeah, I know. I'm gonna need some help. Send Brian or Gene over here."

"Yeah, a'ight," Edward said, then the phone line went dead.

Even though there were powered pole lights mounted near the train tracks, there were some blind spots and that's why I always carried a flashlight with me. Norfolk International Terminal had dozens of dark places where you could hide or hide things. So having this flashlight was essential.

Before I took off in the direction the Asians had run, I sprinted to the metal container to see where they had escaped from. As I approached it, I saw a tiny head peeping out the top corner. I couldn't tell if it was a woman or a man, so I pointed my flashlight toward them. "Get back in there!" I motioned toward the container. They must have understood what I had said, because they disappeared in an instant.

I dashed off in the direction where the others had gone. I only hoped that I found them before anyone else did. Because if I didn't, shit was going to hit the fan really hard, and it wasn't going to look pretty.

I didn't know how insane Mr. Ming could be, but judging from the look he gave me at his restaurant, I knew he wouldn't be happy finding out that we botched this job. And knowing the amount of money he paid us to handle his business, it wouldn't surprise me if he made us pay for our mistakes. I figured that either we got things back intact or we found somewhere to hide until the dust settled.

14

DAWN

Thinking about the job Reese and his fellow longshore-men friends were doing had me on edge. I tried to go to sleep, but I couldn't. I called Reese a few times, but he didn't answer his phone, so I had no other choice but to wait for him to call me back or come home.

Instead of lying around and staring at the fucking ceiling, I got out of bed and made myself a cup of hot tea. Drinking hot tea always helped me calm down. Hopefully, it would still do the trick.

When I crawled back into the bed with my cup of tea, I heard a noise outside my bedroom window, so I rushed over to see if Reese was trying to sneak into the house. But when I got to the window and peeped through, I didn't see anyone. The driveway was empty and there were no cars on the street. But I knew that I had heard something. Then I saw it: a black cat was sniffing around in the fucking trash.

The garbagemen picked up everyone's trash by six o'clock in the morning, so Reese made sure it was front and center so I didn't have to get up early in the morning and do it myself. He was a good man at times. I loved when he'd make breakfast for me some mornings, or when he'd run bathwater for me when he knew I'd had a bad day at work. Those nice things didn't outweigh the fucked-up shit he did: the gambling problem, the infidelity that happened a few years ago, not paying our bills on time, and the fact that he allowed his baby mama to disrespect me a few times in the past. Somehow I forgave him, and accepted his marriage proposal when he asked me to marry him a couple of months later. All in all, I knew Reese would fuck up a wet dream, but in his own little way, I knew that he loved me, which was all I could ask for. Because his love was all I needed.

While I stood there at the bedroom window, I noticed a car had come out of nowhere and parked across the street, in front of my neighbor's house. I looked closer and saw someone in the driver's seat, and it spooked me. My heart leaped from my chest while I stared at the car. Then it started moving slowly. I stepped back from the window and pulled the curtains shut while I peered around the edge of the fabric. "What the fuck?" I said, my words barely audible as I watched the car drive away slowly. I wanted to know who that person was and why their car was parked across the street from my house. Was it someone that Reese owed money to? Or was it one of his fucking mistresses stalking my house? Whoever the hell it was, I didn't appreciate them spying on my house. That ain't cool, and Reese was going to hear about it.

After the car drove completely out of sight, I walked away from the window and sat down on the edge of the bed. I looked at the cup of tea on the table near my bed, but I didn't want it. I wanted answers from Reese, and tonight I was going to get them.

15

REESE

I swear, it felt like I had run at least five miles around the terminal. "Where the fuck are y'all?" I mumbled underneath my breath as I panted. I was tired as hell, but I knew I couldn't stop until I found the people who'd escaped the container. The pressure I felt bearing down on me was a heavy load to carry, but I had to complete my task.

After running around for twenty minutes, my cell phone started ringing. I pulled it from my pocket and noticed it was Dawn calling me again. I knew that if I didn't answer this time, she was going to continue to call me until I finally answered. I took a deep breath and then I exhaled and took the call. "Hello."

"Why the fuck didn't you answer my call earlier?"

"Because I'm working."

"Do you know that I saw somebody sitting in a car watching our fucking house a few minutes ago?" she roared.

I could tell that she was pissed. "What car?"

"I don't know what kind of car it was. But it was a black, four-door car. And when the person driving it saw me looking at them, they drove away. So, tell me who the fuck you know that would do some bullshit like that?"

"Look, I can't answer that because I don't know anyone that would do something like that."

"Was it one of your bitches?" she yelled.

"Fuck no! I don't have any bitches!" I whispered harshly.

"Well, who do you owe money to? It could've been them."

"I don't owe anybody any money," I lied. "Maybe they were watching somebody else's house," I continued, trying to calm her down. With all the shit I had going on out here at this terminal, that shit she was talking about was minor. And I wasn't gonna deal with it now. Or later, for that matter.

"Well, if they were watching someone else's house, then why did they drive away when they saw me looking at them?"

"Dawn, I can't answer that right now. They're gone, right?"

"Yeah, they're gone."

"So then, why are we talking about it? I've got a lot of stuff on my plate right now, so can we talk about this some other time?"

"What's going on? Why do you sound like you're out of breath?" she asked.

"Because I'm running around the pier working," I told her.

"But you drive around in the straddle carrier, so again, I'm gonna ask you why you sound like you're out of breath." She wouldn't let up.

"What's with all the questions, Dawn? You know I'm out here working." I was defensive. She knew I was getting irritated, but that didn't stop her from pressing the issue.

"Yeah, and I also know what kind of job you're trying to pull off tonight, and I know that you don't sound like your usual self."

"Listen, baby, everything is good. I've just got a lot on my plate that needs to be done."

"Have you started on the job?"

I sighed heavily. "Yes, I'm in the middle of it now."

"Okay, well, if you're in the middle of it, then why aren't you in the machine?"

"I was just in the machine. I got out for a moment. But I'm—" I paused. "Hey, you, bring your ass back here!" I yelled, not realizing that I had just let the cat out of the bag.

"Reese, who are you talking to?" she belted out. I could hear the concern in her voice and I could tell that she was alarmed. But I couldn't worry about that now. I had to get these fucking people that were trying to escape before I fell deep into some hot water.

"Dawn, I'm gonna have to call you back," I told her, and I abruptly disconnected our call.

I knew she was going to be upset with me and be worried about what was going on, but I couldn't entertain that thought. My main concern was catching these people before someone else at the terminal did.

Immediately after I hung up with Dawn, she called me back. As badly as I wanted to answer her call, I couldn't. I knew that if I did, she'd slow me down with all her fucking questions. So I turned the ringer off, shoved my cell phone down into my pocket, and raced toward the Asian guy. I ran after the guy for at least two hundred feet before I caught up with him. And when I got within arm's reach, I grabbed him by the back of his shirt and pulled him back toward me. It seemed like everything happened in slow motion. "Where the fuck you think you're going?" I hissed. "What the fuck is wrong with you?"

"*Pu jie,*" I heard him say. I wasn't sure what that meant, but the expression on his face spoke volumes.

"Yeah, what the fuck ever!" I spat, and led him back to the container.

Four seconds into the walk back to the railcar, my cell

phone started vibrating in my pocket. I started to ignore it, but the call might be from Edward, so I pulled it from my pocket and looked at the caller ID. Seeing that it was Brian, I answered it on the third ring. "Yeah," I said.

"Where you at?" he asked me.

"I'm about four hundred feet away from the train tracks. Three of the Asian people climbed out of the first container. But I caught one of 'em."

"Do you know where the other ones ran to?"

"Fuck no! That's why I called Ed and told him to send you over here to help me. Where are you?"

"I'm standing next to your straddle carrier."

"Good. Stay right there and make sure no one else crawls out of there. I'll be there in a few minutes."

"All right," he said.

It took me another two minutes to meet Brian back at the train car, and when I got there he had a lot of questions for me. "Where did you catch him at?" he asked.

"The son of a bitch almost made it to the gate on the west wing."

"Think the other ones made it past the gate?"

"It's hard to say. They could really be anywhere around here," I told him.

"You know we're fucked if Customs or the port police find them before we do."

"Of course I do. That's why I told Ed to send somebody over here to help me find 'em."

"Whatcha going to do with this one?"

"Make him crawl back inside the container."

"You think he's going to do it?"

"He ain't got no other choice. I mean, it ain't like we can walk around with this little motherfucker. Look how he's dressed. He definitely looks like he just crawled off the boat."

"All right, well, let's get him back in there before somebody sneaks up on us."

I looked at the Asian guy and pushed him forward. "Come on so you can get your ass back in that container," I instructed him, even though I knew he didn't understand a word I was saying.

"Think he understands you?" Brian asked.

"Probably not." I continued to push the guy toward the train car.

"Well, get him back inside and I'll go look for the other two," Brian insisted, and then he walked off.

While Brian made his way alongside the train tracks to look for those other two men, I stayed back and forced the Asian guy back into the container through a small rusty hole at the top. It was hard for him to jimmy his way up the side of the container, but after a minute of cursing him out and pushing him upward with all the strength I had, I got him back where he was supposed to be. "Don't bring your motherfucking ass back out of there," I cursed, and then I punched the side of the container with my fists. I got no response from anyone inside the container, but I knew that they wanted out of there, and fast.

Once I had everything under wraps on my end, I climbed back in my straddle carrier and watched both containers from my seat. I needed to appear as though I was working, just in case one of the timekeepers or the terminal managers happened to come over to where I was. I don't need to garner any attention. My boys and I have too much money at stake. They'd kill me if I fucked this job up.

16

DAWN

Somehow I fell asleep after talking to Reese. I didn't get to sleep long, but I was able to close my eyes for a couple of hours. That black car was still fresh on my mind, and I couldn't shake the fact that it might come back. So, I crawled out of bed and snuck over to the bedroom window and peered around the curtains really slowly. I looked at the spot across the street and thankfully the car wasn't there. I even looked up and down the street and didn't see the car, so that gave me a sense of peace. It didn't negate the fact that I wanted to know who the driver of the car was, I was just happy that the car wasn't out there this time around.

I crawled back into the bed and lay there thinking about how the job was going for Reese. Thinking back on how he was talking to me over the phone, he sounded a bit stressed out. Now that I thought about it, he always sounded stressed out when he was picking locks on the containers out there on the pier. But then again, this job had bigger risks than stealing flat-screen TVs and fur coats. I remember back when a few other longshoremen got caught helping people from third-world countries escape from a couple of containers. US Customs and federal agents locked their asses up and gave every last one of those guys five- to ten-year sentences. And then on top of that, those guys had to pay restitution and lost their long-shoremen credentials. I heard a few of them came home a few years ago, but they could never get another job with the union. So their lives are fucked. I'm sure they found menial jobs at your local 7-Eleven or the CVS store. But it's not like working at the terminal. Men who have worked for the union can make a minimum salary of $65,000 a year. Right before my father retired, he made $175,000 a year. He doesn't make that kind of money now, but he gets a nice-ass retirement check and he's living a good life, which is what I want for Reese. I try on the regular to get him to stop stealing from those containers and work hard like my father did when he was working at the terminal. But everything I say to Reese goes in one ear and right out the other. He hates when I compare him to my dad. But I don't do it to insult or belittle him. I say it because my father was a great leader and I want the same thing for Reese. Too bad he never listens.

17

REESE

Brian finally called me after I sat in the straddle carrier for more than thirty minutes. "Where the fuck you at?" I asked him. I was irritated as hell. I wanted to hurry up and finish this job so we could move on to the other work we had to do to get our union check. I'm sure the timekeepers were walking around here trying to see where we were.

"We gotta problem," he said.

"What kind of problem?" I wondered aloud. I wasn't in the mood to hear any more bad news. This situation could not get any worse.

"I caught one of the other Asian dudes, but when I grabbed him he started doing that karate shit on me. The motherfucker was whipping my ass until I slipped and fell down."

"So, what's the problem?"

"I made the mistake of strangling him when I put him in a head lock."

"So, you're telling me he's dead?"

"Yeah, the little motherfucker is slumped over on the ground a few feet away from me."

Hearing Brian tell me that he just snuffed out one of the

Asian immigrants made me sick to my stomach. With the knots turning nonstop in the pit of my stomach, my heart raced at an uncontrollable speed. What else could go wrong?

"Think I should call Edward and tell 'im?" Brian wanted to know.

I was trying to think of a good answer to give him, but my mind went completely blank. I literally lost sight of everything around me until Brian brought me back to reality.

"Yo, Reese, man, I need to know what to do before the timekeeper or one of the terminal managers rolls up on me," Brian pressed.

"Well, I know calling Edward definitely wouldn't be a good idea. So if you think you could pick him up and drag him back over here, then do so."

"And then do what with him?"

"We're gonna have to figure out a way to get him back into one of the containers," I suggested, even though I knew that putting that guy back inside the container wouldn't be easy.

"What should we do about the other guy?"

"He's probably found a way off the terminal, so let's just worry about the guy you got and go from there."

"A'ight. Well, I'ma be there in a few minutes," Brian told me and we hung up.

I was really starting to see why Dawn told me not to get involved with this job the first time I did it. This whole plan had gone straight to hell in a handbasket. And not knowing what to do to fix it scared me to death. I mean, what's the worst could happen if we decided to tell our boss what we were trying to do and this happened? Would we all lose our jobs? Whatever the consequence, I couldn't afford to lose my job, especially over something illegal like this. This would be jail time.

I sat there in the straddle carrier for another five minutes, waiting for Brian to bring that Asian dude back. Before he made it back to where I was, a set of headlights came from nowhere and beamed at me. I tried to partially cover my eyes so I could get a look at who was driving, but I couldn't see through the lights. I sat there in sheer panic, not knowing whether to drive off or jump out of the straddle carrier and run until I couldn't run anymore.

"Please don't let this be the fucking port police," I mumbled as my heart rate sped up. "Come on, Reese, you gotta be calm and stay ahead of whoever is coming your way. Don't let them get the best of you." I continued to mumble to myself as I watched a large vehicle drive in my direction.

It finally stopped about seventy-five feet away from me. I blinked my eyes to get a clearer look to see what kind of vehicle it was, but I had no luck. Then the door on the driver side opened, heightening my anticipation. The driver walked a few feet away from the vehicle and turned on his flashlight and pointed it at me. I shielded my eyes a little more and prayed that I wasn't being approached by a fucking terminal cop. "Reese, is that you?" I heard a guy yell.

I recognized the voice and squinted my eyes, hoping I could get a better look and that I was correct. I opened the door of the straddle carrier and yelled, "Who's that?"

"It's me, Gene," I heard him say.

Boy, what a relief it was to hear him say his name, because I swear, I knew I was about to be doing a lot of fucking explaining. And even worse, cause my wife a lot of embarrassment. She'd been working here for a long time, so I couldn't screw things up for her. Not now. Not later.

I stepped down out of the machine and greeted Gene by the rear right tire. "Where is Brian?" he asked me.

"He ran behind one of the Asian guys, so now he's on his way back here."

"How many of them got out?" Gene wanted to know.

"Three of 'em. I caught one and Brian caught one and the other one got away."

"Edward is going to snap the fuck out when he hears that."

"I know. But that's not all that happened."

"There's more?"

I nodded. "The guy that Brian caught started using karate on him. So Brian got tired of him and choked his ass out."

"Whatcha mean he choked him out?"

"The guy is dead. Brian strangled his ass."

Gene's mouth fell wide-open. "The guy is dead?"

"Yep."

"Where is his body?"

"Brian is bringing it back over here. He should be here any moment," I explained.

"What y'all gonna do with the body when he brings it back?"

"We're gonna try to put it back in the container."

"That's gonna be hard to do."

"So, what do you suggest?"

"Y'all may wanna just hide the body somewhere. Because it's gonna be impossible to get the body inside the container without breaking the seal that has the twenty-digit number on it, unless we crawl on top of the container and push him back through that rusty opening where they have been escaping from."

"I kinda figured that. So I guess the best thing to do would be to hide the body and hope that no one finds it for a long time."

"Let's just store it somewhere and hope the birds eat it up before the terminal cops find it."

"I think that would be good idea. But I wonder will Mr. Ming notice that one of the immigrants is gone?"

"You mean two. The one that Brian killed and the other one that got away."

"Oh yeah, I forgot about that one," he replied.

While Gene and I tried to figure out how to resolve our issue, we heard footsteps behind us. We turned around. "Will one of y'all niggas please help me?" Brian yelled out.

Gene headed toward Brian, and I followed suit. "This little motherfucker is heavy as fuck," Brian complained as Gene grabbed ahold of the man's right arm and the right side of his shirt.

But before they started carrying the body, I said, "Gene said it would make more sense to hide this guy's body rather than try to put him back in the container."

"Where would we hide him?" Brian asked.

"Let's stash his body near the fence at the left exit gate," Gene suggested.

"Nah, let's throw his ass in the water. The port police or US Customs really wouldn't find him there," I interjected. I was confident that my plan was solid, so there was no need to follow up with another idea.

"Yeah, that's a damn good idea," Gene said.

"Yeah, I like that too. So come on and let's get this thing done," Brian said as he looked at Gene and me.

"I ain't gonna be able to go," I said. "You know I've been away from the ship long enough and I know the timekeepers are looking for me and this fucking straddle machine."

"A'ight, well, you go back to the ship and Brian and I will handle this," Gene insisted.

"Whatcha want me to say to Edward if he asks me about the Asian people?"

"Tell 'em two jumped out of the container and we caught 'em and made them get back in it," Brian instructed.

"You don't think we need to tell him about the one that died and the other one that got away?" I need clarity.

"No. Just tell him two got out and we caught them and

made them crawl back inside the container," Brian said adamantly.

"All right," I said, and then I turned my back to them and crawled my ass right back inside of my machine. I powered up the machine again, and while I made my way back to the pier, I watched Brian and Gene tote the Asian guy's body away from the train tracks. I couldn't believe how we fucked up this lucrative job. I just hoped none of this backfired on us because if it did, I knew we would never get another job like this. I could also envision the port police and US Customs watching us like a hawk every day from this day forward. And if that happened, we'd never be able to steal regular shit like TVs out of the containers ever again.

18

DAWN

Lying in bed trying to figure out what was going on with Reese down at the terminal was unbearable to think about. I wondered if something had gone wrong. What if some of the immigrants were dead? Or worse, what if he got caught and was too afraid to tell me? Okay, maybe he didn't get caught, because my father would be the first one to find out and then I would be the second. My father would break his fucking neck to call and tell me Reese was in trouble. He'd even go as far as to drive over here to tell me what happened, so he could rub it in my face and say I told you so.

My family was brutal when it came to Reese. They never made it a secret that they hated him. At one point, my father asked me to choose between Reese and my family. Luckily my mother stepped in and asked my father to drop it. She later told me why she did it. She said she knew I would've chosen Reese over them. She also said that she knew the day I had fallen in love with Reese. She said I had that same sparkle in my eyes that she'd had when she fell in love with my father. My mother was a very understanding woman. I just wished that my father would be the same. I know that's wishful thinking. But who knows, maybe one day he will come around. I guess, whenever the stars aligned in the sky, so would the ill feelings my dad had toward Reese. But until then, I wouldn't hold my breath.

While I stared up at the ceiling of my bedroom, I also thought about the possibility that Reese would change after we have a baby. I mean, relationships change all the time for the better when a newborn baby comes into the mix. So maybe this could happen for us, because I get sick and tired of playing stepmommy to his other kids. They very seldom listen to me. And I know it's coming from his baby mama, so every time I bring it up to Reese, he always acts like I'm overreacting. As far as I'm concerned, his kids never have to come over here again, because I wanna play mommy to my own kids.

I swear, I hope things will change for the better when I bring a baby into the world. If not, then will I have done all of this for nothing? Only time will tell.

19

REESE

Images of Brian and Gene toting that man's dead body across the train tracks wouldn't leave my mind. I couldn't shake it for nothing in the world. Shit! What if they couldn't hide the body? Or what if someone found the other guy who ran away, and he blew our entire plan? Damn, shit would get so chaotic that I wouldn't know whether to leave my job, get fired, or be arrested. Hopefully none of that happened. We get the rest of our money and Mr. Ming gets his containers and everybody is good. "God, please don't let anything else happen. I swear, I will stop gambling and be a better husband to Dawn if you help us with this situation," I prayed, and then I slowly drifted off to looking at the other containers that I needed to move to other locations in the terminal.

Not too long after I pulled back up to my location on the pier, I saw Edward give me a stern stare. He knew I fucked up. I knew that I was about to get chewed out. But I would be the first to tell him that I wasn't the one that fucked this job up. I did what I was supposed to do. It wasn't my fault that those fucking immigrants wanted to get out of that container. Shit! If I had to be in there for close to thirty days, I probably would've done the same damn thing. The weather here was kind of mild, so I knew that it was ten times as hot in that fucking metal box. I didn't put those motherfuckers in there and I didn't let them out. Blame somebody else for that bullshit! Not me, because I had my own set of problems.

Toward the end of the job Gene and Brian finally showed back up to the pier. They both gave me a look that indicated things weren't good with them. I couldn't get out of the straddle carrier to find out what happened since I'd last seen them. So I did one better and called Brian from my cell phone. "What's wrong now?" I asked him as soon as he breathed into the phone.

"We found somewhere to put him, but it won't be long before someone finds him," Brian explained.

"Where did you put him?"

"In an old container near the west side of the pier."

"Did y'all walk back by the train cars?"

"Yeah."

"Did you hear any noise coming from them?"

"No. They were quiet."

"Think any more of them escaped after we left?"

"If they did, then they would've run into me and Gene."

"Have y'all decided if y'all are going to tell Edward what happened?"

"Yeah, Gene said we can't leave him in the dark about it. So, we're gonna tell him right after we clock out."

"A'ight. Well, I'll get with you guys then too," I said.

After I put my cell phone away, I looked back up at Edward in his crane machine. He wasn't looking my way, but I knew he wondered what had gone wrong. I also knew that he was going to be pissed when he found out that Brian killed one of the people. What he was going to do about it, I didn't know. But I knew he would flip the fuck out. Brian might not get any more money because of it. Who knows, all of us might not get the rest of our money.

It depended on what went down when Edward had the meeting with Mr. Que Ming. He could easily tell Ed to get lost because two of his people ran off. Ed would be a fool to tell Que Ming that one of his colleagues killed a guy. Who knew what Mr. Ming would do then? I just knew it wouldn't end well, so I would make sure that I was nowhere around when this meeting took place.

We got those containers on the train in good timing, but our overall job that we get a check from ended a few hours later. I couldn't wait to crawl out of the machine and go home. Tonight was one helluva night.

Edward parked his machine while we did the same. Normally at the end of our shifts, we'd lock up our machines and then we'd head to the timekeeper's office to clock out. Tonight was no different. But instead of huddling around the main building, Edward instructed all of us to meet him by his truck. I knew right off the bat why he wanted us to leave the terminal. Edward was one paranoid cat. He never liked talking where there were cameras because he figured if you have a camera, then there's a huge chance that there's a microphone not too far away. So I didn't question his motives; I did what he asked and we all headed toward his SUV.

"So, tell me what happened," he started off as he looked at every one of our faces. His facial expression was stern; the intimidation was in full effect.

I spoke first so I could use Brian as a way to get the heat off me. "We fucked up. The whole plan we had fell apart."

"What's the status of the other one?" Edward wanted to know.

I looked over at Brian, hoping he would take over the conversation, but he didn't. So I said, "Well, Brian ran after him, so I can't tell you what happened with that."

After I threw Brian under the bus he gritted his teeth at me. Everyone saw him too. But Edward interrupted the hard stare Brian gave me. "So what's up with the guy you went after, Brian?" he asked.

Brian hesitated and then he mumbled, "He's dead."

"He's what?" Edward took a step closer to him. Todd stood there in disbelief.

"He's dead," he repeated. This time it was audible.

"How the fuck is he dead?" Edward roared, but it was only loud enough for us to hear.

"Yeah, how is he dead? What happened?" Todd asked Brian.

"Well, when I caught him, I tried dragging him back to the container, but he started fighting me. So the only way I could restrain him was with a chokehold. But I guess I choked him too hard, and when he stopped kicking and fighting me back, I thought he had calmed down, but he was dead."

"Where is his body now?" Edward asked.

"Gene helped me hide it in one of those old abandoned containers near the west gate."

"Fuck! This can't be happening right now," Edward said as he turned his back to us and walked a couple of feet away. He took off his fitted ball cap and massaged his bald head with his right hand. Then he kicked a small rock that was a few feet away from him.

When he finally turned back around to face us, he placed his ball cap back on his head and said, "You know this changes things, right?"

"It changes how?" Gene spoke up.

"That fucking man is expecting twenty-five people in each container. So the fact that we're delivering one short of what he's expecting isn't going to fly right with him. And to make matters worse, the fact that the missing man is dead is going to be impossible to explain to him."

"Don't tell 'im. Just act like you didn't know he escaped," Brian suggested.

Edward stood there like he was in deep thought. He

stood there for a few seconds and then he finally opened his mouth. "Yes, that's exactly what I am going to do. I'm gonna see him tomorrow, and if he mentions that his cargo is one person short, I'm gonna act like I know nothing about it."

I nodded my head as if to say I agreed with that plan. Gene and Todd nodded their heads too. "Yeah, that's a good idea," Todd said.

"So, what time are you supposed to meet him?" I wanted to know. I had plans for my money, so I couldn't wait to get the rest of it in my hands.

"He told me to stop by his restaurant around the same time we went the first time," Edward told us.

"Is that when he's going to give you the rest of the money?" Brian asked.

"Yep, that's when we get our final payment. He also said that he might wanna use us again. But after what happened with this one guy, I'm not sure if we should do it," Edward pointed out.

"That was just a small thing. At least next time, we'll know how to handle this type of situation if it ever arises," Brian said.

"Let's just get our money first and then we can talk about doing another job later," I said. Thinking ahead wasn't something I did. I learned a long time ago that it's not wise to count your chickens before they hatch.

"You know you're gonna have to move that body again, right?" Edward said while he looked at Brian.

"Move it where?" Brian replied. He seemed irritated by the mere thought of it.

"Off this terminal."

"And take him where?"

"I'm not sure. But we're gonna have to figure it out before we come back to work tomorrow. His body has got to be moved when it gets dark. If that means we have to come into work earlier than usual, then that's what we're gonna have to do. We can't afford to have US Customs breathing down everyone's neck. We got ourselves into this shit, so now we've got to clean up our mess." Edward drilled us like we were his little fucking soldiers.

After he gave us his final lecture we parted ways. I couldn't wait to get home. That seemed like the best place in the whole wide world right now. I needed to unwind and think about our next move. No more fuck-ups!

20

DAWN

When I heard Reese open the front door and walk into the house, I immediately looked at the alarm clock on the nightstand. It was five minutes until six a.m. Reese always came home this time of the morning. Even if I didn't have clock, I could tell the time by his actions, whether it be him coming in from working the night shift or him taking a shower in the afternoon before he returned to work.

Normally I'd wait for him to join me in the bedroom, but I felt like he was going to take too long so I crawled out of bed and met him down in the kitchen. I found him standing by the sink drinking a glass of orange juice. He winked at me as I approached him.

"What's up with the wink? Feel guilty or something?" I asked him, trying to sound tough.

"No, I am not feeling guilty about anything. I'm just happy to see you," he told me, and then he took another gulp of his orange juice.

"How was work? You sounded really freaked out when I last talked to you."

"Things got off to a rocky start, but we were able to get it under control, so everything is good now," he explained. He swallowed what was left in the glass.

"Well, since everything went well, let me see the rest of this money," I said as I held my hands out in front of him.

"We don't get the rest of it until later today. Edward said he's supposed to meet the guy around noon and that's when he'll get the money."

"Well, when you get it, don't go and blow it up on a fucking gambling table." I spat. I knew what he was planning to do with the money. I knew him like a fucking book. He figured that since he gave me the whole $15,000 from his first job, that he could do whatever he wanted with the money from this second job. But not on my watch. He was going to put some of that money away for a rainy day.

"I won't. I'm gonna handle my business with the money. I promise, okay?"

"Okay," I replied, giving him the biggest smile I could muster up. But then I thought about the car I had seen a few hours earlier parked outside. I felt like, since he wanted to clear the air about all the wrong he's done to me, he needed to fess up to that stalker that was posted up in her car watching our house.

"Since you're in the mood to be honest right now, when I told you that someone was sitting in their car watching our house, did you know who I was talking about? Or do you have an idea who it was?"

"No, I didn't."

"Come on, Reese, you're supposed to be honest. I won't be mad at you," I assured him.

"Baby, I swear I don't know who that could've been. That's why I said that they were probably watching one of our neighbors' houses."

"So, it wasn't one of your side bitches?"

"Dawn, I don't have any side bitches. You're the only woman in my life. And I don't want it any other way," he said, looking directly into my eyes. I knew when Reese was lying, and tonight he seemed sincere. So, if he says that that person had to be watching one of our neighbors' houses, then that was what it was.

He changed the subject. "So, what time you gotta be at work today?"

"I'm going in by eight o'clock. We've got a meeting with two of the top administrators, the head terminal manager, and the vice president of the local union. I heard the meeting might last for hours. I hope not, because I'm trying to get off work early today. My mama wants me to go to her doctor's appointment later. She thinks the doctor changed her blood pressure medicine without her knowledge, so she wants me to go with her."

"And what are you supposed to do? You can't make that doctor do something that he doesn't want to do."

"I told her the same thing. But she wouldn't listen. So, I have no other choice but to go with her."

"Why doesn't your sister go with her? I mean, it's not like she has a damn job," Reese commented sarcastically.

"My mom just prefers me. I'm more attentive with her. And she likes that."

"Well, I can't argue with you about that."

"Call me the poster child for the most beloved daughter in the world," I said and chuckled.

"The most beloved wife too." Reese smiled and put the empty glass in the sink.

"Kiss me right here," I told him as I pointed to my right cheek.

He leaned over and kissed me on the cheek and then he smacked me on the butt. "I'm out of here," he said.

"Where are you going?"

"To sleep," he replied, and then he left the kitchen.

21

REESE

Hours later, I was awakened by the constant ringing of my cell phone. I answered the call on the fifth ring. "Hello," I said, still somewhat groggy. I was so out of it that I didn't even look at the caller ID.

"Reese, are you still asleep?" I heard a familiar voice say.

"Yeah," I mumbled.

"Look, you gotta get up. I need you to hear what I'm about to tell you." The voice became more familiar. And then it clicked in my head that it was my wife, Dawn, so I opened my eyes wide enough to let the light in the bedroom wake me up.

"I'm up," I assured her.

"Baby, the port police and US Customs are crawling all over this place because a dead body was found inside of one of the old containers by the west gate."

Hearing that the Asian man's body had been found shook me to the core. I instantly sat straight up. The tiredness I felt when I answered my cell phone disappeared at that very moment. I need to get Brian and Edward on the phone ASAP.

"Was it a white man? Black man? Or what?" I asked, even though I already knew the answer. I just didn't want to jump the gun and give her some information that she wouldn't be able to handle.

"Reese, don't play games with me. You know the guy was Asian. Now tell me what's going on and why that man was dead," she whispered angrily.

"Baby, I don't know why that man is dead. I don't even know who you're talking about. After the guys and I moved the two containers to the railroad cars, we did our other job and that was it." I tried to explain, but she wasn't buying it.

"Reese, I am not stupid. You told me you guys were going to get paid to move the containers with Asian people inside of them. So, tell me what's going on before something happens and I can't defend you."

"Dawn, I swear I have nothing to do with that dead guy. But tell me who found him."

"Two of the terminal inspectors. They were making their rounds around the terminal and that's when they ran across the container. My supervisor just told me that the port police and US Customs are starting a homicide investigation and everyone that worked last night will be interviewed."

"Well, when they come at me, I'm gonna tell them that I don't know shit."

"Regardless if you know something or not, they're coming for you and whoever else was working last night, so you better be prepared," she warned me.

"A'ight, well, let me get off this phone so I can get up and take a shower," I told her. But in reality, I was trying to get her off the phone so I could call Edward. It was almost one p.m., so there was no question in my mind that Edward had seen Mr. Ming by now.

Feeling a thick cloud of anxiety looming over my head, it took me three tries to dial Edward's correct cell phone number. And when he answered I went straight into question mode. "Hey, Ed, what's up?" I started off, trying to get a feel for the mood he was in.

"Well, I just left the big man's restaurant. So, we're good as far as the money is concerned," Edward explained.

"Did you tell 'im about the dead guy?"

"Of course I didn't. As far as he knows, everything is intact. Apparently, he had one of his people go out to the terminal to take pictures of the containers and text him copies. So, as far as I'm concerned, that guy that was accidently killed by Brian escaped on his own and somehow got murdered in the process. And that's the story I'm sticking to."

"So, have you talked to anyone? Todd, Brian, or Gene?"

"No, but why you ask?"

"I take it that you haven't been to the terminal?"

"No, why? Is there something wrong?" he asked me.

"Dawn just called me and told me that two of the terminal inspectors found that Asian guy's body not too long ago."

"Reese, please tell me that you're pulling my leg."

"If I said that, then I'd be lying. But my wife just called me and told me that the guy's body was discovered and now US Customs and the port police are starting an investigation. She also said that they're going to interview every fucking person that worked the night shift."

"Are you fucking kidding me right now!" Edward barked. "This is some bullshit!" he continued as he spewed out over a dozen words of profanity. I could tell that he was about to come apart at the seams and spaz the hell out. But I needed to keep him levelheaded so we could figure this thing out.

"Whatcha think we should do?" I asked Ed. I needed some direction concerning this matter. And since he'd been working at this terminal the longest, I was positive that he'd come up with a plan to stay clear of the cops. It didn't matter if it was US Customs or the port police because at the end of the day, they both had the authority to lock our asses up. Simple as that.

"Look, you're gonna have to let me call you back," Ed told me, and then he abruptly disconnected our call.

I sat in the bed not knowing what to do. One part of me wanted to quit my job and never step foot on the terminal again. But then the other part of me wanted to say *fuck it* and deal with the situation head-on. I mean, it's not like I was the one that killed the guy. Brian did it. So, he alone should take the fall for it.

I knew one thing for sure, Dawn was right when she told me to stay clear of that job. But no, I let greed get in the way and cloud my judgment. I just hoped that the officers would close the case when they realized he was an immigrant with no name or legal papers. I mean, why do anything else? It was his fault that he got into that container. Plus, I'm sure he knew that this journey to the US would be shaky. I'm sure he'd heard other stories about immigrants losing their lives trying to sneak into our country. Why should this time be any different? I say dump his fucking body in the ocean and call it a day's work. Because if the cops did a full-scale investigation, they were gonna end up spending a lot of people's tax dollars. And considering where our economy is now, that would be a bad move. My only hope was that this thing didn't blow all out of proportion, because if it did, Edward, Brian, and the rest of us would be traveling up shit creek without a fucking paddle.

After getting that initial call from Dawn and then having that talk with Ed, I couldn't go back to sleep. Instead, I got out of bed and hopped in the shower. I wasn't in there long because I wanted to fix myself a cup of hot tea. While I was preparing my cup, I heard my cell phone ring in the bedroom. I dashed out of the kitchen to answer it. "Hello," I said, putting the call on speakerphone.

"Yo, Reese, I just got off the phone with Ed. He told me

that we got a problem and that I needed to call you," Brian said.

"Did he tell you anything else?" I needed to know how to break the news to him and if I needed to start from ground zero.

"No. Why?" Brian replied.

I sighed heavily and said, "Look, dude, I just got a call from my wife saying that two of the inspectors found that Asian man's body about two hours ago. And that they're going to start a homicide investigation."

"Are you fucking serious?" Brian sounded panicked.

"Yeah, I am. I just hung up with her not even an hour ago."

"Get the fuck out of here. This can't really be happening right now."

"Well it is, so get with Ed and Gene so y'all can figure out how you're going to handle this situation."

"Whatcha mean, so *y'all* can figure out? You're as involved as the rest of us. I mean, if you had done your fucking part, I wouldn't have had to come and help you catch those motherfuckers in the first place."

"So now it's my fault that the man is dead?" I roared.

"It's as much your fault as everybody else's."

"Nigga, you gotta be out of your fucking mind to say some dumb shit like that. So, on that note, I'm gonna have to talk to you later." I ended the call because this nigga was getting me angrier and angrier by the second. I mean, how dare he say that I was involved with that man's death? I was nowhere near Brian when he choked the life out of him. So, he can take that sob-ass story somewhere else, because I ain't trying to hear it. Not now. Not ever.

Immediately after I hung up on Brian, I fixed my cup of tea and carried it back to my bedroom. I set the cup down on the nightstand and thought about the conversation I had just had with Brian. Was he fucking serious when he said that I was to blame for that guy's murder too? He was the one who strangled the guy, not me. He and Gene disposed of the body, not me. So, why the fuck must I go down with those motherfuckers? I needed to figure out an exit plan.

22

DAWN

I sat at my desk while my coworkers whispered and gossiped about the dead Asian guy. My supervisor, Mrs. Powell, was having a field day with this newfound information. Her cubicle was about thirty-five feet away from me, but I could hear her like she was standing next to me. I heard her talking to someone on the phone.

"I just got off the phone with Linda over there at the main building, and she said that port police and Customs are all over this place. She also told me that those boys in uniform aren't gonna stop this investigation until they find the culprit that did it," I heard Mrs. Powell say. Judging by her responses, there was no doubt in my mind that she was talking to someone in one of the office buildings on this terminal. Mrs. Powell talked for about fifteen minutes. But one thing she said really stuck in my head. So I paid close attention to every word she uttered. "Linda said right after the inspectors found the Asian guy's body, they went on a full-scale search and found two containers on the railroad cars with at least thirty to forty people in each one. And she also said that out of that number, a total of six people were found dead. They think they died because of the conditions in the containers. Can you imagine lying in that small metal box with limited oxygen and food? And then to have to watch people around you die? I swear, this whole thing is a tragedy," she continued, and then she fell silent.

I couldn't tell if I was about to hyperventilate or pass out altogether. Finding out that Customs had found all the freaking Asian immigrants that my husband had been paid to help transport made me sick to my stomach. I fucking told him not to get involved with this whole thing, but he wouldn't listen. And now he might get arrested for his role in this human trafficking conspiracy. What the fuck was I going to do now? I mean, it wasn't like I was going to be able to help him. Now that government officers were involved with this investigation, my hands were tied. I couldn't even get my dad to call in a favor. This whole situation was beyond my control, so I guess all I could do was sit back and watch everything as it unfolded.

When Mrs. Powell finally got off the phone, I got up from my chair and walked over to her cubicle so I could get all the information she knew about the investigation. "So, I hear that Customs just found two containers with people from another country inside of them," I said, acting like I knew what was really going on.

"Yes, my friend Linda from the administration building overheard Customs agents talking to the head captain of port police. She said she heard them say that there were about eighty people divided between the two containers, and six of them were dead."

"Wow! That's so unfortunate. I hope there weren't any children in there," I said, trying to get Mrs. Powell to give me everything she knew.

"No, I'm sure there weren't any children. If there were, she would've told me."

"I wonder how long they were in there?"

"They say the containers were picked up from China. And that trip from there to here took twenty-seven days," Mrs. Powell said.

"Who could possibly sit in that thing for almost thirty days? I mean, wouldn't they have to eat, sleep, and use the bathroom in that thing?"

"Yes," she said.

I shook my head with disgust while I tried to picture the living conditions in those containers. And now that I thought about it more, I felt really fucked up that I used some of the money that was paid to Reese for his involvement. "Did your friend Linda tell you what Customs is going to do with the people that are still alive?"

"No, she didn't. But I'm sure the agents are going to transport those people to a hospital, where a quarantine area will be set up as a precaution just in case any of them are infected with any diseases."

"What about the people who died?"

"I'm not sure how the agents will deal with that situation. But I'm sure they've got a plan in motion."

"Think any of the longshoremen or merchant seamen were involved?" I asked her, trying to sound naïve. I felt like the only way she'd feed me all the information I needed was by acting like I didn't know anything, so that's what I did.

"Of course I do. This same situation happened a little over ten years ago. I don't know if you were working here or not, but US Immigration and Customs Enforcement agents got a tip that forty-six women and three little girls were coming into port from one of the third-world countries. Well, when the ship pulled up, the agents surrounded it and intercepted the delivery of those women, minus two of the kids that died from dehydration and hypothermia. And when they started their investigation, four longshoremen and three merchant mariners got arrested for aiding and abetting illegal immigrants, conspiracy to commit human trafficking, and manslaughter."

"Manslaughter!" I blurted out. I was shocked by the charges that those men had gotten for the role they played. The thought of Reese getting arrested and charged with human trafficking and manslaughter made my heart fall to the pit of my stomach. My legs started buckling underneath me. I knew I would fall to the floor if I didn't hurry up and take a seat somewhere, so I asked Mrs. Powell to excuse me and I scurried away.

"Are you okay?" I heard her ask me while I headed toward my cubicle.

"Yes, I'm fine. I just need to sit down for a minute. My head started spinning, so I just wanna take a seat for a moment."

"Okay. I'm here if you need me," she said.

"Thanks."

I took a seat in my chair and laid my head down on my desk for a few minutes. I closed my eyes for a bit so I could feel like I was hiding in a dark closet. I needed to feel like I was in that small space hiding from the world, and that included Reese. I swear, for the life of me, I couldn't figure out why I didn't stop him from getting involved with this mess before he did the first job. What was I going to do now?

I believe I sat at my desk for ten minutes trying to decide whether or not I should call Reese and fill him in on what Mrs. Powell just laid on me. One part of me wanted to separate myself from this whole saga, but then again, I knew in my heart of hearts that I couldn't sit around and not warn him about what was going to happen. I eventually grabbed my cell phone and walked away from my cubicle. I headed outside and walked over to the smoking stand. Thankfully no one was around smoking a cigarette, so I had total privacy to talk to Reese. After I dialed his number I sat on a bench and waited for him to answer my call.

"Hello," he finally answered.

"We've got to talk."

"I hope you're not calling me with any more bad news," he said.

"Well, I'm sorry, but that's exactly what I'm about to do," I spat. I mean, how dare he act like I'm the bearer of bad news? The only reason I'm calling his dumb ass in the first place is because I don't want him walking around here blind. But this is the thanks I get.

He let out a long sigh. "What happened now?"

"I just heard that as soon as the man's body was discovered, ICE agents ordered a thorough search of the terminal and found over fifty fucking people hiding inside two containers. And that's not all. I also heard that six of them died inside it, and now this thing has turned into a six-time murder investigation."

"Oh my God! No, this can't be happening!" Reese yelled. It sounded like he was about to have a nervous breakdown.

I tried to console him as much as I could. "Baby, please stay calm. Everything is going to be fine," I told him, even though I knew what I was saying wasn't true. Reese was about to be in some very hot water, and I didn't think anyone was going to help him.

"How the fuck can I calm down? Do you know what you're saying? You want me to calm down after hearing that Customs has found six more bodies? My fucking life is over. The feds are going to come looking for me and probably lock my ass up for the rest of my life. Fuck! Fuck! Fuck!" he screamed.

I pulled my phone away from my ear a little bit so his yelling wouldn't damage my eardrums. I couldn't bear it when he started sobbing. I'd never heard Reese cry before. He'd always projected himself as a strong man. Not afraid of anything or anyone. But today I saw a totally different man. I just hoped that he didn't do anything to hurt himself while I was at work. "Baby, I'm gonna come home, so stay there," I told him, while I began to have mixed feelings about everything. Dead people! Really? The mere thought of them made me sick to my stomach. I didn't know how I was going to get past this one.

"All right," he said, and he hung up.

I went back to the office and walked over to Mrs. Powell's desk with this lie about me being sick and needing to take off the rest of the day. Thankfully she had no problems with it and let me go. "Hope you feel better," she said.

"I'm gonna try," I replied, and then I left.

23

REESE

What else could go wrong? My role in this human trafficking had gone from bad to worse. It wouldn't take the agents long to figure out who was involved. I needed to figure out how I was going to minimize my role in it. I also needed to consider going to the agents and telling them what they needed to know so I could work out a deal with them. I'd seen shit like this all the time on cop shows. The first one to go to the police always came out on the winning end. They either got short sentences or no sentence at all. So, maybe that needed to be one of my options. I know niggas might end up calling me a snitch, but that was the least of my worries. I just wanted to be on the streets so I could take care of my wife and kids. All that other bullshit ain't even worth my freedom. Now I know people would look at me and say, *Damn, Reese, what about those people that died? Do you even care about them?* And my answer would be, *I didn't tell them to walk into that container. That wasn't my choice so that's not my problem.*

While I sat around and thought about what would be in my best interest, my cell phone started ringing again. I grabbed it from my bed and noticed that it was Edward calling me. I started not to answer, but then I decided against it. I figured maybe he knew how we were gonna get out of this jam we were in. "What's up?" I said calmly. I didn't want to give him the impression that I was alarmed about this situation.

"Did you hear that they found the containers?"

"Yeah, Dawn just called me and told me."

"Do you know what that means?" Edward asked me.

"Yeah."

"Tell me what it means," Edward instructed me. But I was in no mood to answer questions. I wanted him to get to the fucking point of this conversation.

"It means that the investigation is going to be massive. And we might be getting fired and sent to jail when this is all over," I finally answered.

"Bingo. I'm glad we're on the same page," he replied sarcastically.

"So, have you figured out what we're gonna do?"

"All I can tell you to do is call your lawyer."

"But I don't have one."

"Then you better take this money I owe you and use it to get you one."

"That's it? The only advice you got for me is for me to call a lawyer? Come on now, Ed, we're about to be in some major shit. And all you want me to do is lawyer up? That's fucked up, don't you think?" I snapped. I was getting annoyed by his lack of concern. I didn't run down behind him and beg him for this gig. He recruited me for the job, so he was gonna have to come up with something better. "Look, Ed, I've got mad respect for you, but you're gonna have to come up with a better plan than the one you're laying down in front of me now."

"You better appreciate the fact that I'm gonna pay you the rest of the money that's owed to you. Do you know how many people get robbed in situations like this?"

"I don't care about other people. I thought you and I had an understanding."

"We did. But now things are different. And if you want some advice, call in sick today and lawyer up like I told you to."

"When are you gonna give me the rest of my money?"

"Meet me at Pop's Diner in an hour and I'll give it to you then."

"What about Gene and Todd?"

"What about them?"

"Are they gonna be there too?"

"See, kid, you worry too much about everyone else. Concentrate on your own affairs and you'll be okay."

"Yeah, whatever," I said, and then I hung up.

I swear I can't believe how this nigga just changed on me like that. He used to be like a father figure to me. He went from treating me like his son to treating me like a fucking has-been in the streets. Now how am I supposed to handle this situation? He basically just told me to lawyer up, which means that I should look out for myself because he was going to do the same. But it puzzled me how he changed overnight. Was he like this a few years ago when I first started doing little theft jobs with him? Or had this incident changed him? I might not know the answer that question, but I did know that I was leaning toward going to the agents and telling them everything I knew. The only way I'd change my mind was if Brian took charge and acted like he worked alone. I knew it would be a hard sell to US Customs agents, but what other information did they have to go on?

After I hung up with Edward I called my union manager, Chris Dalton, and told him that I wasn't feeling good so I wouldn't be coming in today. "What's going on? You never call off work," he said.

"I know. But I think I caught the flu bug from my wife,

and now I'm at home trying to nurse myself back to good health," I lied.

"Whatever it is, I hope you feel better by tomorrow," he replied. "Oh, wait, you were working last night, right?"

"Yeah, why?" I asked, even though I knew where this conversation was going.

"US Custom agents and immigration officials found dozens of stowaways in two containers that were taken off a Maersk ship last night. And seven of them were dead. Everyone around here is calling it DOA, dead on arrival."

"That's fucked up. So, what are they going to do with the other people?"

"They transported them over to a nearby hospital. The ones that are dead will end up at the city morgue. And if no one comes to claim their bodies, most likely their bodies will end up in someone's research facility."

"What's the word around there? Anyone got in trouble for it?"

"Agents from every field office in DC are here conducting interviews. I'm sure they'll be coming in here to talk to me and the other gentlemen that are on the clock."

"Damn! That's some weird shit. I can't believe that people would live in those small-ass metal boxes."

"Those metal boxes are bigger than most of the houses those immigrants lived in back in their country."

"Yeah, I guess you're right," I said. "Well, let me get off this phone so I can get this hot tea in my system. And I'll give you a call tomorrow if I haven't kicked this sickness," I continued.

"Sure thing," Chris said, and then we hung up. I set my cell phone down and stood. I knew I needed to get dressed so I could meet Edward and get the rest of my money. Pop's Diner was only a twelve-minute drive from my house. I figured if I got dressed and left in the next twenty minutes, I'd arrive there before him. So that's what I did.

24

DAWN

When I got home from work I saw Reese getting in his car to leave. I grabbed my purse and scurried out of my car. I approached the driver's window and leaned down to ask him where he was going.

"I've gotta meet Edward at Pop's Diner. He's gonna give me my money."

"Well, you and I need to talk, so I'm going with you." I walked around the front of the car. After I climbed in the passenger side, Reese backed out of the driveway and headed in the direction of the diner.

A quarter of a mile into the drive, I broke the ice and started talking about the shit that was going on down at the Norfolk International Terminal. "Have you thought about what you're going to do?" I asked him.

"No, I haven't. I did call the union manager, Chris, and told him I wouldn't be coming in."

"Why would you do that? Now the other longshoremen are going to think you've got something to hide," I spat. Other than taking on that human trafficking job, I felt like this was the stupidest thing he could've done.

"They aren't going to think anything. I told Chris I was

sick and that I was going to call him tomorrow if I don't feel any better. He said okay."

"Who cares what he says! He's a nobody at the terminal. The other workers run all over top of him. He has no backbone whatsoever."

"Look, Dawn, just calm down. Everything will work out."

"Easy for you to say. You don't have everybody breathing down your neck and judging everything you do. Do you know that my father has some of the guys down at the terminal watching you?"

"Who cares! And anyway, that's old news."

"I care. I get tired of going to visit my family and your name always comes up. I'm tired of defending everything you do!"

"Well, stop defending me."

"But you're my husband! That's what I'm supposed to do."

"So then, why are you complaining about it?"

"Because for once I wanna be able to brag about what a great husband you are and how excited I am that we're finally having a baby together."

"Can we please talk about this shit later?" he snapped.

I could tell that he was irritated by me backing him into a corner. But how else would we resolve our issues? Every time something comes up, he pushes it under the rug and frankly, I am tired of it. "No, we can't. I'm tired of talking about shit later. We need to deal with this now."

"And how do you propose we do it?" he replied sarcastically.

"Well, first of all, we gotta lay our differences out on the table and then deal with them one at a time."

"Easy for you to say."

"No, it's not easy at all," I said, and then I paused for a second. "Reese, you have no idea how hard it is for me to sit around and watch you create havoc in your life. You didn't have to take on this last job. You were doing all right with the flat-screen TVs and the iPhones. But no, you had to be greedy and take on a job that had serious consequences if you got caught."

"No, I wasn't all right with the fucking TVs and the other stuff, because every time I got rid of the shit and counted up the profit, I only ended up with pennies on the dollar."

"But whose fault is that?"

"Whatcha mean, whose fault is it?"

"Reese, you make over eighty-five thousand dollars a year, and I make over fifty grand, so there's no reason why we should be in debt. And with as long as we've worked at the terminal, we should be sitting on a nice nest egg."

"Blame that on your fertility treatments."

"Are you fucking kidding me right now?" I roared. I wasn't going to back down this time. The fact that he was blaming my fertility treatments for our financial debt had my blood boiling.

"Then what is it?"

"It's your fucking gambling that's got us in the poorhouse."

"Yeah, I knew you were going to say that. But it's all good. I'll wear that one."

"You're fucking right, you're gonna wear it. It's your fault!" I shouted, and then I turned my head to look out the side window.

"If you're gonna fuss all the way to my meeting with Edward, I can turn around and take you back to the house, because I'm not going to be able to deal with you and him at the same time. I swear, my head feels like it's about to burst wide open."

I turned my attention back toward Reese and said, "How fucking convenient!" I rolled my eyes and gritted my teeth at him, then shifted my attention back to whatever I could see out the window. But I really wanted to slap the shit out of him and let him know that I was tired of his bullshit once and for all. Luckily for him, I took the nonviolent approach and counted to ten. Otherwise, I would've caused him to have a car accident.

25

REESE

I was so glad Dawn closed her fucking mouth. I swear, I was two seconds from putting her ass out on the side of the road. Dealing with her mouth and all this shit going on at the terminal was enough to make a nigga commit suicide. I mean, I didn't know how much more of this I could take. I needed somebody to give me a break.

Driving the rest of the way to the diner in silence gave me some time to think about what I was going to tell Edward when I saw him. The bullshit attitude he was giving me over the phone earlier was unacceptable. Hopefully he had calmed down a little and had some useful information to give me about how to handle our situation when the shit hit the fan. If he didn't, then I wasn't sure how this meeting was going to end.

When I arrived at Pop's Diner, I noticed that Edward hadn't gotten there, so I parked my car and waited for him to show up. After sitting there for five minutes, Dawn got restless and decided to go inside. "Want something while I'm in there?" she asked me after she opened the car door.

"No, I'm good," I told her.

Without saying another word, she closed the door and walked away from the car. I watched her as she headed toward the front door of the diner, and all I could think about was how much I'd fucked up her life. She was right, my gambling was the main reason we were in so much fucking debt. I could've manned up and agreed that I was the cause of our money problems, but my pride wouldn't let me. Since I was a child I was always told that I was dumb and I'd never amount to anything. So, to hear the same thing as an adult had further damaged my self-esteem. How could I rebound from years of mental abuse? Was it even possible? I really wanted to know.

Dawn came back from the diner with a bag in her hand. As she walked toward the car, she never looked at me once. I knew then that she was severely angry with me. "Whatcha get?" I asked her, trying to see if she'd even talk to me.

"A slice of key lime pie."

"Oh."

"Want some?" she asked me, pulling the pie out of the bag.

"Nah, I'm good." I wasn't in the mood to eat anything. I just wanted to see Ed, get my money, find out what he was going to do with this situation, and then take my ass home; in that order.

"Are you sure?" she asked me again. This time she was cutting into the slice of pie with a fork.

"Yeah, I'm sure," I assured her, and then I looked down at my wristwatch.

"What time did he say he was going to meet you here?"

"He told me he was going to meet me in an hour. But it's been an hour and fifteen minutes now."

"Call him and see if he's on his way," she suggested in between chews of her food.

"Nah, I'm gonna give him ten more minutes. But if he's not here then, I'll call him."

"Does he know about ICE finding those other people?"

"Yeah, he knows."

"What did he say about it?"

"He didn't have much at all to say."

"What do you mean?"

"He simply told me to take the money he's giving me and hire a lawyer."

Dawn dropped her fork on her lap. "That's it? That's the only fucking advice he had for you?" she snapped.

I nodded.

"That low-down, country-ass nigga! I now know why I never liked him. He's all smiles when he's breaking into those containers and getting his cut. But as soon as it gets hot, he runs out of the kitchen. I swear, when I see him today I am going to have a few choice words for him. Fucking loser!"

I sat there in complete awe, watching my wife spaz out. I rarely saw this side of her. She goes in headfirst and doesn't come up for air until she's done. I smiled at her because it was good seeing her jump to my defense. She would fuss me out when I fucked up, but she'd really go crazy when she found out someone else was trying to play me to the left. I loved the spunk Dawn had about her. She was definitely a winner. I just hoped that I didn't cause her to leave me after all this shit went down.

Dawn finally calmed down and ate the rest of her key lime pie. She and I talked about the different patrons that walked in and out of the diner. She cracked a few jokes here and there. I gave her a half smile sometimes so she would think that she was lightening the mood.

Dawn looked at the clock on the dashboard. "I don't appreciate the fact that that nigga ain't here yet. Got us parked out here like sitting ducks."

I looked at the dashboard too and picked up my cell phone from the cup holder. "Yeah, he is disrespecting the hell out of us right now," I agreed as I dialed his phone number.

"I can't wait to hear his weak-ass explanation as to why he's not here!" Dawn retorted.

I sat there waiting for the phone to ring so I could put the call on speaker, but it didn't ring. Edward's phone went straight to voicemail. "*This is Ed, leave a message at the tone*," the voicemail greeting said. I disconnected the line and dialed Ed's number again. But once again, the call went straight to voicemail.

"Did it go to voicemail again?" Dawn asked.

"Yeah, it did." I hung up and called him for the third time.

"He either has you on his block list or he turned off his phone," she added.

"We might be trying to call each other at the same time," I said, trying to convince myself that this was true. I guess I needed to hear the words out loud. Because in reality, I knew he turned off his phone. But why would he, when he told me to meet him here?

Hoping that Edward would eventually answer my call, I redialed his number again. But like the first four times, it went to voicemail. "Shit! Shit! Shit!" I roared, and slammed my cell phone against the steering wheel. "I swear, if this motherfucker doesn't stop playing games with me, I am going to fuck him up really bad!" I was so angry I felt spit spewing out of my mouth.

"Baby, please calm down!" Dawn said, trying to comfort me. She tried hugging me, but I pushed her arms away. I wasn't in the mood for a hug. I wanted my fucking money and I wanted Ed to tell me how we're going to come out of this thing without any cuts and bruises. But no, that motherfucker wants to have me sitting out here like I'm a fucking joke to him. I swear, when I see that nigga I am going to hurt him really bad. Mark my words on that.

It took me another minute or two to get my mind right,

and when I thought I was stable enough to drive, I put my car in drive and headed back home. Dawn talked most of the way about how I needed to go and pop up at Edward's house and ask for my money. I thought about doing that before she even suggested it, but I hadn't thought through how I was going to address him when I saw him. I was somewhat sketchy on that part, so I said I'll sit on that idea until I plan it out the best possible way.

Hopefully, all of this is was just one big misunderstanding and Edward was on his way to the diner and I'd missed him. Because if it was what I thought it was, it was going to be some people singing and some flowers bringing when I got through with that piece of shit.

26

DAWN

Riding around with Reese, I forgot that I had promised my mother I would take her to her doctor's appointment. So when she called to remind me, I felt like shit when I told her that something came up and that I couldn't go with her.

"What do you mean you can't go? I'm supposed to be at the appointment in the next forty-five minutes," she said, sounding disappointed.

"Mom, I'm sorry. But something came up, so I can't go to your doctor's appointment."

"But you promised."

"Mom, I know I did, but . . ."

Reese said, "Take her. I'll drop you off at the house so you can get your car. That way I can go and take care of some stuff on my own."

"Is that Reese in the background?" my mom asked.

"Yes, Mommy, it's him."

"Is he the reason why you can't take me to my doctor's appointment?"

"No, Mommy, he's not the reason," I said, and then I paused. "Look, I'll be at your house in twenty minutes." I rubbed my right hand across my eyes.

"Are you sure? Because I'll ask your father to do it. Now I'm sure he'll do it, but he's gonna really be upset because I'm asking at the last minute."

"Mommy, don't worry about it. I'm on my way," I assured her.

"All right, well, I'll be waiting."

"Okay. See you in a few minutes."

When Reese dropped me off at the house, I gave him a kiss and got out of his car. I headed straight to my car. Reese sped back off down the road. I'm sure that he was going to pay Edward a visit, I was just not sure how it would end.

It only took me ten minutes to get to my mother's house. I beeped the car horn so she could come outside and get in the car, but my car horn fell on deaf ears. Calling her cell phone was my next option, so I went with it and thankfully it worked. "Mom, I'm outside, so come on before we be late," I told her.

"Okay, I'm on my way outside now," she replied.

I heard some rustling noises and then her phone went silent. She appeared at the front door less than a minute later, and what do you know, my father was on her heels. He got to the car first and opened the passenger door. "Have you heard about the immigrants?"

"Dad, I work there. So of course, I heard about it. Everyone at the terminal is talking about it."

"Honey, move out of the way so I can get in the car," my mom said to my dad as she pulled him back from the door and got inside.

"You know they're saying that some of the guys on the night crew are involved?" my dad continued, but in an indirect way. He was basically telling me what was going on, hoping that I would add what information I knew.

"I heard that too." I was really short.

"Reese works the night shift, right?"

"Dad, what kind of question is that? You already know that Reese works night shift," I replied. I was getting kind of annoyed by his manipulating tactics.

"Honey, leave her alone. We gotta get going before I be late for my appointment," my mother interjected. It seemed like she was more ready to go than I was.

"Oh, stop it, Bonnie, your doctor's office is three blocks away. You'll get there in plenty of time," my father replied sarcastically.

"You know what, Dad? Mom's right. We gotta get out of here."

"All right, I'll leave this alone for right now, but when you bring your mother back home, I want you to come in the house so we can talk."

"All right, Dad, I'll see you when I get back," I told him, even though I had no intention of seeing him, period. After I dropped my mother off, I was going straight home so I could help my husband deal with the bullshit issues he's got. Spouses are supposed to stick together, no matter the cost.

27

REESE

Edward lived in a ranch-style house in Norfolk, off Military Highway. He told me he bought his wife their house back in the late seventies for thirty-two grand and now it's paid off. The outside of the house looks generic. But when you enter his home, this man has all new living room and bedroom furniture, top-of-the line kitchen appliances, granite countertops, hardwood floors, flat-screen TVs, and a high-tech security system. Believe me, if anything new comes from overseas in those metal containers, Edward is going to be the first one to get it. No ifs, ands, or buts about it.

I pulled up curbside to his home and I didn't see his truck, but I saw his wife's car parked in the driveway. I also saw movement from the front seat of the car in my peripheral vision. When I turned my focus in that direction, Edward's wife peered over the roof of her car. "How you doing?" I yelled from my car window.

"I'm fine. Now how can I help you?" the Mrs. Weezy look-alike from the TV series *The Jeffersons* replied.

"I'm looking for your husband. Is he home?"

"No, he's not."

"Do you know when he'll be back?"

"No, I don't. But if you give me your name I will let him know that you stopped by."

"I'm Reese. I've come to a couple of cookouts you guys had." I tried to jog her memory. But it didn't work.

"Okay, Reese, I will let him know that you stopped by," she said.

And just like that, she grabbed the few bags she was retrieving from the car when I first pulled up and walked into her house and closed her front door.

"Fucking bitch!" I mumbled under my breath. I mean, she didn't have to be so nasty. I hadn't done shit to her old ass. Edward was probably fucking around on her so she's taking it out on everybody around her. Oh well, old lady, get over it.

While I drove away from Edward's house, I decided to call Brian to see if he had heard from Ed. He answered my call on the second ring. "What's up?" He got straight to the point. He sounded aggravated too.

"Heard from Ed?"

"Not since earlier. Why?"

"Because he was supposed to meet me at Pop's Diner so he could pay me the rest of my money."

"Call 'im."

"I've tried that. His cell phone keeps going straight to voicemail."

"Maybe he's at the terminal in a blind and his calls aren't going through," Brian offered.

"Trust me, he's not at work. With all the agents running around there, Ed may not show up to work for another week."

"He's not scared of those agents."

"Well, he should be, because shit is about to hit the fan."

"You think Customs is going to come fucking with us behind a boatload of refugees from a third-world country?"

"Of course I do."

"Ed says that he's got a contact person in the Customs office, so we don't have anything to worry about."

"Brian, that's some bullshit and you know it. Let me ask you something."

"What?"

"Did he give you the rest of your money?"

"No. He said he's going to give it to his Customs contact so they can destroy any evidence that would implicate us in their investigation."

"Nigga, you need to wake up!"

"Look, Reese, I don't know what you got going on with Ed. But I'm good on my end. So, let me get off this phone. I gotta get ready so I can head to the terminal."

"You might not want to do that," I warned him.

Brian chuckled. "Man, I am not letting nobody scare me from showing up to work. I've got money to make."

"A'ight, well, you go ahead, dummy. Don't call me when port police lock your ass up!" I said, and then I abruptly ended my call with that fool.

I couldn't believe the conversation I just had with Brian. If he thought that Edward was going to save him then he was sadly mistaken. But what really worked me up was how Brian believed that Edward was going to give his cut of the money to a so-called contact at the Customs office. I wondered if Ed sold that bullshit-ass ticket to Todd and Gene. I guess the only way I was going to find out was if I reached out to those niggas.

I looked into the contacts in my cell phone and found Gene's number first, so I called him. His phone rang seven times, but he didn't answer it. So of course, I called it again, and this time it rang five times and then it went to voicemail. Now the first thing that came to my mind was that either Edward or Brian had told him not to take calls from me. If that was in fact true, then I hoped all three of those niggas burn in hell. Not taking calls from me would be some immature shit. And the thought of it made me sick to my stomach. I hoped that I was not jumping to conclusions. But in the end, everything would be revealed in its own time.

I thought about going back home to clear my head. But something inside me convinced me to reach out to Todd, so I did. Fortunately for me, he answered on the first ring. It was a big relief to hear his voice. "Hello," he said.

"Hey, Todd, this is Reese. Got a minute?"

"Absolutely. Do you know I've been trying to get your new number all morning?"

"Who did you ask?"

"I tried to get Brian and Edward, but they said that they didn't have it."

"Are you fucking wit' me?" I asked him. What he was saying wasn't making sense to me.

"No, I'm not. When Edward called me and told me that Customs found the two containers and that some of the people inside were dead, that fucked me up. So, I was like we all need to get together and try to come up with a plan of attack before the agents get a chance to talk to us one by one. But Ed totally disagreed. He said that I shouldn't worry about being implicated because I didn't get my hands dirty."

"What did he mean by that?"

"He basically said that since I didn't help to bring those containers down from the ship this time around, and didn't help catch the Asians that got out, I don't deserve the rest of the money."

"Oh, that's the grimy-ass shit!"

"Yeah, it is. But you best believe that I am going to make sure that he doesn't get away with this shit!" Todd said.

"I'm wit' you on that. I almost cursed that nigga out. As a matter of fact, he was supposed to meet me at this food place so he could give me the rest of my money. But the motherfucker never showed up. Yo, I promise you, as soon as I see that nigga, I'm gonna fuck him up."

"Whatcha think we should do?"

"Todd, I swear if I had the answer, bro, I would give it to you right now."

"Are you going in to work this evening?"

"Nah. I've already called out."

"Well, I'm gonna go in."

"You sure that's a smart thing to do? You know Customs agents are going to be interviewing everybody that worked last night."

"Remember, Edward said that I didn't have direct contact with the containers last night, so I don't have to worry about falling into the investigators' trap. And besides that, I think he is going to show up to work, so I wanna be front and center when I run into him."

"Well, you be careful. And again, if you see that nigga, call me ASAP."

"Roger that," Todd said, and then we ended the call.

After talking to Todd, I felt like I had accomplished something. Not only did I get more information than I had before, I finally got the feeling that somebody was on my side and that they would fight as hard as I would. Now all I needed to do was get the rest of my money from this nigga so I could pay off my bookies and use the final portion to retain an attorney. I hope I found the right attorney, because if I didn't I was gonna be riding up shit creek without a paddle.

28

DAWN

My mother talked me to death about Reese and what was going on down at the terminal, all the way to her doctor's office and while we waited in the lobby for her name to be called. There was another elderly woman sitting in the waiting area. She was with her husband. He sat in his chair pretending to be asleep, but that didn't stop his wife from running her mouth. And when they called his wife's name, he wouldn't move out of that chair. "Charles, let's go, they're calling my name," she told him after she stood up.

With his eyes still closed and head tilted backwards on the headrest, he said, "Well, go ahead. I'm gonna sit right here until you're finished." And he did not budge.

I laughed because what he displayed was typical behavior from a man. I also laughed because he kind of reminded me of Reese. Just wanted to sit around and not do much when it concerned me. But if someone called him to come gamble or help rip off a container full of laptop computers, he was there.

Before the lady disappeared into one of the examination rooms, I couldn't help but recognize how lonely she looked. I would bet every dime I had that she wasn't happy. I didn't wanna be like that. I wanted to be happy, but the question was, would Reese stop putting himself first and put me in that seat?

Six minutes into our wait time, my mama struck up another conversation about Reese. I instantly became annoyed, but I knew that she was worried about something happening to me if Reese got arrested and lost his job. "Your father thinks Reese is behind that human trafficking scheme," she started off.

"Mommy, I really don't feel like talking about that right now."

"Why don't you wanna talk about it? Talking is a way of therapy."

"I'm not interested in getting therapy right now."

"Then what are you interested in?"

"I'm interested in making sure you see your doctor and go home," I replied sarcastically.

"Dawn, let's not be pessimistic. You know your dad and I are worried about you, especially after finding out what's going on down at the terminal."

"What's going on down at the terminal has nothing to do with Reese."

"Did he tell you that?"

"Of course he did."

"So I guess that means that you thought he had something to do with it too?"

I looked at my mother like she had just lost her damn mind. She just threw a trick question at me and I didn't even see it coming. I now see that my dad's skepticism had been wearing off on her. "What kind of question is that?" I asked her, but at the same time I was trying to come up with a plausible answer.

"You know your father has a lot of friends down at the terminal. If he wants to know something, those friends jump to the occasion."

"That's because they have no freaking life."

"I don't know if I agree with you there, but I do know that when something goes on down at NIT, your father knows about it before the port police find out about it."

"Good for Daddy," I replied sarcastically.

"So, does Reese know who's involved with the scandal?"

"If he does, he didn't tell me," I lied. I couldn't let on that I knew anything about what was going on.

"Well, all of it is a shame. I just can't figure out why people will climb into a metal box like that for twenty to thirty days at a time. Can you imagine how hot it was, and how bad that thing smelled?"

"I'm trying not to," I replied without looking at her. I pretended like I was looking for something in my purse.

"Well, I sure feel sorry for those people that died. They probably starved to death or died of dehydration and a heat stroke."

"They probably did," I continued, as if I wasn't interested in continuing this conversation.

"I asked your father what's gonna happen to the longshoremen after the agents find out who they are. And he said that they're going to jail for sure," my mother said, as she continued to ramble on. I swear, I was two seconds from telling her to shut the fuck up already. I didn't bring her to her doctor's appointment so we could talk about this fucking human trafficking investigation. I only brought her here because I promised her that I'd do so. Anything outside of that was extra shit that I didn't sign up for.

Thankfully the nurse called her to come back to one of the examination rooms, because if I had to sit and listen to her talk about what my father said, I was going to lose my fucking mind.

Back in the examination room, the physician greeted us, took my mother's blood pressure, and then he went through all the formalities concerning my mother's health issues. We sat with the doctor all of seven minutes, and then he sent us on our way. I was quite happy that this visit didn't take as long as I thought it would. "That visit went by fast," I commented as my mother and I exited the main door of the office building.

"Oh no, that's nothing new. He always gets me in and out, that's why he's been my doctor for so long."

"I don't blame you," I said as I escorted her to my car. "So, what are we doing now?" I asked as I opened the car door for her.

"I need to prepare lunch for your father, so take me back home," she instructed me.

I sighed heavily. "As you wish."

Surprisingly, the drive back to my parents' house wasn't as stressful as it was when I first picked my mother up. On the way there, she and I talked about our new president, Donald Trump, global warming, and we even talked about all the reality shows that are on television.

"Do you watch that TV show *Mary Mary?*" my mother asked.

"Yeah, sometimes, why?"

"I think the show is really nice. It's a far cry from that other mess on TV—young girls fighting each other and sleeping around with each other's husbands."

"They say drama sells," I commented.

"I hear your father say all the time that all money isn't good money."

I burst into laughter. "Ma, listen to you sounding all hip and stuff."

She smiled at me. "Honey, I'm just telling you how it is. I may be old, but I've got plenty of sense," she concluded.

When my mother and I arrived back at her house, she begged me to come inside to get a slice of her German chocolate cake. "No, Mommy, I'm good. I had a slice of key lime pie earlier."

"Well, come inside and get a piece to take home with you. Get a slice for Reese too. You know your father and I won't be able to eat all of that cake," she insisted.

"Can you tell me why you baked it in the first place?" I wondered aloud as we sat in the car, parked in the driveway of her house.

"Because it's your father's favorite cake. But you know if he eats it all, his sugar levels could go up," she explained. I swear, she was trying with all her might to get me in her house. But I knew it was a setup. She knew my father was waiting for me to bring her back home so he could grill me about everything going on down at the terminal. He knew I knew what was going on behind the scenes. But he also knew that it didn't matter what he said, that I was not going to sell Reese out.

While I continued to refuse my mother's invite to get a slice of her cake, my fucking sister pulled up alongside me in an all-black Jeep Wrangler my parents bought her. She was such a fucking spoiled-ass brat. It's pathetic at times seeing her use my parents for her personal gain. "Mommy, let me get out of here, because I am not in the mood to be going a second round with your other child," I said, and put the gear in reverse.

"So you're not gonna come say goodbye to your father?"

"Tell 'im for me."

My mother sighed. "All right. But you know he's not going to like this."

"He'll be all right. Trust me," I insisted while I watched her get out of my car.

"You ain't coming in the house?" my sister yelled as she walked around the front of my car. She smiled while she approached the driver's door.

"Yeah, I've got some errands to run," I lied.

"I tried to get her to come in the house and get a couple slices of cake, but she said she didn't want it," my mother interjected after she closed the passenger-side door.

"That's because she's trying not to see Daddy."

"I saw Daddy earlier when I picked Mommy up, thank you," I replied nastily.

"Well, excuse me for breathing."

"You're excused," I said, and started backing my car out of the driveway.

"We know you ain't gotta run no errands. You just trying to rush home to your man," my sister yelled out.

I didn't even dignify her comment with a reply. You piss people off more when you don't feed into their mess.

29

REESE

I was sitting on the sofa watching television and drinking a beer when Dawn walked into the house. She looked flustered when I looked at her. "You all right?" I asked her.

She dropped her purse and car keys on the table by the front door and let out a long sigh. "You will not believe how my parents ambushed me when I pulled up in their driveway," she said as she flopped down on the sofa next to me.

"I can imagine," I told her, and then I turned my attention back to the TV.

"You know he asked me if you were involved in that thing with the Asian people."

"Come on now, that was expected. I would've thought something was wrong with him if he didn't."

"He said that the people down at the terminal are pointing fingers at the niggas you work with."

"And what did you say to him?"

"I told him that I knew for a fact that you weren't involved in that."

"What else did he say?"

"I really don't think it's worth repeating. He has his

opinions about how you should be and how you should treat me, and you have yours. So let's just leave it at that."

"What is your mother saying about all of this?"

"She only repeats what my dad drills in her head. You know whatever my dad says or does, she rides with him."

"Why can't your parents act like my grandmother?"

"And how is that?"

"She knows how to stay out of our fucking business."

"She only does that because you've fed her a bunch of lies about how perfect our lives are."

"That's a damn lie. I don't ever tell her shit. I can't say the same for you."

"Oh, fuck off, Reese! That's a low blow."

"No, what's low is how disrespecting your sister is. I know for a fact that she had something negative to say."

"I didn't see her when I first picked my mother up. I saw her for about two minutes when I was dropping my mother off. Alexia tried to talk slick by saying that I was rushing home to be with you."

"Next time she mentions me, tell her to get her own man and stop worrying about me!" I spat. That fucking bitch always gotta say something negative about me. Dawn doesn't see that her sister wants me. I would bet every dollar in my pocket that if I gave her some dick she'd probably act better. I wouldn't have another problem with her ass.

"Enough about her. Have you talked to Ed yet?"

"Fuck no! I went by his house, but he wasn't there. I saw his wife. She gritted on me when I pulled up and asked for him."

"That's because he probably fed her a bunch of fucking lies."

"Yeah, I felt the vibes."

"Have you talked to anyone else?"

"Yeah, I got in touch with Todd, and you won't believe the shit he told me."

"What did he say?"

"He told me that Ed reached out to him and told him about the investigation, but he told Todd he didn't have anything to worry about because he was busy pulling other containers off the ship and had nothing to do with the immigrants."

"And?"

"And because he didn't have direct contact with the containers, he's not getting the other ten grand that was promised to him."

"Are you serious?"

"As a heart attack."

"That's fucked up!" Dawn commented, nodding her head and looking disgusted.

"Yeah, it is. But don't worry. That motherfucker is going to get his. Watch!"

"Well, since Todd isn't going to be tied to the investigation, what is he going to do?"

"He didn't say. But he did say that he's going to work today. I told him that if he sees Edward, tell him to call me."

"What did he say?"

"He said he would."

"What are you going to do if he calls you?"

"I'm gonna run up on him and whip his ass. And then I'm gonna take my money from him."

"You know if you do it at the terminal, port police is going to lock you up."

"At this point, Dawn, I couldn't care less what those motherfuckers do to me. I just want the chance to beat his ass, and then they can haul me off to jail for however long they want me there."

"I don't like hearing you talk like that. Don't say that. I want you home with me."

"I wanna be home with you too. But shit never works out the way you plan it."

"You're right. But there is also a thing called self-control. We've all been given that power. Whatever action we display creates a reaction."

"Can't argue with that. But I still say that I'm going to fuck that nigga up when I see him, so get my bail money ready," I said and took another sip of my beer.

"I am so glad you got all the money from the first job."

"Yeah, me too."

"What are you going to do with that five thousand Ed already gave you?"

"I'm not sure," I told her and then I fell silent for a moment. "Have you spent all of that fifteen grand I gave you?"

She looked at me suspiciously. "Why you ask?" She knew I had something up my sleeve.

I broke down and told her. "Because I might need some of it back."

"Well, I'm sorry because that's not gonna happen, Reese."

"Why not?"

"Because first of all, I used most of it, and what I have left, I'm gonna use for the rest of our bills."

"Yeah, a'ight. Whatever!" I really wasn't trying to hear anything she had to say. I was going to get some of that money back.

"Be honest and tell me why you want some of that money back."

"You don't need to know all of that," I replied, trying to be evasive.

"What do you mean, I don't need to know all of that? I know about everything else."

"Look, I owe a couple of people money, all right!" I forced myself to say.

"So you got into another card game and lost, huh?"

"Yeah, something like that," I replied nonchalantly.

"Wait! So that's it? You just lost money in a card game and you're okay with it?" she responded. I knew she was about to go on the warpath. But I nipped it right in the bud. I wasn't about to let her stress me out more than I already was.

"Look, Dawn, I don't know what you're trying to get out of this argument you're trying to start, but I refuse to let you take me there. Before I sit here and let you scream on me for money I lost in a poker game last week, I will get up and take my ass in our bedroom and drink my beer in peace. I can't let you stress me out more than I already am. Whatcha trying to do? Make me lose my damn mind?"

"No, I'm not. But when are you gonna start taking responsibility for your actions? If you keep gambling our money away, then we're gonna eventually have to file for bankruptcy."

"But that's what you fail to understand. I'm not gambling up your money, I'm using my own."

"Correction: When we got married, your money went from yours to ours."

"Whatever," I said and stood up from the sofa. I grabbed my beer and made my way right to our bedroom. But as I was leaving the living room, I looked back at her and said, "Don't come following me with that drama."

"It may be drama for you, but it's called *grow the fuck up and handle your business like real men do*," she yelled at me while I continued toward the bedroom.

I didn't say anything in return because I knew that's what she wanted. But I refused to give in to her. My main focus right now was trying to get my money from Ed and hopefully figure out a way to get out of this jam. Anything outside of that, I refused to give it any energy.

30

DAWN

I swear, the way I feel right now, I could call the cops on that ungrateful-ass nigga and not even feel bad about it. How dare he say that the money he makes is his? Whether he realizes it or not, we are in this together. So, if he doesn't get his mind right, then I'm going to give him exactly what he wants. He spends his money on what he wants and I do the same. But the kicker in all of this is, if his silly ass goes to jail and he runs out of the money that he says is his, then too bad, because I'm going to keep all my hard-earned cash in my pocket. Let's see if he likes it then.

A couple of hours went by and the entire house was silent. Reese was in our bedroom doing God knows what, while I was out here in the living room trying to figure out what position I was going to play if Reese and his fucking longshoremen friends got arrested and thrown in jail. I knew my father was going to try to talk me out of sticking by Reese's side. Now if the cops arrested him tonight, then I knew for a fact that I'd leave that nigga out to dry. But if it happened a few days later while I was in better spirits, and he promised to change his ways, then the cops couldn't get shit from me. They wouldn't even get hello.

I thought Reese had taken a nap because I didn't hear any movement in the bedroom while I was lying down on the sofa, until he opened the door to the bedroom and closed the bathroom door. A few minutes later, I heard the toilet flush and then I heard the water from the sink. On his way out of the bathroom I heard him go back into the bedroom and close the door. I started to get up and go to the bedroom to see what he was doing, but then I decided against it. I refused to let him see me sweat. The whole disagreement from earlier did nothing but show me that I was dealing with a selfish nigga, and as long as we were together, things were going to be his way, regardless if I liked it or what. It was a fucked-up arrangement, but hey, what could I do about it?

Tired of lying on the sofa, I got up, went to the kitchen, and made myself a turkey sandwich. It wasn't anything fancy. All I wanted to do was put something in my stomach to stop it from growling.

"Whatcha making?" Reese asked as he walked quietly into the kitchen. I had no idea that he was about to join me, so he damn near gave me a heart attack.

"Wooo, you just scared the shit out of me!" I blurted out after I whirled around from the countertop.

"Sorry about that," he said as he looked over my shoulders. "Oh, you're making a turkey sandwich," he continued, and then he turned around and walked over to the refrigerator.

"Did you get some sleep?"

"Nah, I watched TV the whole time. I even tried to call Ed too. But his phone is still going to voicemail."

"Have you heard back from Todd yet?"

"No. He said he's gonna call me if he runs into Ed," he replied as he grabbed a beer from the refrigerator. After he popped the top he headed to the living room. I heard him sifting through the channels of the television, so I knew he was going to be in there for a while. He finally settled on one of our new channels. I heard the meteorologist giving the forecast for the day, so I kind of tuned it out. I wasn't interested in how warm it was going to be today. I was more concerned about the elephant in the room, and if Reese and I didn't get on the same page about everything going on, then we were gonna eventually fall apart.

After I prepared my sandwich, I opened the utensil drawer to look for a knife to cut it in half when I heard Reese say, "Oh shit! Dawn, come in here and look at this."

I left the utensil drawer open and made a dash into the living room. I stood there next to the sofa that Reese was sitting on and looked at the television. My heart sank in the pit of my stomach when I saw a news crew filming a reporter standing in front of Norfolk International Terminal. Reese turned up the volume so we could hear every word the reporter had to say. *"In breaking news this afternoon, a murder investigation was launched early this morning after seven men were found dead in two shipping containers. This tragedy was a human trafficking deal gone wrong. I spoke with Gerry Mills, who is an area port director, and he says that this type of thing doesn't happen here at NIT. He also said other stowaways in the containers were still alive, and they have been transported to an area hospital. The carrier that transported these Asian immigrants was the Orient Overseas Container Line. There's been some speculation that that vessel was tied to Asian organized crime groups, so the authorities are looking into that theory. Translators were called in to help open dialogue between the authorities and the immigrants and hopefully this will help further the investigation and bring them closer to making arrests. If you have any information concerning this unfortunate tragedy, please call the tip line."*

Reese and I looked at one another after the news journalist ended her story. "Oh my God! They are really making this a murder investigation. But who are they going to charge? The people that own the ship, or what?" I asked him.

Reese buried his face in his hands and held them there for almost ten seconds. I took à seat next to him and put my arms around him. "I hope they aren't trying to charge us with murder," he said.

I tried to console him. "But you didn't murder anyone, so they can't be talking about you."

"What if they are?" he asked, lifting his head and giving me eye contact.

"I guess we're gonna have to get you the best attorney in the area."

"Fuck! Fuck! Fuck!" he roared, and abruptly stood up. "Why is this shit happening to me? I can't get a break to save my fucking life!" His voice boomed as he started pacing the living room floor. I sat there not knowing what to say or do because he was right, he couldn't ever get a break. But what he failed to realize was that he couldn't do the same things and expect different results. I wanted so badly to tell him this, but as soon as I opened my mouth it would start a huge argument.

"I gotta call Todd back," he said and pulled his cell phone from his pocket. I watched him as he dialed Todd's number and put the call on speakerphone. I was shocked when Todd answered Reese's call on the first ring. "Man, you're gonna live a long time. I was just about to call you," I heard him say to Reese.

"Have you seen Ed?"

"No, I don't think he's coming in today. But there's about four news crews in front of the terminal talking about the Asian people Customs found in the containers."

"I just saw that on TV. Is any of the other guys there?"

"No. I haven't seen Brian or Gene. I think they called off too."

"I can't believe this shit is happening. We were all just laughing and high-fiving each other when Ed gave us the five grand, and now none of those niggas will even answer their fucking cell phones."

"Yeah, this shit is fucked up! I told you if I see Ed's punk ass I'm gonna give him a piece of my mind and demand that he gives me my money immediately."

"Has anyone from Customs or Immigration tried to talk to you?" Reese asked him.

"No. But I've been getting a lot of stares from these other guys around here."

"Well, get ready, because if you're getting stares, port police will be asking you to come to their office to talk to you."

"I'm ready. But again, if I see Ed, I'll call you back."

"Thanks, man."

"No problem, Reese. Keep your head up."

"I will," Reese said. He hung up and stuck the phone back into his pocket.

"Whatcha going to do now?"

"I don't know," he replied. He walked back into the kitchen and grabbed another beer from the refrigerator. He pulled the cap off and stood there with his back against the countertop and went into a daydream stance. I couldn't tell you what he was thinking about. But I knew it had something to do with possibly being charged with murder. I felt like even if Edward gave him the other $10,000 he owed Reese, that money still wouldn't be enough for what Reese needed to do. I just hoped that Ed turned out to be a stand-up guy and paid him. I really did.

31

REESE

Those motherfuckers are really going to try to lock my ass up. Is it lawful to charge someone for a murder when they didn't kill someone? This is total bullshit, and I refuse to go down by myself because I didn't shoot or stab anyone. So why try to lock me up forever when my only job was to transport two containers from one side of the pier to the railroad cars not even five hundred yards from the ship? This whole thing is totally fucked up, and I can't let it go down like that.

"Whatcha thinking about, baby?" Dawn asked me from where she was sitting on the sofa.

"I think I might need to go and talk to the Customs agents and tell them what really happened," I replied, watching her to see if her facial expression would change.

"Are you saying this because you're afraid that after they find out that you were involved they may try to give you a lot of time?" she wanted to know.

I hunched my shoulders. "I think I will go to them and tell them that I didn't know that people were inside of the containers and that I was only transporting the containers because I was told to do it."

"Do you think they will believe you?"

"If I sound convincing enough, they probably will. I mean, I see it on TV all the time when cops offer people deals if they help them with their investigation. And sometimes those people don't even go to jail."

"If you decide to do that, don't you think it would be better if you get an attorney to go with you?"

"I don't need a lawyer to go with me to talk to the cops. That would be a waste of money. If that's the case, then why talk to the cops in the first place? I think the only way I would need a lawyer is if the cops don't wanna cut me a deal."

"Look, you can do whatever you wanna do. But I think it would be better if you walked in there with proper counsel so they won't try to railroad you. Believe it or not, those cops don't give a fuck about you, for real. They just wanna get this case solved and have someone to take the fall. That's it. And after they lock up whoever they wanna lock up, they're gonna get their medals and go home and eat dinner with their families and call it a day."

"Why you gotta be so negative? I knew I shouldn't have told you. I knew you were going to shoot my idea down."

"Reese, I'm not being negative and I'm not trying to shoot your idea down, baby. I just don't want you to take the bulk of the heat from your so-called buddies. They're the ones that don't give a fuck about you," she spat as she stood to her feet and started walking toward me.

"Just let me handle this, all right!" I told her as she stood before me.

She took a deep breath and then she exhaled. "All right. But don't come crying to me when it doesn't go right." She turned around and left me standing in the kitchen.

I stood there and watched her as she walked away from me. She could be a fucking smart-ass when she wanted to be. If she'd give her ears the same chance as she gave her mouth, she'd probably learn something. I mean, I didn't do that second job with Edward and the other guys just to walk away with $5,000 and then give it away to a lawyer. Is she insane? That's hustling backwards. And I don't hustle backwards. I'd rather gamble it up in a poker game before I do that. Now that I think about it, I just may do that. I just need to figure out how to get the money back from Dawn.

32

DAWN

I wished I had a girlfriend I could call and talk to about the shit I was going through with Reese. I remember when Alexia used to be my best friend, but unfortunately that relationship has changed. She's not the common denominator in the rift between Reese and me, but she definitely adds to it.

Right now, I'm sitting in the house by my lonesome wondering where Reese has gone. He never lets me know anything, which is something I should've nipped in the bud a long time ago. But it's all good. Things will change, whether he and I like it or not. My only concern is that I'm prepared when it happens. I don't do well when things come at me unexpectedly. But if they do, Lord, please take the wheel.

I couldn't believe how it got dark so fast. It seemed like I just left the doctor's office with my mother. And now it was after eight o'clock at night. I hadn't heard from Reese in several hours, so I didn't know where he was and if he was okay. I grabbed my cell phone from the coffee table in the living room and dialed his number. It rang one time and then it went to voicemail. I disconnected the call and dialed his number again. Unfortunately, it went to voice-mail for the second time. "Reese, there you go with that not-answering-your-phone shit again," I hissed, gritting my teeth. There was no question in my mind that he turned his phone off so I wouldn't be able to contact him. And if that was the case, then that would prevent Ed or the other guys from getting in contact with him too. Whatever reason he had was stupid, and I was livid at this point.

I gave up on calling Reese anymore. I figured if he wanted to talk to me, then he'd pick up the phone and call me. As soon as I placed my phone down on the coffee table it started ringing. I snatched it back up because I knew it was Reese and I was going to give him a piece of my mind. But when I looked at the caller ID and saw it was my supervisor, Mrs. Powell, my heart rate shot up that instant. I was a bit hesitant to answer her call, but I did after the phone rang four times. "Hello," I finally said.

"Is this Dawn?" she asked.

"Yes, ma'am, Mrs. Powell, it's me. Is everything all right?" I replied. The butterflies in my stomach were fluttering around like crazy.

"Yes, sweetie, everything is all right. I just wanted to call you to see if you're feeling any better from earlier."

"Yes, I feel a lot better now. Thanks for calling to check on me."

"No problem. So, I can look forward to seeing you tomorrow?"

"Yes, I will be there."

"Great. But before I go, there's been a lot going on since Customs agents found those immigrants in those containers. News reporters were parked in front of the terminal all day. And I know your husband works nights, so has he said anything to you about the investigation?"

"We talked about it a few times after seeing it on TV, but other than that, no," I lied. I knew Mrs. Powell was fishing for information. But she ought to know that I was the wrong person to ask. I would never sell my husband out like that. Was this bitch crazy?

"Well, according to my sources, a couple of the container checkers and the terminal manager are saying that the guys that work with your husband may be in on the scandal."

"If Reese's longshoremen buddies did have something to do with it, this is my first time hearing it."

"Well, whoever was involved will be charged with the murder of all the people who died in those containers."

"Are you talking about the people that put those people in those containers, or are you talking about the longshoremen that pulled the steel containers off the ship?" I asked her. I needed clarity so I could give Reese the information he needed when he came home.

"Both."

"Both?" I replied sarcastically. "Why would the agents charge the longshoremen when they didn't make the people get inside of the doggone container? I think that's wrong on so many different levels."

"Well, from my understanding, the longshoremen that are involved will get charged because they knew the people were in the container and didn't report it."

"But how can the agents say that the longshoremen knew the people were inside?"

"Because on the manifest, those containers were supposed to be stacked on one part of pier, but the longshoremen carried them to another part of the terminal with hopes that they could hide them."

"I see what you're saying, but I don't agree with it. I think it's a bunch of BS if you ask me," I commented. And was frankly ready to get off the phone. The thought of Reese going to jail didn't sit well with me.

"Well, hopefully none of our crew members are involved; that way they won't be arrested or lose their jobs."

"Yeah, I feel you," I told her. She and I said a few more

words to each other and then we hung up. I placed my cell phone back down on the coffee table, got up from the chair, and slipped on a pair of my Nike running shoes so I could get in my car and drive around to see if I could find Reese. I was not going to sit in this house any longer without knowing where he was. Besides that, I needed to talk to him. He needed to know about the conversation I just had with Mrs. Powell, since he thinks he knows what's really going on. Sounds like he may actually need a lawyer, being as how murder charges are going to be handed out like government cheese.

I didn't waste any time leaving the house after I grabbed my handbag and car keys. Within a minute and a half, I was in the garage and in my car with the garage door opening up. As I backed out, I noticed a car parked on the opposite side of the street again. And when I blinked my eyes, I realized that it was the same fucking car that was there before. My heart dropped into the pit of my stomach. "Who the fuck is that?" I whispered as if I someone could hear me.

I stepped on my brakes halfway down the driveway and sat there to see what the driver of that car was going to do. But they didn't do anything. They just sat there. This scared me in a very alarming way. "Why the fuck are you just sitting there? Who are you fucking watching?" I continued to whisper as my heart rate sped up.

After sitting there for more than two minutes, I took my foot off the brake and started backing my car out of the driveway a little more. I watched the silhouette of this person like a hawk. But there was still no movement on their part. This really freaked me out because when I was looking at them from my bedroom window they drove away the moment they saw me watching them. But now it seemed like they wanted to play a cat and mouse game. "Fuck it!" I said and pressed my feet against the accelerator. My car sped backwards out of the driveway. I turned the steering wheel to the left, which brought me a few feet away from the other car. But just as I put the gear in drive, the car pulled away from the curb and sped by me. I turned my head to get a look and noticed that it was a dark gray, S500-Series Mercedes-Benz. The plates on the vehicle were from New York. It was going too fast for me to get a look inside. "Motherfucker!" I yelled. I quickly turned my car around. I was determined to find out who this person was. And why they were parked in the same place as they were the last time. More importantly, why did he ride off?

I turned my car completely around and sped off after the car, and made a right at the next corner. But the car was nowhere in sight. "Are you fucking kidding me right now?" I roared. I was pissed and scared at the same time, knowing that I lost out on finding out who was in that Mercedes-Benz. And why were they parked outside? What were they doing? And who were they watching? I needed some answers and I needed them now.

Trying to come to grips with what had just transpired made it hard for me to navigate my car from point A to point B, so I pulled my car over to the side of the road and tried to call Reese. "Please answer my call, Reese. I need you right now," I mumbled after dialing his number. But before I could blink an eye, his voicemail picked up on the first ring once again. This made me angry. So angry that I sat in my car and started crying. I didn't deserve the way Reese was treating me. I've always had his back in every situation. I've always sided with him when my father started to attack him. I protected him like I was the husband and he was the wife. And look at this situation: Why should I have to chase down a car in my neighborhood because I think we're being stalked? This is something Reese should be handling. Not me. So why the disconnect? I swear, I'm at my wit's end with this guy.

After I sat there in my car and cried myself to death, I

called Reese's grandmother. Thankfully, she answered the phone. "Hi, Mrs. Mary, how are you?" I asked her.

"I'm doing well, baby. How are you?"

"I'm okay. But I'm also looking for your grandson. Have you talked to him today?"

"No, I haven't. I called him twice today because he was supposed to stop by and see me. Is everything all right?"

"Yes, everything is fine, Grandma Mary. I called him a couple of times and his cell phone keeps going to voicemail. That's why I called you to see if you've heard from him."

"No, baby, I haven't. But if he calls me I'll tell him to call you."

"Thank you so much."

"You are most certainly welcome," she said, and then she paused. I thought she had disconnected our call, but then again, it didn't sound like it.

"Grandma Mary, are you still there?"

"Yes, baby, I'm still here."

"Oh, I thought you hung up."

"Oh no, baby, I'm still here. So, how are your parents?"

"They're great. I will tell them that you asked about them," I answered. I was ready to end the call with her, especially since she had no knowledge of where Reese was. I really didn't have any more use for her.

"Don't you have a sister?" she continued.

"Yes, I do."

"Well, how is she doing?"

"She's doing well, Mrs. Mary. Hey, listen, can I call you back? My mom is trying to call me on the other line," I lied, hoping she'd believe me.

"Oh yes, honey. You go ahead. And tell your mother I said hi."

"I will."

"Okay. Well, take care."

"Thanks," I said and finally disconnected the call.

Since Reese hadn't reached out to his grandmother, I knew that he was up to no good. Ever since I've known him, he's always avoided her when he was about to do something that she'd disapprove of. It was like when he talked to her, she'd be able to tell that he was about to do something stupid. It was almost like she could read his mind or could tell by his body movement when something was off with him. She's known about his gambling problems for as long as I've known. So if she ever found out that he was involved with that human trafficking investigation, it would break her heart. I only hoped that she never found out.

33

REESE

Dawn didn't know that I took the $5,000 I gave her to hold for me, plus another $3,000 she had stashed in her sock drawer, and now I was on my way to another gambling spot so I could double the money.

I decided to head on over to a spot I used to go to a few years back, run by this OG named Pork Chop. Pork Chop was an old man, but everyone respected him. His gambling spot was located off Brambleton Avenue. This was no ordinary gambling spot. And he didn't allow young guys to come in his domain. You had to be at least thirty years old and you gotta come in his place with at least $1,000 to sit at a table. I won money in his establishment a few times. As a matter of fact, I won more money than I lost there. So I figured tonight would probably be a good night to win some more money.

Pork Chop's spot was situated in the middle of the block. Players that wanted to join his game had to park their cars off the street, and when they got to the house they had to enter from the back. I couldn't believe that this operation had been going on for the past seven years, and not one police raid. There was talk that he paid a couple of local cops to look the other way.

Pork Chop had his son Jamil working as his security. And obviously that was working for him, because no one had ever tried to rob their spot. "Long time, no see," Jamil said as he let me in the house through the back door.

"Yeah, brother, where you been?" Pork Chop asked.

"Workin' a whole lotta hours. Trying to get wifey pregnant," I replied.

"So what are you trying to get into tonight?" Pork Chop wanted to know.

"I got a few grand with me that I am trying to spend."

Some random guy said, "Well, come on over here and sit down at this table." I had never seen this guy before. I took him for a newcomer, until Pork Chop warned me about him.

"Reese, you gotta watch this guy. He's been known to walk away from these tables with a lot of honest men's paychecks."

"Well, he ain't walking away with mine," I announced as I took a seat at the table. After I sat down, I sized this fellow up. "What's your name?" I asked the five-foot-five, out-of-shape character. He looked like George Jefferson from *The Jeffersons* TV show. He had the height, the receding hairline, and complexion.

"My name is Butch. What's yours?"

"People call me Reese. I used to come here all the time."

"Yeah, he sure did. But he put me down and started hanging with his longshoremen buddies at the other gambling spot," Pork Chop interjected.

"Come on, Chop, you know it wasn't even like that. Wifey started giving me a lot of grief because I was spending up the house money."

"How is she doing, anyway?" Pork Chop asked.

"You need to be asking me how I'm doing," I said, while I pulled five hundred-dollar bills from my pocket and placed them on the table in front of me.

Jamil laughed. "It ain't that bad, is it, brother?"

"If it ain't, it sure feels like it."

"You were down at NIT, right?" Pork Chop asked me.

I let out a long sigh. "Yeah, I'm down there," I replied. "Put me down for a hundred," I told the dealer, and then I waited for him to deal me my cards.

"What's this I hear about the port police finding dead Asian people in those containers down at the pier?"

"Yeah, they found some people down in there. Some dead, some alive. So now they're trying to find out how those people got inside the container and who was behind it," I explained while I sifted through the cards I was just dealt.

Pork Chop pressed the issue. "Do you know who's behind it?"

I wanted to say, *yeah, nigga, I know who's behind it, but I ain't gonna tell you.* "All in," I said, talking to everyone at the poker table. And then I looked at Pork Chop and said, "Nah, I don't know who's behind it. The guys at NIT are pretty tight-lipped about everything that happens at the pier."

"Do you think that the port police is going to really hand out murder charges to everyone that was involved?" Pork Chop wanted to know.

"Who knows what those people are going to do," I replied nonchalantly. And then I looked at everyone at the table and said, "Bump," letting them know that I was raising my stakes.

Pork Chop and his son Jamil asked me a few more questions about the investigation going on at the pier, and I answered them. After that, nothing else was discussed except for the poker game. In the beginning, everything was going my way. I was up by seven grand, but after being there until five o'clock in the morning, I walked away with nothing. I didn't have one dime when I left Pork Chop's spot. A wave of disappointment and embarrassment overcame me. I sat in my truck outside of Pork Chop's spot for nearly an hour trying to figure out what I was going to say to Dawn when I got home. There was no doubt in my mind that she was going to curse me out. But maybe after I explained to her that I felt bad for not getting the rest of the money from Edward and that's why I did what I did . . . Would she accept that answer? I wasn't sure. But I would find out sooner than later.

I finally made it home. It was 5:40 a.m. when I walked through the front door. The sun was coming up and so was my wife. She must've heard me unlock the front door because I saw her racing toward me as soon as I crossed the threshold. She was dressed in her nightclothes, but she looked like she was ready for war. She didn't waste any time questioning me. "Where the hell have you been all night?"

"I went over to one of my homeboy's house so he could give me some advice on how to handle the situation," I lied, giving her my most sincere expression.

"So why was your phone off? I called you over a dozen times tonight. Made me think something happened to you, and that's not fair," she said, folding her arms across her chest.

"Honestly, I didn't even know my phone was turned off."

"You are a fucking liar!" she spat, as she unfolded her arms and took two more steps toward me. I knew then that any moment she was going to swing on me. So I took a couple steps backwards. "Hold up now. I'm telling you the truth," I lied once again.

"Reese, we've been married a long time. So I know when you're lying. And you're lying right now."

"Why are you coming at me like that?" I raised my hands up in front of me to prevent Dawn from attacking me.

"Whatcha scared for?"

"I'm not scared . . ."

"Well, nigga, you need to be, because I'm about two seconds from fucking you up in this little room."

"Why you don't believe me? I can give you his number right now and you can call him."

"You think I'm stupid, don't you? I know you already called him and asked him to vouch for you just in case I want to call. That's the oldest alibi in the book. But it's all good, I'm not even going to argue with you anymore. I'm done with this," she said and then she turned around and walked away.

Now, I didn't know what she meant by that, but for the first time in years I believed her, and that scared me. I guessed she was at her wit's end with me. And if that was the case, I was fucked.

Instead of following her to our bedroom, I pulled a blanket from the hallway closet and found me a spot on the living room sofa. This wasn't the first time I had to sleep on the couch. And I know it's not going to be my last. Hopefully she wouldn't find out that I took the money back. Because if she found out before she left to go to work this morning, I knew she was going to make the rest of my day a living hell.

34

DAWN

That son of a bitch thought that I was naïve. I knew he wasn't at his friend's house because the only friends he had were the guys at NIT. So where the hell was he? From past experiences, when he wanted to stay out all night, he was either at a gambling spot or with another woman. Now, I could have pressed the issue and made him tell me where he really was, but I decided against it. I'd had enough of Reese's lies. When I heard them they drained me of all my emotional and mental energy. And I couldn't have that. Not now. Not tomorrow or the day after. I'm putting my foot down today. And that's final.

I went into the bathroom and took a quick shower. After I picked out what I was going to wear I got dressed, went into the kitchen, and made me a hot cup of tea, and then I grabbed my house and car keys and left the house. On my way out, I noticed that Reese was snoring extremely hard. When this happened, it was a sure sign that he had been up all night. I say whatever goes on in the dark will eventually come to the light. He would be exposed before it was all over.

I dreaded going into the office today. The questions that

Mrs. Powell asked me made me feel uneasy. And the possibility that she was going to ask me a lot more questions when she saw me in the office this morning gave me a strong case of anxiety. I wanted to tell her to leave me alone about the investigation, but I knew I wouldn't do it because it could hurt her feelings. She and I have always had a good relationship and I would like that to continue, but if she continued to press me for more information, I was gonna have to tell her to monitor her business. I knew she wasn't gonna like it, but she would be okay when it was all said and done.

As soon as I parked my car I noticed that I was the only one there. I was happy because I had a few more minutes to myself before all my coworkers walked into the office and graced me with their presence. Well, that's what I thought, until a coworker of mine named Kelsey Nelson walked her happy ass into the office. Kelsey was a young white girl with a whole lot of stuff to prove. I didn't know her correct age, but she looked like she was in her mid to late twenties. She also looked like a *Baywatch* lifeguard. She had the tan thing going on and always talked about how she loves to hang out at the beach. I think she's an airhead. All she ever talked about were her tanning appointments, how she and her boyfriend were going hiking. And when they were done hiking they were going to hang out at the beach. Her life was pretty boring to me. While she's at the beach or hiking, I'll be at home Netflixing and chilling.

When she walked into the office she greeted me. I said hello and then I pretended to be busy immediately thereafter. Her cubicle was only three over from mine. So after she set her things down she walked out of her cubicle and started walking in my direction. I watched her in my peripheral vision and prayed that she wasn't coming to my work space to talk. Unfortunately for me, that's exactly what she did.

She entered my cubicle. "Hi, Dawn, how are you?"

"Great, Kelsey. How are you?" I replied, hoping she wasn't going to be here for long.

"Shocked to see you here so early this morning."

"Yeah, I normally don't come in this early. But I had some accounts that I needed to close, so I decided to come in a little bit earlier just in case my workload gets busy later on today."

"You leave early yesterday?" she asked. And for a moment there I thought she was being nosy so she could pry into my personal life. But when she mentioned that a lot of guys from the night shift had been called in to be interviewed by port police and US Customs agents, I lightened up a little.

"Have they arrested anyone?"

"Not as of yet. But from what I hear, people will be getting charged before the day is over with."

"Who told you that?"

"Everybody's talking about it."

"Did they say who?"

"No. But we all got a feeling who they will be."

"Who?"

"Well, one of the people we know is going to get arrested is your husband."

"My what?"

"Your husband."

Taken aback by Kelsey's accusation, I had to turn my chair around and face her head-on. "Are you fucking with me right now?" I hissed. I swear, I wanted to jump on her, pull all of her hair out. How dare this bitch confront me like she's giving me some information about the investigation and in the same breath tell me that she knows that Reese is involved? Is this bitch that bold?

"No, I'm not fucking with you. But I will say that I'm

being real with you, while Mrs. Powell and everyone else around here tiptoes around you like they're afraid to speak their minds."

"Are you done?" I asked her. I mean, was this bitch really serious right now? She had some huge balls coming at me with her newfound information about Reese. Did she want a medal for her findings? Or was she trying to insult and embarrass me? Either way, the bitch was out of line.

"Yes, I'm done," she replied confidently.

"Well, good. Then carry your ass back to your cubicle before I drag you back over there myself," I snapped as I gritted my teeth. She got the message and left my cubicle at once.

Kelsey didn't say another to me, nor did she make any eye contact for the rest of the day. I guess her bold ass got the hint. Thirty minutes after the altercation with Kelsey, Mrs. Powell and all the other employees started coming in one after the other. When Mrs. Powell saw me, she smiled and waved. I returned the smile and hand gesture, but I had a sour taste in my mouth from the information Kelsey gave me about everyone in this office.

Not too long after Mrs. Powell and the other employees walked into the office, I noticed everyone in there started looking at me and whispering. This definitely pissed me off. I was so livid that I got up from my desk and walked over to Mrs. Powell's cubicle. She was busy with a phone call, so I waited there until she was done. She looked at me a few times as if she was wondering why I was standing there. Not to mention, I was invading her space, but I didn't care. I wasn't leaving until I got a chance to have a talk with her.

After I'd been standing there for about a minute and a half, she got off her call and turned her chair around so she could face me. "Dawn, is everything all right?" she asked.

I wanted to say, *bitch, don't play with me. You already know what time it is. And you know why everyone is whispering behind my back*. "No, everything isn't all right," I started off saying. "Kelsey walked over to my cubicle before you came in this morning and told me that everyone in here thinks that my husband had something to do with that investigation that's going on now. And I'm really pissed off about it."

"Well, I'm sorry if she did that. And as far as everyone in here thinking your husband had something to do with the human trafficking investigation, that's not true. But if it is, that's because they formed their opinion on their own. Trust me, we haven't been walking around in this office here, smearing your husband's name or reputation. As a matter of fact, I can't see where Kelsey got that information from."

"Let's find out," I said and turned my head in the direction of Kelsey's cubicle. "Hey, Kelsey, can you come over here for a minute?" I yelled. I wasn't concerned about how loud I was or who looked up. I was only concerned about finding out who was talking about me behind my back. That's it.

Kelsey stood up and walked over to Mrs. Powell's cubicle. As soon as she approached us, I said, "Remember you told me that port police were going to make an arrest today and one of those people that were going to be arrested was my husband?"

Kelsey hesitated as she looked at Mrs. Powell's face.

"Yes or no?" I pressed her.

She looked at me and said, "Yes."

"Okay, and didn't you say that everyone in here knew that my husband was involved in that murder investigation?"

She hesitated again.

"Don't look at Mrs. Powell. Just answer my question. Yes or no?" I hissed. I wanted to expose this bitch and any other bitch in this office for talking about me and my husband behind our backs. I mean, I couldn't care less if I didn't fuck with any of these women in here. But these people walked around here like they were my best friends, so I needed to put their asses on front street and let them know that I see them for who they really are.

"Yes, I said it," she finally said.

"Now tell Mrs. Powell who you heard it from." I was not going to let this gossip go until I exposed everyone.

Kelsey looked at Mrs. Powell again. "Why do you keep looking at Mrs. Powell?" I asked her. I felt something wasn't right with these two fake-ass bitches.

"Because she's the one who said it," Kelsey finally answered.

"Oh, really?" I said and turned my focus toward Mrs. Powell, who was by this time trying to pick her bottom lip up from the floor.

Mrs. Powell finally opened her mouth to speak. "Wait, I can explain."

"I'm all ears," I assured her.

"Can we talk about this in the supply room?" she asked me.

"Hell no! Don't be trying to go into hiding. We're gonna talk about this right here. Now, tell me why you said what you said about my husband."

"I was only repeating what I was told by another office manager."

"Oh, so your buddy over at the other building is running her mouth too, huh? Well, let me tell all of you something." I turned my volume up so everyone in the entire office could hear me. "It's really messed up how y'all jump to conclusions about stuff you don't know anything about. Yes, my husband works night shift and he operates a straddle carrier, but he does not operate the machinery that takes containers off the ship. So, as far as I'm concerned, my husband hasn't done anything wrong. Now if you wanna take what I'm saying and twist it up, then so be it. None of y'all pay our bills or put food on our table, so your opinions of him don't matter to me. I will ride with my husband on this until I find out otherwise, so until that happens please mind your business." I went to my cubicle, grabbed my things, and walked back out of the office.

I knew I wasn't supposed to just walk out of the office without getting permission, but I knew I wouldn't be able to stay in there another minute. I can't believe that I work around so many fake people. I thought that at least five out of the eleven people in there were my friends. I guess not. So what am I gonna do now? With everything weighing heavily on my heart, I didn't know if I could face those people again. It hurts when you think someone has your best interests at heart and then at the last minute you find out that it's the total opposite. How could I come back from that? And if I couldn't, would I be able to move to a different office? I swear, Reese had really done it this time. First at home and now at the office. What else could happen?

The moment I exited the parking lot of the terminal, I decided to go to my parents' house instead of going home. I didn't want to see Reese. Not now, anyway. As soon as I pulled up to the parents' house, I saw Alexia taking mail from the mailbox. She stood at the curb and sifted through the mail like she was looking for something. "Lord, please don't let me get into an argument with this chick today," I prayed, and then I stepped out of the car.

"Whatcha doing over here? Aren't you supposed to be at work?" she asked me.

"I took off," I told her. "Anything in there for me?"

She sucked her teeth. "Girl, please, you know you ain't got no mail over here." She turned around to head back into the house.

I started walking behind her. "Who's in the house?"

"Mom and Dad are both in there."

"Mom cooked?" I wanted to know because I was a bit hungry, since I hadn't eaten anything all morning.

"She made pancakes for Dad, but I don't know if there's any left," Alexia replied as she walked onto the porch and opened the front door. When we entered the house, she ruined my surprise by announcing that I was with her. I wanted to choke her. "Mom, Dad, Dawn is here!" she yelled.

I pushed her a couple of steps forward. "You always gotta mess up something," I pouted.

"Oh shoot! My bad," she said as she continued to lead the way down the hallway.

Like always, my mother was in the kitchen, cleaning, while my father read the newspaper at the kitchen table. He laid the paper down when I entered the room. "Goodness, gracious, what brings you here?" he asked me after he cracked a smile.

"I just wanted to stop by since I wasn't doing anything else," I replied as I leaned over to my dad and kissed him on his cheek. I walked over to the kitchen sink and kissed my mother on her cheek as well. "I'm hungry. Any more food left?" I inquired, looking around in spots of the kitchen were food would be, like the stove, the oven, and the microwave.

"No, baby, it's all gone. But I can whip you up some eggs and toast," my mother offered.

I opened up the refrigerator and said, "No, Mommy, I'm good. I'll just eat this bowl of fruit you got in here."

"Yes, why don't you eat that," she encouraged me.

I grabbed the bowl of chopped strawberries, kiwi, and mangos from the top shelf of the refrigerator, took a fork from the drawer, and then I took me a seat at the kitchen table. "What's going on, Daddy?" I asked him right after I put a piece of strawberry into my mouth.

"I was about to ask you the same thing. Have you been keeping up with the news?" he answered, while looking at the local news section.

"Why? What happened?" I asked. I was not trying to get caught up giving out any information unless asked. And even then, I probably wouldn't do it because I have a very judgmental set of relatives. They don't hold back any punches.

"There was a report that Edward Cuffy was found sitting in the driver seat of his truck, dead."

Shocked by the sudden information about Ed, all I could do was sit there in awe. How did this happen and why? "When was this? Did they say when and where they found his body?" I wondered aloud.

"Wait a minute, you don't know anything about this?" my father asked.

"No. I don't. This is my first time hearing this."

"Well, they found his truck in the parking lot of Mount Trashmore. A woman doing her morning run noticed that there was something off with him, so she called 911. And when they showed up, that's when they realized that he was dead. Apparently, he was shot in the chest a few times," my father explained.

"Oh my God! This is awful. Reese is not gonna believe this," I said as I looked at my parents. Alexia was standing next to my mother, so I gradually looked at her too.

"The port police is going to think this is really strange, because first they found Asian people hiding in those containers and now one of the guys that they suspect had something to do with their case is dead. This is definitely gonna raise a lot of eyebrows. So you may wanna get Reese on the phone right now and let him know what's going on, if he doesn't already," my father said excitedly.

"He's asleep now, so I'm just gonna go home and tell him."

"He probably already knows," Alexia interjected.

"He was asleep when I left for work this morning, so I know he doesn't know," I replied, looking directly at Alexia. I needed to let her know that she really doesn't know everything that goes on in my life.

Finding out what just happened to Ed gave me a sick feeling in my stomach. And then I became nauseated, so I pushed the bowl of fruit aside and stood up from my seat at the table. "Leaving already?" my mother asked.

"Yes, Mommy, I gotta go home and let Reese know what's going on."

"Why don't you take the bowl of fruit with you?"

"I just lost my appetite. Put it back in the refrigerator. I'll come and eat it later," I told her, even though I had no idea if I was coming back or not. My main focus was to get home so I could sit down and have a long conversation with my husband. The fact that Ed's body was found with gunshot wounds to his chest made me wonder if Reese was involved in his death. I swear, if I found out that Reese killed Edward, I was going to leave him on the spot. I can't be married to a murderer. Yes, I love him, but I would never sit around and act like that shit is cool. I figured if he could murder someone over money, then he could also murder me and God knows who else. I just pray that this isn't true.

35

REESE

"Reese, you need to get up," I heard Dawn say, faintly. I thought I was dreaming until she started shaking my body. That's when I realized that she wanted me to wake up. "What's wrong?" I asked her in a groggy manner, while I tried to focus my eyes at the lights that blinded me.

"We need to talk."

"About what?" I wanted to know. I was irritated by the fact that she woke me up after I'd had only a couple hours of sleep. I turned on my stomach and covered my head with my pillow.

"Edward is dead," she said.

When I heard her say the word *dead*, I instantly thought I was still asleep. So I lifted my head up from the pillow and looked at Dawn where she sat on the edge of our bed. "Did you just say that Edward is dead?"

She nodded her head.

I turned completely around and sat up in the bed with my back against the pillows. "Who told you that?" I asked.

"It's in the newspaper and on the news," she explained.

I didn't say another word as I reached for the remote control for the TV. I powered it on and started sifting through all the news stations.

"It's probably not going to be on TV now. Wait, hold on," she continued as she pulled her cell phone from her purse. I saw her logging onto the Google site. She typed in a few things and within in a matter of seconds she had pulled up the news feed with the headline, HUSBAND, LONGSHORE-MAN OF 25-YEARS FOUND DEAD IN PICKUP TRUCK.

I grabbed the phone from her hand. "What the fuck is going on?" I said, my words barely audible.

"I wanted to know the same thing," she commented and gave me a weird look.

"Why the fuck are you looking at me like that?"

"Did you do that?"

"Are you out of your fucking mind?" I barked. I wasn't feeling her at all with that question. How the fuck could she sit in my face and ask me a question like that? Was she on drugs or something?

"No, I'm not out of my mind. It's a simple yes or no an-swer," she pressed.

"Fuck no! I didn't do that," I told her while I held the phone with one hand and pointed to it with the other one. "I mean, come on, I was pissed off with that nigga for standing me up and not paying me my money, but I wouldn't kill him behind it. We've been knowing each other for too long," I tried to explain to her.

"Well, who do you think would do this?"

"I don't know. I mean, how did they say he died?" I asked Dawn while I searched the news story for the cause of death.

"My father told me that he got shot."

"Hold on, wait, your dad knows about this?"

"Yeah, I just left their house. He was the one that told me first."

"I bet he thinks I had something to do with this too, huh?"

"No, he doesn't. After he told me about Ed's body being found in his truck near the walking trail at Mount Trashmore, he asked me if you had already heard about it. And I told him that you hadn't."

"I can't believe that," I said nonchalantly as I handed the phone back to her. For the first time, Dawn's parents weren't pointing fingers at me. But I knew that would be short-lived. They hated me and nothing was going to change that. "I wonder if the guys know about this," I said, and reached for my cell phone near the lamp on the nightstand. While I dialed Todd's number, Dawn didn't move one inch. She sat there and watched me while I waited for Todd to answer his phone.

Like clockwork he answered on the first ring. "I know what you're calling me for," Todd said.

I put our call on speakerphone before I uttered one word. I wanted Dawn to hear the entire phone call, since she was a little leery about my involvement in Edward's murder. "So, you heard too, huh?" I finally said.

"Yeah, my buddy Stan that works on the morning shift called me about thirty minutes ago and told me."

"So, when you worked last night, Edward never showed up?"

"No, he didn't. The only person showed up was Brian. And as soon as he clocked in, a couple of guys said that port police escorted him to their office. I can't tell you how long they were in there, but I can say that when I clocked out this morning, I was told that Brian had already gone."

"Think Brian did it?" I threw the question out there. I had no idea how Todd was going to answer it.

"I don't know," Todd replied, not taking the bait.

"What about Gene? Remember you said that he didn't show up last night."

"That's a hard one too. You just can't tell what a man will do in desperate times. I mean, I was mad at the nigga because he still owed me money, but I wouldn't kill him for it."

"Yeah, I feel you. I said the same thing. But the real

fucked up thing about it is that the nigga died before we got the rest of our money," I stated, and then Dawn gave me a disappointed look. I ignored her.

Todd chuckled. "That's funny because I thought the same thing."

"Think we ought to pay his wife a visit and ask for the rest of our cash?" I suggested.

This time I didn't look at Dawn. But I felt a sharp and evil stare coming upon me. When she realized that I was purposely dodging eye contact, she gave me a light punch in my arm. "Stop it," she hissed.

"Ouch! That hurt," I replied under my breath and grabbed my arm with my other hand.

Todd chuckled again. "Nah, I don't think that would be a good idea. We might have to take one for the team on this one," he said.

"Yeah, all right. But check it out, what if he got robbed for the money? If that's the case, then who knew that he had the money, other than us?"

"Gene and Brian."

"Exactly. It has to be one of them." I needed Todd to side with me on this.

"Well, whoever it is, the cops will find them."

"We'll see. So, let me ask you—d'you think it would be inappropriate if I decide not to go to his funeral? I mean, the nigga did talk shit to me and told me that I was on my own after some of the people were found dead."

"He basically told me the same thing. But in good conscience, I can't not go. That would be fucked up on my part. And what kind of message would that send the cops?"

"You know me, I couldn't care less about the message I'm sending. If you wanna know the truth, I think he got what was coming to him," I said, and right after I said it, Dawn punched me in my arm again. "Ouch, stop doing that," I whined.

"You all right?" Todd asked. I figured he heard me flinch at the pain my wife was inflicting on me.

"Yeah, I'm good. My wife punches me in the arm every time I say something she doesn't like."

"Maybe you ought to take heed."

"Yeah, a'ight. Well, I'ma get off this line. But if you hear or see Brian or Gene, let me know."

"Will do," Todd said.

From the moment I ended the call, Dawn was all over me like a cheap suit. She started cursing me out. "What the hell is wrong with you? You're acting like you're happy that he's dead. You can't walk around here with all the bitterness in your heart because he owes you money. Shit! You heard Todd: Ed owed all of you guys money. But guess what? You got another chance to go out there and work for some. He doesn't, because he's lying on a hard metal table, being cut open as we speak so the county morgue can do their autopsy. So, you need to get it together and stop with all that negative shit you got going on inside of you. It's not healthy."

"Dawn, I'm not trying to hear that," I told her and scooted off the bed. I went to the bathroom to take a leak. But that didn't stop Dawn from hanging around at the bathroom door after I closed it.

"You really need to do some soul searching, because if you don't you're gonna die a miserable old man," she yelled through the door, and then she punched it. I heard her mumble something while she walked away. But I didn't feed into her. I let her carry her ass down the hallway.

36

DAWN

Who the fuck did I marry? I was beginning to see Reese for who he really was. Come on, have some respect for the dead. I shook my head with disgust as I walked toward the kitchen. I had lost my appetite earlier at my parents' house. But after dealing with Reese's bullshit, I somehow became hungry again. I went into the kitchen and grabbed milk and a bowl of cereal. After I grabbed a spoon from the utensil drawer I took a seat on one of the bar stools. Reese joined me a few minutes later. Surprisingly he didn't try to apologize, but he was curious as to why I wasn't at work. "I left to keep from cursing my supervisor out," I replied, gritting my teeth.

"Why were you gonna curse her out?" he asked me while he pulled a bottle of water from the refrigerator.

"Because I found out that she was talking about you to everyone in the office after I left early yesterday," I replied between chews.

"That fat bitch! I knew I didn't like her for a reason," he said, and then he took a couple of gulps from his bottle of water.

Before I could utter another word, our doorbell rang. We weren't expecting any visitors, especially this time of the morning. I put the spoon down in the bowl and sat still on the bar stool while Reese tiptoed out of the kitchen and into the living room. I sat there quietly, trying to think who could be at the door. Reese was at the door and peering through the peephole. I watched him as he looked back at me. What he said, I wasn't ready for. "It's the cops," he whispered.

At that moment, my entire body froze. I was completely paralyzed, wondering why they would be here. It could be for no other reason but to arrest Reese for being involved with the human trafficking scheme. And all I could think about was that those cops were going to take Reese from the house and lock him away with no bail. Just the thought of him leaving me in this way gave me a sick feeling in my stomach. How was I going to help him get through this? I guess now would be the best time to call a lawyer.

"Don't answer it," I whispered to him.

Reese walked a couple of feet away from the door while the cops rang the doorbell a few more times. "If I don't answer it, they'll probably wait in their car for me to leave the house," he whispered back.

"Just don't leave the house," I whispered again.

"No, I'm gonna answer the door. Maybe this is the sign I need to talk to them and give them my version of what happened with those containers. And maybe they can give me a deal," he said, trying to rationalize the situation.

But I still wasn't convinced. I slid off the bar stool and tiptoed toward him. When we were face-to-face I said, "No, no, no. You will do no such thing. You need a lawyer with you before you open your mouth and say anything," I insisted.

"Yeah, all right," he said. He turned back toward the front door and yelled, "Who is it?"

"Virginia Beach homicide detectives," we heard one guy reply.

I was livid. I almost wanted to scream. Reese never lis-

tens to shit I have to say. Now he was about to be hauled
off to jail because he thought that if he told the investigators what they wanted to hear, he would get a get-out-of-
jail-free card. In my eyes, cops don't care about any of us.
Their main objective is to solve their cases, no matter the
cost.

I stood there and watched Reese as he opened the door
and faced two homicide detectives. For the life of me, I
couldn't believe that he did it. "How can I help you gentlemen?" he said.

Both detectives were Caucasian men. One of them was
stocky and overweight; the other one was a medium-size
fellow. They were both dressed in slacks and suit jackets
and dark sunglasses.

"Can we come in?" the stocky guy asked.

"Sure," Reese replied, acting nice and accommodating.
I wanted to slap him in the back of his fucking head and
tell him to wake up.

"Can I ask why you guys are here?" I blurted since
Reese was busy kissing their asses.

"And you are?" the stocky detective asked me.

"My name is Dawn and I own this house that you're
standing in," I replied. I mean, what gave him the fucking
right to ask me who I was? I'm sure he knew my name already, but wanted to be an asshole about it.

"Nice to meet you, ma'am," he said, and extended his
right hand. I shook it even though I didn't want to. The
other detective extended his hand so I could shake it too.
"My name is Detective Wise," the stocky guy said.

"And my name is Detective Rose," the other cop said
after Reese closed the front door and locked it. Immediately after Reese walked away from the front door, both
detectives turned toward him and shook his hand too.

"So, what's this about?" Reese asked them.

"We're here because we're investigating the murder of
Edward Cuffy," Detective Wise explained.

"Yeah, my wife told me about that this morning. So, what's happening now? Do you have any suspects?" Reese asked him.

"Right now we don't, but that's why my partner and I are doing a full-scale investigation so we can get some justice for Edward Cuffy," Detective Wise said.

"Can we have a seat?" Detective Rose asked.

"Sure." Reese scrambled to rearrange the pillows on the sofa. It was obvious that he wanted to make these guys feel as comfortable as possible. But I couldn't care less.

After the detectives took a seat next to each other, I sat on the love seat while Reese stood alongside me.

"So, what do you need from us?" I asked.

"Well, Detective Rose and I want to know where you were late last night," Wise said, looking straight at Reese.

"I was at a friend's house."

"What's this friend's name and where does he live?" Detective Wise continued.

Reese looked like he was about answer the detective's question, but then he hesitated. I can't tell you why he did it, but I do know that it didn't sit well with the cops or me.

"Well, his name is Pork Chop and he lives in Norfolk," he finally replied.

"What time did you go there?" Detective Rose interjected.

"About nine o'clock last night."

Rose pressed the issue. "What time did you leave?"

"Probably around five thirty this morning," he replied.

And while he was talking I felt the blood boiling in my veins. The second he uttered Pork Chop's name, I knew that he was gambling. Pork Chop has been in business for a long time and local dummies like my husband are always drawn to that place so they can give up their fucking money. So now, I asked myself, where the hell did he get the money to gamble? He hadn't gotten paid yet this week. Had he gotten an advance from Pork Chop himself? I knew one thing, I would find out after these fucking cops left.

"Did you go anywhere else?" Wise asked Reese.

"Nope. I left my house and went straight there. And after I left there I came straight back here," Reese assured them.

"Have you and Edward ever had any conflict? Disagreement or altercation?" Rose interjected.

"No, we haven't. He was my friend. Like a father to me," Reese told them. But he was lying his ass off. I guess he didn't want them to know that Edward owed him $10,000 from that botched human trafficking job. Shit, tell them. I mean, it's not like they won't find out about it later.

"Can you tell us how long you've been knowing him?" Rose asked.

"Since I started working at NIT."

"Can you think of anyone that would want him dead?" Rose asked.

"No. I can't."

"When was the last time you saw him?" Wise chimed in.

"The night we all clocked out at the terminal, which was two days ago."

"When was the last time you spoke with him?" Rose asked.

"Yesterday morning. We were supposed to meet up at this diner but he never showed up."

Rose's questions continued. "Why was he going to meet you there?"

"To talk and get a bite to eat."

Wise jumped back in. "You're saying that you two agreed to meet at a diner so you guys could sit down, talk, and eat, but he never showed up?"

"Yep, that's what I am saying," Reese assured them.

"What's the name of this diner?" Wise asked.

"Pop's Diner."

"Where is this diner?" Rose asked.

"Off Liberty Street."

"What time was this?" Rose continued.

"Like about one in the afternoon."

"I was there with him, so that's about the right time," I interjected.

"How long did you guys stick around until you realized that he wasn't going to show up?" Wise said as he looked at me and Reese. He looked at Reese's expression and then he looked at mine.

"Maybe thirty to forty minutes," I answered.

"Did you call to see why he never showed up?" Rose asked.

"Of course I did. I called him over a dozen times, but it kept going to voicemail."

"Did you send him a text or leave him a voicemail message?" Wise chimed back in.

"I don't remember. But I think I did. I also stopped by his house. His wife was outside by her car. And when I asked her was he home, she told me no. I told her to let him know that I stopped by and she said okay."

"You said that you two work together. Did he show up to work yesterday?" Rose asked.

"I didn't go to work at all yesterday."

"And why not?" Wise asked.

"Because I wasn't feeling good."

"Did you call out of work?"

"Of course I did."

"Why does it matter if he called in to work yesterday?" I wanted to know. I felt like that was an irrelevant question. Shit! Go out there and find the real fucking killer.

"We're just trying to establish a time line, ma'am," Rose answered.

"Yes, I understand that, but whether or not he called into work is reaching, don't you think?"

"That all depends on how you look at it," Rose replied.

"It's okay, baby. I don't have anything to hide."

"Is this it? Because he and I have some things we need to do," I said, giving them a stern look. I wanted them to know that I knew my constitutional rights, so I could end any interview or home visit anytime I wanted to.

Wise spoke. "We have just one more question."

"What is that?" I asked.

"Detective Rose and I are aware of a human trafficking case that was just opened by US Customs agents, so my question to you is, aren't you, Edward Cuffy, and a couple of other gentlemen currently being investigated because of it?"

Before Reese could get a word out, I stood to my feet and said, "Okay, now it's time for you guys to leave. We appreciate you stopping by. And if there's anything else you may need in the future pertaining to Edward Cuffy's murder, feel free to ask. But other than that, this interview is over."

Both of the detectives stood to their feet. And as they walked toward the front door, they handed Reese their business cards. "Thanks for stopping by, you guys," Reese said as the men left.

Immediately after they stepped onto the front porch, I walked in front of Reese and slammed the front door. Reese looked at me like I was crazy. "What's wrong with you? You didn't have to be nasty to them."

"Fuck them!" I roared as I walked away from the front door.

"You could've handled that a better way, Dawn," Reese said as he walked behind me.

I started walking down the hallway toward the bedroom. "So, you were at Pork Chop's gambling spot, huh?"

Reese hesitated to answer my question, so I knew this conversation was about to be turned upside down. I stopped in the middle of the hallway and turned around to face him. He stood there with the dumbest expression he could muster up. "Did you take some of that money I had hidden away?" I asked him in the calmest way I knew how.

"Yeah, but I'm gonna get it back."

"Are you fucking kidding me, Reese? Get out of my house right now!" I snapped. "Get out of here right now, you fucking loser!" I screamed, and pushed him backwards as hard as I could. He stumbled.

"And go where?" he spat as he stood there before me.

"I don't care, Reese! Just get out of here!" I roared, and then I turned around and stormed down the hallway toward my bedroom. I heard Reese walking behind me but he wasn't saying anything. When I got to the room I stood at the bedroom door as he entered. "Pack your shit right now and get the fuck out of here!" I continued. I wasn't backing down. I was over it with this guy. He had made a fool of me for the last time.

"Can we please talk about this?" he asked me as he stood at the foot of our bed.

"There's nothing to talk about. We are over our heads in debt. You gave me that money to pay our bills. Not to mention, you owed me eight hundred dollars for my fertility treatment."

"Why are you acting like I took all the money back? I only took a third of it."

"You are a grimy-ass nigga! You know that? And you wanna talk about it? Talk about it and say what? That you're going back to the gambling spot tonight and that you're gonna win all our money back? Bullshit! I'm so tired of your fucking lies, so I want you out of here. Now get your shit and go!" I was not backing down from Reese today. I was at my wit's end with him. So, he's gotta go. Get out of my face right now.

"Dawn, I am so sorry!"

"Get out, Reese! I have nothing else to say to you," I barked, still standing at my bedroom door.

After standing there for another minute and a half

pleading with me, he finally got the message that I didn't want him around. I watched him as he pulled a few shirts and pants from the walk-in closet, grabbed a travel bag, and started placing his clothes in there. When his packing was coming to a close, I walked out of the room and headed back down the hallway. I went straight to the front door so I could make sure that Reese was going to leave.

I waited another few minutes before Reese joined me in the living room. He had his big travel bag thrown across his shoulders while he toted the medium one in his hand. "So, how long do you want me gone?" he asked.

"Reese, I don't want you coming back. I don't want to be in this marriage anymore."

"So, what are you saying?"

"I'm filing for divorce."

"Come on, Dawn, it hasn't gotten that bad, has it?" He dropped both of his travel bags on the floor in front of him.

"Reese, I am done with you and I don't wanna be married to you anymore," I told him, giving him the sincerest expression I could muster up. The small amount of respect I had for him was now gone. The mere sight of him disgusted me, so this was it. I was putting the nail in the coffin.

Reese reached toward me like he wanted to embrace me, but I stepped back, preventing him from doing so. "Reese, don't touch me. Just leave."

He finally got the hint that I didn't want him anymore and picked his things up from the floor. To make this transition swift, I opened the front door for him so he could leave.

"Baby, I love you so much! And if you can find it in your heart to forgive me, I promise I will give up gambling and I will be a better husband to you," he said. I guess this speech was his last-ditch effort to get me to change my mind. But I wasn't listening to his bullshit! It was the same song and dance, and I'm over it. Over him and over all the shit that comes with him.

"Leave, Reese," I said with finality.

"Will you at least think about it?" he wanted to know, his facial expression that of a man in dire need.

"Reese, I'm not going to tell you again." I raised my voice, hoping he'd take heed to my warning.

"A'ight, I'ma leave. But I'm going to my grandma's house if you need me."

"Yeah, whatever."

Reese finally walked out of the house, and when he did I closed the door and I locked it. Part of me was hurt because I really wanted our marriage to work. But at the same time, I couldn't continue to allow that man to drag me through the mud. He had ruined everything I brought to this relationship. I had carried him so long, and the debt he had put me in was insane. I was embarrassed by the way my life had turned out because of him. My parents were right when they said that I needed to leave him when he started acting reckless. But no, I wanted to stick by my man and show him that I was a ride-or-die chick. Look where that got me. On a one-way trip down skid row. How stupid was I?

37

REESE

How the hell did I get put out of my own house? Granted, I didn't put the money down on it, and my name wasn't on the loan, but I paid those fucking mortgage payments. So, do I still have the right to be there? What the fuck am I going to do now?

I threw my two travel bags in my truck and drove out of there. During the drive to my grandmother's house, all I could think about was if Dawn was really serious about divorcing me. She had never, ever talked about leaving me before, or divorcing me for that matter, so should I believe her? I swear, if she left me I would go fucking crazy. I knew I wouldn't be the same. Dawn has always held me down, even in our rough times. To have her walk out of my life wouldn't be something I could handle, especially with all this shit going on with the human trafficking investigation. I mean, what if I got locked up? Would Dawn come see me? Or make sure my commissary was always plentiful? I couldn't live without that woman, so I had to figure this out.

It didn't take me long to get to my grandmother's house. I called her phone as soon as I pulled up into her driveway.

"Hey, Grandma, I'm outside," I told her after she answered the phone.

"Are you getting ready to come inside the house?" she asked me.

"Yes, ma'am, I just wanted to let you know that I just pulled up and that I will be in the house any minute."

"Okay, baby, I'm in here," she told me.

I grabbed my belongings and headed inside the house. Like always, my grandmother was in her bedroom sitting in her lounge chair, watching TV. She smiled as soon as she saw me. "She put you out the house, huh?"

I sighed heavily. "Yes, ma'am, she did."

"Do you want to talk about it?"

"There's not much to talk about. I think she's gonna leave me," I replied as I leaned against the wall in her bedroom.

"Do you cheat on her?"

"No. I got us in a lot of debt and she's not happy about it."

"How much debt are you two in?"

"A little over fifty thousand dollars."

"You have got to be joking, son. How did you do that?"

"Credit card debt, mortgage payments, and other bills."

"Now I see why she wants to leave your butt. You can't put that much strain on a woman, especially in these times. Folks are losing their jobs and their homes because they can't afford to pay their bills anymore. You're gonna have to clean your act up and do it fast."

"I think it's too late for that."

"What makes you say that?"

"Because she said she's gonna file for divorce."

"If I don't know anything else, I know that that woman loves you. Give her a few days to cool down. She may come around. But if she doesn't, God will give you the strength to get through this time."

"I hope so," I said, trying to think positive.

"Where are your things?"

"I left them at the front door."

"Well, you can take your old room. But you're gonna have to make your bed on your own. Grandma don't make beds for grown folks anymore."

I cracked a half smile. "I really love her, Grandma."

"I know you do, son. But you're gonna have to let God work this out for you."

"Sometimes God takes too long. And what if He doesn't?"

"Then it wasn't meant to be."

"If it wasn't meant to be, then why did we get married in the first place?"

"Because you did it on your own. Who knows, she may not have been the woman that God had for you in the first place. Have you wondered why it's been impossible for you two to have a child together? It's probably not in God's will."

I know my grandmother means well, but I wasn't trying to hear anything she had to say. I wanted my wife back. I wanted to be home with her. Not here with my grandmother, listening to her tell me about how God's will works. Now don't get me wrong, I grew up going to church, so I believe in God. But sometimes it's hard to talk to God and understand when He gives you answers. Sometimes I think that when I pray to Him I don't get answers. So what am I supposed to do? Just sit back and not do anything? Not doing anything isn't a part of my DNA. I guess that entitles me to do what I think is best for me.

"Yeah, we'll see," I finally replied.

"What's going on down there where you work at? Is it really true that y'all found some dead Asian people in a few of those containers?"

"Yes, ma'am," I replied nonchalantly, because I wasn't in the mood to talk about what's going on down at the terminal. I came here to get away from it.

"Why were those people in there in the first place?" she inquired. My grandmother was an old woman from the

South. Even if I told her why those Asian people were found dead, she still wouldn't comprehend it. So I thought for a second and said, "They were poor and they didn't have a place to live, so they crawled into those steel containers and their oxygen ran out and they died."

"Oh my, that's horrible."

"Yeah, I know. That's what everyone around the terminal is saying too."

"Well, I hear they are trying to get someone to take the fall for those people," she continued.

"Because that's just how society works. When something goes wrong, someone always has to take the fall for it," I explained to her. And it seemed like as soon as I finished my response she wanted to go deeper into that situation, so I changed the subject entirely. "Have you had lunch yet?" I asked her.

"I just had a cup of coffee and a bagel. Why?"

"Because I was gonna go out and get you some of that hot fried fish from your favorite spot."

My grandmother started smiling. "You sure know the way to my heart."

I smiled back. "That's right," I said. I walked toward her and gave her another kiss on her cheek. "Stay right here and I'll be right back."

"And where am I gonna go?" She cracked a smile.

"I don't know. But you know you women sure know how to sneak off to places when you want to."

"That's what I used to do in my younger days. I can't do it now. Ole grandma sits in her house all day long and minds her own business. That's my life," she said and waved me off.

Before I left the house, I took my travel bags into my old bedroom. I looked around the room and noticed that nothing in it had changed. She still had the full-size bed in there, along with the old dresser and mirror. The comforter, the sheets, and the pillows were all the same too. I remembered when I was a child sleeping in this room. The memories of having to be in this room all day because I was on punishment were very vivid. I also remembered hiding in here, underneath my bed, when my mother used to try to take me home with her. I didn't want to be with her and her abusive boyfriend. Living with my grandmother was the best thing my grandmother could've ever done for me. I was able to sleep in a warm bed and eat hot meals for breakfast, lunch, and dinner. At my mother's small, rat-infested house, it was dark. Listening to her and her boyfriend fighting and not knowing if I was going to miss a meal for the day wasn't what any child should have to endure. Seeing my mother locked up in jail was probably the best thing for the both of us. She never meant me any good. In fact, I believe that if she was still on the streets now, I wouldn't be where I am today, great job security and married, even though both of those things are in jeopardy. I think I probably would've been in jail by now. Who knows, I could have been dead too. All my friends from my mother's neighborhood are either dead or in prison serving ten and twenty years for selling drugs. I also had a homeboy I grew up with who is in prison, like my mother, for murder. So, my life could've easily mirrored their lives. Once again, I thanked my grandmother for everything she has done for me. She kept me from going to jail when I was growing up and now I needed to figure out how to keep myself from going to jail.

38

DAWN

I can't believe that I just put Reese out of the house. Was that the right thing to do? Was I overreacting? Should I have done it in a different way? Or should I have given him another chance?

But now that I mulled over it more, I think I definitely made the right decision. Reese was going down a slippery slope and he was taking me with him. I mean, come on, why the fuck did he give me money and then take it back? What the fuck was going through his mind? I couldn't keep living like this. My family had bailed me and him out of every situation we'd been in, and it wasn't fair to them, so putting him out was the best thing I could do. Now I needed to call my mother for a second opinion.

I called her cell phone and prayed that my dad didn't answer it. I kept my fingers crossed until I heard her voice after the third ring. "Hello," she said.

"Hi, Mom."

"Hi, baby, are you okay?"

"Is Dad around?"

"He's outside in the garage. Would you like for me to get him?"

"No. I called to talk to you. I just didn't want Dad around listening."

"What's wrong, baby?"

"I just told Reese that I am filing for divorce, and I put him out of the house."

"Oh, darling, what happened?"

"Mom, I'm just tired of trying to make this marriage work. Every time I move us one step forward, he's always pulling us two steps backwards."

"What did he do?"

"He gave me money to catch up on some bills, but as soon as I turned my back he went into our savings and took most of it back without telling me."

"What did he do with the money?"

"He gambled it up."

"Oh, honey, I am so sorry to hear that."

Hearing my mother try to comfort me made me break down and cry. It seemed like I let the floodgates open. "Mom, I can't figure out why he's always screwing up things in our relationship."

"Well, baby, I can't answer that question. But I always knew that when you were tired of his mess you were going to do what was best for you."

"I am so mad at myself for wasting my time with him."

"Don't beat yourself up, baby. You had to get to this place you're in right now, so you make the best decision for your life."

"But why couldn't he do right by me? I'm a good woman, Mommy."

"I know, baby."

"I swear, I regret the day I met him."

"I told you not to beat yourself up. It's not your fault. You sacrificed a lot of yourself for this man. And the fact that he doesn't appreciate you is sickening."

Listening to my mother tell me how great I was touched

my heart. And she was right, I wasn't being appreciated. Reese hadn't shown me any gratitude for a long time. But yet and still, I stuck it out with him. I lied to my parents from day one about how great my relationship with Reese was. They knew I was lying, but they left it alone. They even rode with me after I married Reese. My father paid for the bulk of the wedding expenses at the last minute, when a couple of Reese's checks bounced. I was mortified, but like the great man my father is, he stepped in and made everything right.

"Who are you talking to?" I heard my dad ask my mother. I could tell that he had just walked into the room.

"Mom, do not tell Dad it's me," I whispered through the receiver as if my father could hear me talking.

"You know I don't lie to your father," my mother replied.

I swear, I was so fucking pissed off that my mother threw me under the bus like that. "Really, Mom? That's what we're doing?" Here I was, trying to have a heart-to-heart with her, and as soon as my dad walked into the house she started getting all righteous and shit. Ugh! She was such a fucking sucker for my father.

"Is that Dawn?" I heard my father say.

"Yes, Joe."

"What's wrong now?" my father continued to pry.

"Mom, I'm hanging up now," I replied sarcastically. And before she could say another word I disconnected our call. I was so irritated that my mother sold me out like that. She ain't gonna like it, but I'm putting her on ice for these next couple of days.

39

REESE

Ten minutes into the drive away from my grandmother's house, I picked up my cell phone four times, intending to call Dawn. But each time I decided against it. I figured that it was too soon to try to talk to her, and my feeling of rejection weighed on me too heavily.

While I had my cell phone in hand, it started ringing. When I look at the caller ID I saw the call was coming from Norfolk International Terminal. I answered it on the second ring because I knew it was my manager calling.

"Hello," I said.

"Reese Spencer?"

"Yes."

"My name is Bradley Nelson and I am a US Customs agent at NIT."

"How can I help you?"

"I'm sure you heard that the Immigration Unit and our field office are investigating the recent discovery of seven Asian refugees that were found dead in two of NIT's metal containers."

"Yeah, heard about it. What's up?"

"As you know, we are interviewing everyone that works

third shift at NIT. We're gonna need you to come down to the terminal so we can interview you."

"I called in and told my manager that I was sick, so can this wait until I come back to work?"

"No, I'm afraid not. We'd appreciate it if you can come down here within the next hour."

"What happens if I say no?"

"Then we will show up at your house and escort you back down to NIT ourselves."

"From the tone of your voice I feel threatened."

"Mr. Spencer, we're only trying to do our job. And if you make it hard for us to do that, that will make your life hard."

"Yeah, whatever. I'll be down there in thirty minutes."

"Well, I guess I'll see you then."

Instead of replying, I hung up my cell phone. I can't lie when I say that I was scared shitless. I thought I could avoid this investigation at least a couple more days. But the US Customs agents had another plan for me.

The drive to NIT was dreadful. I wanted to turn my car around and go back home at least six times. But then I thought, what good is that going to do me? Agent Nelson sounded like an asshole, so I knew if I didn't show up he was gonna do exactly what he said he would. And I couldn't have that. So, I prepared for what I was going to say when I saw him.

It was obvious that he was going to have me by the balls when he found out my role in this botched human trafficking scheme, so my only choice in the matter was to tell him the truth. This might help my chances of not going to jail. And I would soon find out.

When I arrived at NIT, I parked my car in the parking lot in my normal spot. Like clockwork, everyone who worked the third shift always parked in the same spot, so when I did the same I didn't recognize any of the cars there. It felt like I was here by myself. And it seemed like it all happened overnight: No Edward. No Todd. No Brian. And no Gene. It was just me.

I got out of my car and walked to the main building, which was where Immigration and US Customs agents were housed. My stomach felt like it had over a dozen knots jumping around with no place to go. I gave myself a pep talk. "Calm down, Reese, you can do this."

Right before I entered the building, I took a deep breath and then I exhaled. "Just be honest and candid and you'll get through this."

Upon entering the building, I walked up to the receptionist's desk and told the woman sitting behind it that my name was Reese Spencer and that I was there to see Agent Nelson.

"Take a seat, and I will let him know that you are here," the older Caucasian woman said.

I took a seat in the waiting area. I tried to rehearse what I was gonna say, but I was thrown off track when I saw a black man, dressed semi-casual, escorting Gene Harris to the area of the building where I was sitting. Gene didn't see me. But I saw him shake the guy's hand and walk off. At that very moment, I was paralyzed. One part of me wanted to run away as fast as I could, but then the other part of me convinced me to stay, because I figured since Gene had already talked to the agent, he had one leg up on me. He might even have a get-out-of-jail-free card. Whatever he had, he got it before I did, so now was the time for me to look out for me. Fuck everyone else. I was not going to jail for the rest of these niggas, and they would soon find out about it.

As Gene walked away from the agent, I had to let him know that I was there and that I saw him. Niggas always want to be slick. But I saw him. "Gene, what's up? I've been trying to get in touch with you," I yelled across the lobby as I stood up.

When Gene looked at me, he acted like he'd seen a

ghost, and to put icing on the cake, the nigga just waved me off like I was a groupie or something. I laughed it off. I wasn't gonna let that nigga piss me off. I was just appreciative that I saw where he was coming from. It's every man for himself.

After Gene walked off, that same guy that escorted him started walking over to where I was standing. When he got within arm's reach, he extended his hand. "Reese Spencer?" he asked.

"Yeah, I'm Reese Spencer," I said, extending my hand for him to shake, even though I know he already knew who I was. His handshake was very firm. He instructed me to follow him down the hall.

"I'm gonna take you to our conference room," he told me.

"All right, cool," I said. But I was a nervous wreck. Here this guy was, acting normal like we were going to have a casual conversation, but I knew that if he could slap the handcuffs on me right now, he would.

"Want anything to drink? Coffee? Tea?" he offered right after we entered the conference room.

"No, I'm fine, thank you." I took a seat in a chair next to the conference room door. I figured if I sat there I wouldn't have far to walk when I was ready to leave.

"All right. Give me a second to round up my other partner and the agents from Immigration and I will be right back," he assured me.

As soon as he left, my heart took a nosedive into the pit of my stomach. Was I making the right choice by coming here to talk to these guys without an attorney? Dawn said I needed an attorney. But how could I afford one now? I'll tell you what, after I give these guys the information they need, it will be smooth sailing. Once all of this is over, I will prove to Dawn that I am right and she is wrong.

I sat in the conference room for at least three minutes before I was joined by a total of four agents. There were two agents from Immigration standing before me and two more agents from US Customs. All four of them introduced themselves to me and shook my hand. Agent Nelson's investigative partner's name was Agent Campbell and the two agents from Immigration were Agent Miles and Agent Scott.

"All right, Mr. Spencer," Agent Nelson started off, "I told you to come in today because we are investigating the human trafficking case that started a couple days ago. And it is imperative that we all rally around each other so we can get through this and figure out what went wrong," he continued.

"So, what do you need to know from me?" I asked him.

"We need to know what you know. We need to know what happened the night the containers came in. We already know who pulled them off the ship, so all we need to know is who moved them to the wrong location of the pier and why," Agent Nelson said.

"Is that what Gene told you?"

"Don't let our interview with Gene distract you from giving your side of the story," Agent Nelson replied. "Now we're going to start recording this entire interview, so if you need some time to answer our question, just say so, because we will not turn this recorder off until the interview is finished. Do you follow me?"

"Yes, I do. But can I ask you a question?" I said.

"I'm listening."

"What am I going to get for my statement? I mean, I know how this thing works. Something illegal happens and whoever talks to the cops first and gives them what they asked for, y'all give 'em a get-out-of-jail-free card. So, I was thinking, would I be able to apply for one of those?"

"I don't know about a get-out-of-jail-free card, but I'm sure we can come up with something, just as long as you haven't killed someone."

"Oh, hell no! I'm not into that."

"Well, then you should be okay. I'm turning on the

recorder now." Agent Nelson started off. "My name is Agent Nelson and today is April 10, 2018. The time is 1:23 in the afternoon, and I am conducting an interview in an effort to solve the case involving seven Asian refugees who died while traveling from Korea inside a metal container. I have Reese Spencer at this interview because he is a person of interest. I also have Agents Miles, Campbell, and Scott, who may chime in as needed. Anyone have any questions?" Agent Nelson said.

"No," said Agents Campbell and Miles.

"I don't have any questions either," Agent Scott replied.

"Great. So, Mr. Spencer, can you tell us what were you doing on the night of April 8, 2018, after you clocked in to begin your workday?" Agent Nelson began.

"Well, after I clocked in I headed over to my station on the pier and met up with Edward, Brian, Gene, and Todd."

"What did you do after you met them?"

"Well, Edward pulled all of us into a huddle and told us that he ran into a Chinese guy named Que Ming who said he'd pay each of us fifteen thousand dollars if we helped take two containers off the ship. So Ed took the money and told him that we'd do it."

"Was this the group's first job?"

"No. This was the second time we did it."

"What do you know about Que Ming?"

"I don't know shit about him except that he owns a few Chinese restaurants and a few charter buses that drive back and forth from here to New York."

"Do you know where he lives?"

"Nah, I don't."

"So, what was your job in his whole operation?"

"Well, after Ed took the containers off the ship, it was my job to take the containers over to the railroad car, so that's what I did."

"Did anything unusual happen?"

"I don't understand what you mean by that," I told him. It sounded like he was trying to trip me up.

"What happened after you picked up the containers and moved them?"

"Nothing, I just moved them," I said, but I knew where he was going with this. He wanted me to confess to seeing people trying to escape out of the container.

"So, you didn't see any of the immigrants while you were moving the containers to the other side of the pier?"

"Oh, that's what you're talking about?" I tried playing dumb. "Yeah, I did see a couple of them escaping."

"How many were there?"

"Two."

"Two men, women, what?"

"I think they were men. Remember, it was dark, so I couldn't really get a good look at their physical attributes."

"Are you sure you saw two?"

"Yes, I'm sure."

"Okay, well, tell me what you did after you saw them trying to escape."

"I called Ed first and told him what was going on and that I was going to need some help. He told me okay. A few minutes later, Brian came over to where I was and helped me round those two people up. I managed to get one of the escapees back in the container, but Brian didn't have so much luck."

"What do you mean by that?"

"What I'm saying is that while Brian was trying to catch that other guy, he made the mistake of choking him to death."

"Did you see him choking that guy to death?"

"No, I didn't see him in the act. But when I saw him dragging the man's lifeless body back to the railroad cars, I asked him what happened. And that's when he told me."

"What happened next?"

"Well, we knew that he wasn't going to be able to put the man's body back into the container, so he figured that hiding the body somewhere on the terminal would be a better idea, and so he did it. And by the time he decided to do it, Gene had come over to where we were and helped Brian hide the body."

"Did you see Gene hide the body with Brian?"

"No, but I saw Gene as he helped Brian carry the body toward the front gate of the terminal."

"After catching that one Asian fellow, why did you put him back into the container?"

"Because that's where he came from."

"It didn't occur to you that what you were doing was illegal?"

"You mean taking the containers to the railroad cars? Or making the guy get back into the container?"

"Both. But the most severe is the one when you made that person get back into the container."

"What was I supposed to do? Make him get in my truck and take him home with me?"

"No. You were supposed report this whole operation to us."

"Come on, now, I don't know where you're from, but where I'm from, snitches get stitches."

"But you're in here with us now."

"That's because you told me to come down here."

"Don't bullshit us, Reese! You came down here because you're trying to save yourself from going to jail."

"Did you give this same spiel to Gene while he was in here spilling his guts to you?"

"I told you before, don't let Gene's presence here distract you. We're talking to you. No one else right now," Agent Nelson scolded me. "Now, tell us where that fifteen thousand dollars is."

"I never got it."

"What do you mean, you never got it?"

"Edward told us that as soon as the job was done, Mr. Ming was going to pay us."

"That's not what we heard."

"What did you hear?"

"We heard that Mr. Cuffy gave all of you guys five thousand dollars up front for this last job and that you were going to get the rest of the money owed to you when the job was completed. Is that true?"

"Yeah, that's how it was supposed to happen," I agreed.

"Tell me Todd Dale's role in this operation," Agent Nelson said.

I thought for a moment and then I said, "Well, he didn't do anything really. He uses the same machine as Edward does, so he was working down at the other end of the ship."

"Did he take the five thousand that Edward passed out to everyone?"

"Yes."

"And have you talked to him since this investigation started?"

"Yes, I talked to him a couple of times."

"What did you guys talk about?"

"I called him first and asked him had he heard from Ed, because Ed was supposed to meet me and give me the rest of my money, but he didn't show up. And Todd said that he was waiting to see Ed too."

"You do know that Mr. Cuffy is dead, right?" Agent Nelson said.

"Yeah, I do. So, the second time I talked to Todd he asked me did I know about the murder, and I told him that my wife had just told me about it."

"What else did he say?"

"Nothing. That's it."

"How was Todd's relationship with Mr. Cuffy?"

"Look, man, everybody was cool with everybody. None of us was beefing before this thing happened or after. We just wanted to get paid. That's it."

"When was the last time you spoke with Brian Butler?"

"Not since he and Gene disposed of that man's body. I tried calling him a couple of times, but his cell phone keeps going to voicemail."

"Where is the money that Edward gave you?"

"I took it to a gambling spot and blew it. I thought since I wasn't getting the other ten grand, I might as well try to make up for it in a couple hands of poker."

"You're saying you gambled all of that money up?"

"Yes, I did."

"Did your wife know about the human trafficking operation?"

Before I answered this fool's question I looked at him like he had just bumped his damn head. Did he really think I was going to throw my wife under the bus? Was he fucking stupid? Whether he knew it or not, I knew how this game was being played. If I confessed that I told Dawn about it beforehand, then she'd become an accomplice. And I couldn't have that. They might throw her ass in jail or hit her in the head with over ten years of probation and make her pay a whole bunch of restitution. So, the answer was no. She had no knowledge of my involvement nor did she know that the ship was coming in with the Asian people on it.

"Listen, Agent Nelson, I wouldn't have dared to tell my wife about this whole thing because for one, she would've talked me out of it, and if I wouldn't have listened to her, she would've given me an ultimatum. Either her or that job."

"Does she know that we called you in for an interview?"

"No."

"Why not?"

"Because I don't want to stress her out about something I got myself into."

"So, when will you tell her?"

"When I think the time is right."

"Can you tell us where Brian Butler is?"

"I wish I could, but I can't."

"Why not?"

"I don't think anyone knows where he is."

"Well, do you have any further words before we end this interview?" Agent Nelson asked, giving me the floor.

"Yeah," I said, and then I paused and all eyes were on me. "Well, I'd like to start off by saying that I didn't know that after I did this job with Edward and the other guys that it would turn out like this. All we were told to do was move the containers to the railcars. That's it. And for doing that, we were supposed to be paid fifteen grand each. We were just guys trying to make a quick buck. And I know that our actions don't minimize our role in it, because some of those people died and I feel really bad about it. But at the same time, we didn't put a gun to those people's heads and pull the trigger. I mean, if I could turn the clock back, I would. I also would've reported it to you guys as well. So, I'm sorry."

Agent Nelson let out long sigh and then he said, "My name is Agent Nelson and my interview with Reese Spencer has just ended. The time is 3:02 and I'm signing out."

After Agent Nelson stopped the recorder he looked at me and said, "I'm going to take this tape to my supervisor and have him to listen to it. But let me ask you, would you be willing to testify in front of a jury and help us build a case against Mr. Que Ming?"

"No question. Sure. I'll do everything you want me to do," I said willingly.

Agent Nelson and the other agents shook my hand and thanked me for coming in today. I couldn't believe that this interview turned out the way it did. I know one thing, whatever they tell me to do, I'm going to do it, if it means that I stay on the streets. I can't do a day in jail. Not while my wife is out here on the streets. No way! I refuse to let another nigga take my wife from me. She's the best thing that ever happened to me. I guess now what I need to do is figure out how I am going to get her back before she files for divorce. It's either now or never.

40

DAWN

When I heard the knock at my door and the words, "Dawn, open this door, it's your sister out here," I rose up from the living room sofa because I knew it was Alexia.

Immediately after I opened the front door she pulled me into her arms and held me tight. "Mama told me you're filing for divorce."

"Yep, that's what I plan to do," I replied after she released me from her embrace.

"So, what happened?" Alexia wanted to know while she watched me close the front door and lock it.

"What hasn't he done?" I answered sarcastically as I walked back over to the sofa and took a seat.

Alexia sat next to me. "So, what made you come to this decision? I mean, I know he had to have done something as recent as today for you to call our mama."

"Well, what happened was he gave me money to pay the fees for my fertility treatment and pay some bills with the rest of it. Well, as soon as I turned my back, he goes and takes most of the money back. And then on top of that he blew it up on a fucking card game. I swear, Alexia, I am done with him. This was the last straw for me." I started sobbing. His behavior and lack of regard for me was starting to break me down, which is why I started crying.

"Sis, don't cry. It's that nigga's loss. Not yours," Alexia said, trying to make me feel better. She leaned forward to wipe the tears that were falling from my eyes.

I sniffled a bit and then I said, "I think now is the time that I cut all my losses and move on with my life, because if I allowed Reese to come back home so we could work this out, he'd go right back to doing the same shit again. And I can't have that type of drama in my life. I'm not trying to go backwards, I'm trying to move forward."

"Does he know that you're gonna file for divorce?"

"Yeah, I told him right after I told him to get out the house."

"Has he tried to call you?"

"No. And I'm glad too. I just wish he would go on about his life and leave me alone. I'm getting too old for this shit!"

"Think he might be staying with his grandmom?"

"I'm sure he is. But I couldn't care less."

"That's right, sis, stand your ground and leave that nigga once and for all." Alexia cheered me on and then she said, "You know Dad is happy as hell that you're finally leaving Reese."

"I'm sure he is," I said while the tears continued to fall from my eyes. "Hand me a tissue from that box on the coffee table."

She handed me the box, I took a tissue and began to wipe the tears away from my eyes and cheeks.

"Have you thought about what you're gonna do with this house?" Alexia wanted to know.

"Damn, Lexi, I just put the nigga out of the house."

"I know. But I know how you are, and if that nigga gets on his knees and starts begging, you will let him back in the house. And I can't have that. It's time for you to move on with your life and get with a man who will appreciate you."

"I want that too. But I'm not gonna be able to fall out of love with Reese overnight, Alexia."

"Well, if you start right now, then you'll be well on your way," she replied, giving me a snide look.

I ignored her comment and said, "You know what?"

"What?"

"I sat here earlier and wondered if that nigga is sitting around crying like I'm crying over him."

"Girl, please, niggas don't sit around and cry. They off to the next bitch! Trust me, I know."

"I wonder what his grandmother is saying about all of this."

"She's probably not saying anything. You know how old people are, they couldn't care less about what young folks like us do."

"Yeah, you're probably right," I replied nonchalantly.

"Thought about who you're gonna hire to rep you in your divorce?"

"Damn, Lexi, I just decided today that I'm going to file for divorce."

"Well, if you want me to help you, I'll be more than glad to find one for you."

"I'll let you know." I turned my focus to the television because I noticed that my favorite movie, *Shawshank Redemption*, was on. I wasn't fully engaged in the movie, but it was enough that it took my mind off Reese for a few minutes at a time.

When Alexia realized that I'd rather look at TV than talk about Reese's no-good ass, she left me alone so I could watch the movie. During commercial breaks, she would say little things like, *I can't believe that you're gonna be in this house all by yourself.* And then she said, *I'm glad that Dad helped you get this house instead of Reese, because if he did, Reese would try to take half of what you'd sell the house for.*

Without saying one word, I just nodded my head like I agreed with her. I knew my sister all too well. If I would've fed into her comments, we'd be having a full-fledged conversation right now. This was her way of getting information out of me without seeming to be nosy.

Surprisingly, she watched the entire movie with me and then she watched a few of my taped reality shows too. She cooked a pot of spaghetti for us. But I only ate a few forkfuls while Alexia ate two plates of it. And before we knew it, time had flown by and it was dark outside. "I'm so tired," I announced while I was lying down on the sofa.

"You ready to go to bed?" she asked me.

"Yeah, I think it's time. Maybe after I get up in the morning, I'll feel better than what I feel like now."

"If you want me to stay with you tonight, I will."

"No, you don't have to, Lexi. I'll be all right," I assured her.

"Are you sure? Because you know I don't mind."

"I'm sure," I told her as I stood up from the couch. A few seconds later, I escorted her to the front door and opened it. I followed her out.

"Where you going?" she asked me.

"I'm walking you to your car, silly."

"You don't have to. I'm a big girl."

"Lexi, I'm already out here, so come on." I grabbed her by her arm. As soon as we walked off the porch, I stopped in my tracks when I noticed the same car from all the other times was parked on the opposite side of the street again. "Oh my God!" I said, staying completely still.

"What's wrong?" Alexia asked.

"You see that black car parked on the other side of the street?"

"Yeah, why?"

"Whoever it is keeps parking there, but as soon as they figure out that I'm on to him or her, they drive away."

"The windows are tinted really black. Are you sure some-one is in the car?" Alexia said, squinting her eyes.

"Yes, I am. You don't see that head in the driver seat?" I raised my hands a bit and pointed toward the car.

"Fuck that! We're walking over there to see who it is," Alexia said and took off, holding on to my arm.

"Are you crazy? I'm not going over there with you." I rebelled and snatched my arm away from her. That didn't stop Alexia though. She raced across the lawn and headed directly toward the car. But before she stepped onto the street, the engine started up and whoever was behind the wheel sped off. Alexia's crazy ass started running behind the car.

"Where the fuck you think you're going? Bring your ass back down here and show your face like a man!" she roared.

I was both shocked at Alexia's reaction and scared that someone was really there to watch me, and that also made me feel uneasy. "Lexi, come back before they turn around," I yelled.

"That's what I want them to do. Bring that ass back!" she yelled back at me.

Instead of going back and forth with Alexia, I ran into my house, grabbed a duffel bag from my closet, and started packing any- and everything within reach. I didn't care if it matched or not. I knew I had to get out of my house and that was what I did.

By the time Alexia walked back into the house, I already had my bags at the front door. She looked down at the floor and said, "Whatcha doing?"

"I'm getting the hell out of this house. I'm not staying here by myself, so let's go," I told her as I picked my things up from the floor.

Alexia helped me with my bags as we exited my house. I closed the front door, locked it, and made my way off my front porch.

"Are you riding with me or no?" she asked me.

"I'm not leaving my car here. I'm taking it with me," I replied as I approached it. I opened up the back door and threw all of my things on one side of the back seat, while Alexia threw the things she was carrying onto the other side.

"I'm gonna let you pull out first," she told me.

"All right," I said, and hopped in my car. I started up the engine, put my car in reverse, sped out of the driveway, and headed in the direction of my parents' house.

41

REESE

Leaving the terminal after talking to those agents, I developed mixed feelings. One part of me was glad that I got all this shit off my shoulders. But the other side of me is kind of scared that everything I told them could backfire on me. I needed to stay a free man, so whatever I needed to do to make that happen, I would do it.

When I returned to my grandmother's house earlier with another order of fried fish, I gave her the food and then I retreated to my childhood bedroom and tried to get a nap in, but it didn't happen. What happened was that I binged on old episodes of *Good Times* and *Sanford and Son*. This took my mind off Dawn for a little while, that is until the last episode ended.

Lying there on that small-ass bed was making me feel very uncomfortable. So I got up, grabbed my cell phone from the bed, and walked outside to my truck. I hopped on the back of it and sat on the hood. I played with my Instagram page for a while, looking at old photos of me and Dawn. I knew seeing her smiling in those pictures was going to persuade me to call her. And what do you know, that's what I did. "Dawn, please answer the phone," I begged while I anxiously listened to her phone ringing. I

started thinking all kinds of things. Maybe she was looking at the caller ID and refused to answer my call. I even
thought about her leaving her phone in another part of the
house so she wouldn't be able to hear my call.

The line rang exactly seven times before it went to
voicemail. I was pissed off, so I disconnected the line and
redialed her number. This time her phone went straight to
voicemail. "Hi, you've reached Dawn. I'm not available
right now. So, leave me a brief message and your number
and I will call you back," it said and then the voicemail
bell chimed. But once again, I didn't leave a message. I
wanted to talk to my wife, not a fucking machine. So, for
the third time I redialed her number, with no luck. My call
went straight to voicemail. This time I had no other choice
but to leave her a message. "Dawn, I know I've done a lot
of fucked up shit and you should've left me a long time
ago. But, baby, please give me another chance. I swear, I
will change. I will be that husband you always wanted me
to be. I will stop gambling. And I will start going to church
like you always wanted me to do. I will do anything you
ask me to do. I promise. I love you, baby, so please call me
back," I said, and then I ended my voicemail message.

I tried calling Brian's number again, but for some reason
his phone line wouldn't ring. It also didn't go to voicemail
either. "What the fuck!" I mumbled. "I know this nigga
did not block my number," I said aloud as I cleared the
line and redialed his number. But once again, it wouldn't
ring, and that's when I knew for sure that he blocked me.
"Fucking loser!" I cursed out loud. I was beyond pissed
off at this point. But there wasn't anything I could do. I
guess all I could do now was play the waiting game.

I went back into my grandmother's house and joined
her in her bedroom. Like always, she was sitting in her
chair, watching TV. She smiled at me as soon as I walked
into her bedroom. "You were in your room for a very long
time. Did you get some sleep?" she wanted to know.

"Nope. I sure didn't. But I would've loved to get some."

"Have you talked to your wife?"

"No, ma'am. I tried to call her a couple of times, but she wouldn't answer her phone."

"Well, that's just because she's hurting right now, baby. Just give her some more time, she may come around."

"But what if she doesn't?"

"I already gave you the answer to that question. And I also told you to give this situation to God too. Have you done it?"

I sighed heavily. "Yes, Grandma," I lied.

"Well, then I don't need to say another word," she told me, and then she smiled.

When I was about to say something else, a breaking news segment popped onto the television. *"This just in, a black male named Brian Butler was found dead in his home earlier today. The cause of death was two gunshots to the back of his head. The victim was found by his girl-friend when she came home several hours ago. The girl-friend asked that we withhold her name while she and his family mourn. So far, we know that Brian Butler was a fa-ther of two. He worked as a longshoreman at the Norfolk International Terminal for over a decade. He was loved by everyone that came in contact with him, so people are baf-fled at the fact that he was killed execution style. I spoke with one of the homicide detectives with the Norfolk divi-sion and he said that they don't know who murdered Mr. Butler, but that they will do everything possible to bring his killer to justice. If you have any information concern-ing this unfortunate tragedy, please call the tip line at 888-LOC-KUUP."*

"What is going on down at that terminal you working at? It seems like everybody is getting killed. You might wanna start working somewhere else. Because I would hate if someone called me and told me that someone killed you."

"Grandma, no one is going to kill me."

"Why you so sure? They're killing everybody else that works with you."

"Grandma, no, they aren't," I assured her, with the idea of making her less nervous. But she was right. Everyone around me was getting murdered. Was I next? If I was, then when was it going to happen? But more importantly, who was going to do it? I swear, I couldn't walk around not knowing what was going to happen next. It was obvious that whoever killed Edward and Brian killed them because they had to have done something wrong or screwed someone over. And if that was true, I needed to find out what was going on.

After finding out that Brian had just gotten murdered, I knew I needed to get Todd on the line. "Grandma, hold that thought, I'll be right back," I told her.

"You leaving the house?"

"No, ma'am, I'm going to my room to make a call," I replied, and then I made my exit.

As soon as I walked into my bedroom, I pulled my cell phone from my pocket and dialed Todd's cell phone number. "Todd, you better answer this damn phone," I said, thinking about what I was going to say. But as fate would have it, he didn't answer his phone either. "Damn!" I barked, hoping that his fate hadn't been sealed by Que Ming's hitmen. But then what if he wasn't answering my call because the cops got to him? That would be some fucked up shit. I mean, am I the nigga they don't fuck with anymore? Or was I a lame-ass chump because I was given a job to do and I screwed it up? Whatever the reason was, that shit was foul.

42

DAWN

En route to my parents' house, Reese tried calling me, but I kept sending his call to voicemail. After his third attempt, he finally left me a voicemail message. I pressed the voicemail key to listen.

Everything he said sounded good, but I didn't believe a word of it. He'd given me this same speech before. But this time I refused to waver. I wanted to be happy, and being with Reese wasn't going to give me the life I deserved. To be candid, he'd lost me for good this time. And there was no turning back for me.

Alexia and I finally made it to my parents' house. It felt so good to walk into a house and be surrounded by the people that I knew loved me. My mother was so happy to see me. But when I walked into the den to see my dad, he was watching TV. His face was literally glued to it. "What are you watching?" I asked him.

My dad grabbed the remote control from the coffee table in front of him and used it to turn the volume down. "The cops just found another one of your husband's friends dead," my dad said.

I stood there in utter shock. "Are you serious? Was it just on the news?"

"Yes, it just went off. And I would bet you that their deaths got something to do with the fact that port police and the Customs agents found those people in those containers."

"You think so, Daddy?"

"Sure, I do. You can't mess with those people from another country. They will eat you alive, especially if you're messing with their money."

"What money are you talking about?" I asked him.

"Whoever's idea it was for those people to come to this country in those metal containers was someone very powerful. And if someone very powerful lost a lot of money when those people didn't make it out of the terminal, your husband's friends were killed for that reason. Your husband better be careful, because he might be next."

"Dad, I think you're overreacting," I said, because he was really freaking me out. I didn't want to hear about Reese's friends being murdered and that it could be related to the human trafficking case. Did he know it would tear me up inside if I found out what he said was true? I knew Reese and I were going through a lot right now, but I didn't want to hear that there was a possibility Edward and Brian were killed because of those dead refugees. I swear I would lose my damn mind if something happened to Reese while we were going through our problems. I didn't think I'd ever be able to forgive myself for putting him out of the house. Okay, I know he screws up everything he touches, but when things count, the majority of the time he comes through. And if I could hold on to that, and get down on my knees and pray to God, then I believed that our situation would eventually work out.

Alexia entered the room. "What's this I hear that somebody got killed?" she asked.

"I was telling your sister here that another one of her husband's friends was found murdered in their house earlier today," my dad reiterated.

"Really? Who was it?"

"Reese's friend Brian."

"Oh, wow, that is sad," Alexia commented.

"Did they say how he died?"

"Yeah, he got shot in the head," my father said.

"Goodness gracious. It seems like whoever killed him was trying to send a message."

"I said the same thing," my father said.

"Where did they find him at?"

"His girlfriend found him in the house when she came home from work earlier today." My dad continued to explain everything he'd heard from the news broadcast.

"You think Reese knows about this?" Alexia asked me.

"I'm not sure. But it wouldn't surprise me if he does," I told her.

My dad changed the subject. "Are you really divorcing him?"

"Yes, I am, Dad."

"Now that you're leaving, aren't you glad you didn't have a baby by him?" My dad pressed the issue about Reese's and my relationship. What can I say? My dad is a very nosy man.

"Kinda sorta," I replied nonchalantly, because I really didn't want to talk about my marriage at all. I was more interested in the fact that Reese's friend Brian had just been killed. And if my father was right, Reese's life might be in danger too. My family wasn't gonna like this, but I was gonna have to call Reese and warn him about what I knew. I mean, if I didn't and something happened to him, I wouldn't be able to live with myself. "I'll be right back," I told my sister and my father.

"Where are you going?" my dad wanted to know.

"I've gotta make a phone call."

"To who?"

Instead of answering his question, I looked at him and said, "Do you really want to know who I'm about to call?

Because the last time I checked, I was a grown woman and I don't really have to answer to anyone."

"Oh Lord, she's getting defensive. And I know what that means," Alexia commented.

"What does it mean?" my father asked her.

"She's getting ready to call her husband."

"You know what, Alexia? I notice that every time we get around Mom and Dad, you always want to be extra messy."

"No, I don't."

"Then what do you call it?"

"Look, I'm just trying to look out for your best interests," she said, and then she changed the subject by saying, "Oh yeah, Daddy, did Dawn tell you that she has a stalker?"

My dad looked at me and said, "Dawn, is that true?"

"Daddy, I don't know who it is."

"What do you mean, you don't know who it is?"

"I've spotted a black car parked across the street from my house tonight and a few other times before that, and every time I let the person behind the wheel know that I see them, they always drive off."

"And this happened several times before?"

"Yeah."

"Why did you wait all this time to tell me?" My dad was becoming more furious by the minute.

"Because I got sidetracked with the news about Reese's friend. But I was going to eventually tell you."

"Daddy, I don't think she needs to go back to that house alone. Especially since she and Reese are divorcing. Anything could happen to her," Alexia said as my mother entered the room.

"What's going on?" she asked.

"Well, Dad just saw the news about another one of Reese's friends getting killed," Alexia said.

"Oh no, that's a travesty. What's going on down there at that terminal? Joe, you might need to call one of your

friends down there and find out what's really going on."
She turned toward me. "When did you get here?"

"A few minutes ago."

"She only came here because there's a stalker on the
loose in her neighborhood," Alexia blurted out.

"You're kidding, right?" my mother asked Alexia, and
then she looked at me. "Are you in danger too?"

"Mom, I don't know. But I think so," I replied, not
knowing what to say to her. I was kind of confused about
my situation.

"What happened?" my mother asked me, and then she
looked at Alexia for her to answer the question too.

"There's a car that sits on my block every other night
and watches my house. But when they find out that I see
them, they pull off before I can see who they are," I replied.

"Oh no, Joe, do you hear this? We can't have our
daughter living in that house all by herself."

"I told her that," my dad responded.

"Do you have a description of the car?" my mother
wanted to know.

"All I know is that it's a black car. A Mercedes-Benz," I
said.

"Baby, you're gonna need to file a police report," my
mother said.

"I think so too," my sister agreed.

My mother, my sister, and my dad convinced me to file
a police report. Although I wanted to go into another
room and call Reese, my dad and my sister escorted me
out of the house and down to the nearest police station.

When we arrived, I spoke with a detective in depth
about the times when I saw that car. I had to give precise
times and days that those incidents happened. I also had to
give a reason why I thought the driver was a stalker. The
report itself didn't take long. And when it was over, I felt
good that I made the report.

"Aren't you glad you came down here to file that report?" my dad asked me.

"Yeah, I am. I just hope that after doing this, I won't see that car popping up around my house anymore," I told him.

"Well, look at the bright side, you're at the house with your sister, me, and your mom, and nothing is going to happen to you while you're here with us."

"You can say that again," I commented, giving only a half smile.

On the way back to my parents' house, my dad stopped by the gas station so he could fill his car up with gas. While he was filling up his tank, Alexia got out of the car to go in the store and I waited in the car. I watched my dad for a few seconds to see how far he had gotten with the gasoline, and I looked at the front door of the store, calculating how long it would take my sister to buy whatever it was that she needed before she returned to the car. And when I realized that I had a two- to three-minute window to get Reese on the phone and say what it was I had to say, I grabbed my cell phone from my purse and began to dial Reese's cell phone number.

"Dawn, is that you?" he answered.

"Yes, it's me."

"Oh my God! I am so glad you called me back. It feels so good to hear your voice."

"Listen, Reese, I didn't call you to talk about us. I only called to see if you heard about Brian's murder."

"Yes, I saw it on the news not too long ago."

"Look, I don't know what's going on with you and everyone around you, but you need to look over your shoulder. I think that whoever killed Edward and Brian may come after you next."

"Don't worry about me, I'm good. I went to the terminal today and talked to the agents that are investigating the case. And because I'm cooperating with them, they said they can get me a good deal that will allow me to avoid going to jail if I testify in the case."

"Do you think that is wise?"

"Dawn, that's the only option I have."

"Be careful. Because whoever is doing this is not playing games. And I would hate to get a phone call saying that something happened to you. It would break my heart," I told him.

"Where are you?"

"I'm with my dad and my sister at the BP gas station off Virginia Beach Boulevard."

"Why are you with them, if you don't mind me asking?"

"Reese, that car showed up at the house again tonight. It was parked in the same spot as it always is. Luckily, Alexia was at the house with me when it happened. When she was about to leave the house, I decided to go with her so I wouldn't be home alone."

"Baby, I am sorry you are going through that."

"I'll be okay. My dad convinced me to go to the police station and make a report. So that's what I did," I explained to him. As soon as I uttered that last word, my dad was getting back in the car. "Hey, listen, I'm gonna have to call you later," I told him abruptly. I didn't want my father to know that Reese was on the other line.

"Wait. Why are you hanging up so soon? Don't you think we need to talk?" he pressed me.

"Right now is not a good time," I said nonchalantly, trying to sound as though I was talking to someone other than Reese. But it didn't work.

"Who are you talking to, baby girl?" my dad interjected. I gotta say that he is the nosiest guy in the world.

"Dad, please don't ask me any questions right now," I said, looking in my dad's direction.

"Yeah, tell him to mind his own business," Reese yelled from the other end. I could tell he was getting really irritated by my father's behavior.

"Don't talk to me like that. I am your father, young lady," my dad barked.

"When is he going to shut up?" Reese was still yelling.

"All right, look, Reese, let me call you back," I said.

"Yes, tell him you will call him back. You're with your family right now," my dad kept interjecting. He was running me fucking crazy with it.

"No, I am not hanging up, Dawn. I know shit ain't right with us right now, but you're still my wife."

"Is he giving you a hard time?" my dad said.

And before I could answer him, Alexia hopped back into the car. "Dad, why are you fussing?"

My dad had turned around in the driver seat so he could look back at me. "Your sister is on the phone with that loser husband of hers. She keeps telling him that she's going to call him back, but he won't get off the phone."

"Just hang up on him," Alexia blurted out.

"I know that ain't your sister running her mouth! Tell that bitch to mind her fucking business too," Reese screamed through the phone.

"Reese, please let me call you back."

"No, I wanna talk to you now."

"Hang up on him," my father belted out.

Instead of telling my father, Alexia, and Reese to all be quiet, I ended the call with Reese.

"Are you guys happy now?"

"Yes, I'm happy," my father said.

"I'm trying to figure out why you were carrying on a conversation with him, especially after all the crap he's taken you through," Alexia said.

"You wouldn't understand," I commented.

"You are so right. So, explain to me why you're taking a call from the man you're leaving? If it were me, I would've changed my cell phone number the moment he walked out the front door. I wouldn't have any words for that guy.

He's a pathetic human being. The quicker you see that, the better off you'll be."

"What, are you a relationship expert now?" I replied sarcastically.

"I'm whatever you want me to be," Alexia replied, and then she turned back around in her seat.

"FYI, the quicker y'all stop telling me what to do, the sooner I will come together with you guys. So, stop pushing me away, okay?" I said to them. But I know my words went through one ear and out the other. They'd better heed my warning because I was going to say it only once.

43

REESE

Dawn's old-ass father has become a thorn in my side. I hate that nigga with every fiber in my body. He can't stop poking his nose in our business. I swear, if I was in front of that motherfucker right now, I would hit him one good time in the mouth. That punch alone would knock all his teeth out of his mouth and prevent him from ever talking again.

Does he realize that Dawn is my wife? Does he realize that he's coming between us? From day one, that motherfucker has poked and pried into our affairs. He thinks that because he helped me pay for our wedding he could do or say anything he wants. It's my fault because I should've sat him down a long time ago and gave him the rules and things that I wasn't going to take from him. But no, I lay back like a passive-ass nigga and allowed that old-ass dude to do what he wanted. How would he feel if I always got into his and his wife's business? I bet he would shut me down at the first sign that I was going to be trouble for him and his wife. Well, see, that's the same respect I'm supposed to get, regardless if Dawn and I get a divorce or not. Speaking of which, I know he's happy as hell that Dawn wants to divorce me. He may not realize it, but I'm gonna win my wife back. And sooner than later, that's gonna happen.

It took a while to do it, but I finally calmed down after that altercation I had with Dawn's father and her sister. After Dawn ended our call, I held my cell phone in my hand for an hour, hoping that she would call me back. Unfortunately for me, she didn't. And I'm sure her family had something to do with it. So, as I placed my cell phone down on my bed, it started ringing. I picked the phone back up and looked straight at the caller ID. The phone number wasn't visible, so that seemed odd. But I answered it anyway, just in case it was Dawn blocking the number she was calling from.

"Hello," I said.

"Hey, Reese," the caller said.

I stood there for a second, waiting for the voice to register in my mind. "Todd, is that you?"

"Yeah, man, we need to talk."

"I tried calling you again, but your phone wasn't working," I told him.

"I know. I had to get rid of that phone. Hey, Reese, we need to talk."

"Sure. I'm listening. What's up?"

"Not over the phone. Can you meet me at the Starbucks coffee spot on Military Highway in twenty minutes?"

"Okay, I'll be there. But did you hear about what happened to Brian?" I blurted out before Todd disconnected the call.

"Yeah, I heard about it and that's why I called you. Remember, twenty minutes," Todd repeated.

"I'm leaving the house now," I assured him, and then we hung up.

Getting a call from Todd threw me for a loop. Not wanting to talk to me over the phone kind of spooked me. I wanted so badly to find out what he wanted.

On my way out of my grandmother's house, I yelled, "Hey, Grandma, I'll be right back. Okay?"

"Okay. But be careful driving out there. People are dangerous," I heard her yell back.

After I reassured her that I would, I made my exit. "What could Todd have to say in person that he refused to say over the phone?" I mumbled to myself. I hopped in my truck and sped out of my grandmother's neighborhood.

It took me less than fifteen minutes to get to the Starbucks where Todd told me to meet him. Surprisingly, he was there the moment I pulled into the parking lot, and waved me over to his car. I looked in both directions after I stepped out of my truck. I wanted to make sure I wasn't being ambushed by Todd or anyone who might be lurking behind one of these buildings. I saw that the coast was clear, so I hurried over to his car and got in.

As soon as I sat down in the passenger seat, I noticed how paranoid Todd was acting. He kept his eyes locked on the rearview mirror and occasionally he'd look out the driver-side window and the passenger side. "What's going on, Todd?" He was taking the word *paranoia* to the next level.

"Our lives are in danger," he said.

"What the fuck you mean, our lives are in danger? What's going on? And how do you know this?"

"Before Edward was killed, he told me that Que Ming was a very dangerous and powerful man. You saw how he looked at me when we were at his restaurant. So there was no room for error after we agreed to do the job for him. When we took his money, we were indebted to him. There was no turning back. But we fucked up and didn't deliver his goods to him. Immediately after that happened, targets were put our backs. Now I didn't know this then, but after

Edward and Brian turned up dead, I knew what Edward had told me in the beginning was true."

"Have you seen anyone hanging around your house?" I asked him. I wanted to know if he was having the same problem as Dawn.

"No, not that I've noticed."

"So, what you think we should do?"

"It's up to you, but my family and I are leaving town for a while. Well, at least until all of this blows over."

"What are you going to do about your job? You just gonna walk away from it?"

"Listen to me and listen good. I have a few days of vacation time and medical leave, but if I'm forced to go beyond that, I'll do it and won't give a damn what the union says. I'm more concerned about being alive. I can find another job somewhere else if need be."

"I understand whatcha mean," I told him. "Have you told Gene about this?"

"I've been trying to get in touch with him, but he still won't answer his phone."

"Don't worry about him. I saw him down at the pier. He's working with Customs and Immigration agents. He gave them the motherload about me, you, and Que Ming, so they are on the hunt and gonna start bringing in everyone that knew about this whole operation," I explained.

"They can do what they want. But they're gonna have to find me first, cause I'm getting out of here first thing in the morning. As a matter of fact, I'm gonna leave before the sun rises. I've got to make sure that no one is following me or my family."

"Have you thought about where you're gonna go?" I only asked him to get an idea where I could go if I decided to leave too.

"I prefer to keep that under wraps. I can't jeopardize putting my family in harm's way."

"I get it."

"So, are you leaving town or what?" Todd wanted to know.

I hesitated a moment before I answered him. I wanted to say yes, but since Dawn and I weren't in a good place in our marriage, I wasn't sure if she would go with me. "Yeah, I think I'm gonna leave too," I replied, even though I wasn't quite sure.

"Good for you. Well, I'm gonna get out of here. Got a lot of shit to do before I leave. So, you take care of yourself, and if we never see each other again, stay safe."

"Yeah, Todd, you do the same." We shook hands.

Before exiting his car, I looked out the back window and the passenger-side window to once again make sure the coast was clear. "A'ight, I'm out of here," I announced, and then I hopped out of the car.

The second I got back into my truck, I hauled ass out of that parking lot and headed back in the direction of my grandmother's house. But that's not really where I wanted to go. I needed to get out of town, like Todd was getting ready to do.

Dawn needs to come with me. But how am I going to convince her? Will she listen to me if I tell her everything Todd just told me? Or will she think I'm trying to manipulate her into coming with me? With the negative influence coming from her family, I know it's going to be hard to even get her on the phone, never mind the part about getting her to leave with me. But I'm a swift guy and I've never given up on anything, so I will get my wife out of harm's way, whether she likes it or not.

During transit back to my grandmother's house, I tried to call Dawn a few times, but like all the other times, she didn't answer. As a matter of fact, I could tell that she had turned off her cell phone because it kept going straight to voicemail. This pissed me off, because I knew her family told her to block my calls. I wasn't going for that, so I decided to stop by her family's house unannounced. The worst thing they could do was call the cops. But before they came, I would get a chance to talk to Dawn, by any means necessary.

It didn't take me long to drive to Dawn's parents' house. I was there in less than seventeen minutes flat, but the anxiety I felt during the drive was overwhelming. Between the conversation I had with Todd about Que Ming, and the probability that Dawn's family would not let me talk to her, the situation weighed heavily on my heart. I know it seems like everything I touch falls apart, but I can also build shit too. Even though I didn't do what I was supposed to do by Dawn, I did provide her with a married life. When she would bring up the subject about us getting married, I used to shoot it down because I knew I wasn't ready. I had just gotten out of the relationship with my kids' mother, plus I was having money issues. But Dawn kept forcing it by making sure we were exclusive. And then one thing led to another and here we are today, going through problems that I saw coming a long time ago.

When I pulled my truck up to her parents' house, I parked curbside. I noticed her car in the driveway next to Alexia's Jeep. I wanted so badly to stab her tires up, but I held my composure and focused on the mission at hand. "Okay, Reese, you can do it. Just act respectful no matter what her father, her sister, or her mother says when they find out you're here," I uttered under my breath.

Upon exiting my truck, I took a deep breath and then I exhaled. As I approached their house, I tried rehearsing what I was going to say if Dawn's father answered the door. I also rehearsed what I was going to say if Alexia answered the door. I've never had any beef with Mrs. Bryant, so I decided I'd play things by ear with her.

I stepped onto the front porch, walked up to the door, and rang the doorbell twice. I don't know why, but my heart started beating out of control. Maybe it was the fact I had no idea how this meeting with Dawn's parents would turn out. But then again, it could be the fact that I was afraid that she'd reject me. Whatever it was, I wasn't comfortable with this feeling. "Who is it?" I heard Dawn's father ask.

"I'm here to see Dawn," I yelled from the other side of the door.

"Who did you say you are?" Mr. Bryant asked.

It was evident that he hadn't heard my first answer, so I said, "Is Dawn here?" I changed my voice, hoping her dad wouldn't recognize me.

A couple seconds later the front door opened. Mr. Bryant stood on the other side of the threshold like he was the king of the castle. He held his head up high and he poked out his chest more than I'd ever seen him do in the past. He smiled at me because he knew he had the upper hand and I was at his mercy, so I stood there and waited for him to open up the dialogue.

"What are you doing at my house? Didn't my daughter tell you that she's filing for divorce?"

"Mr. Bryant, I know I haven't been the best husband in the world for Dawn and I don't deserve to talk to her after all the stuff I put her through. But would you please let me speak to her for a couple of minutes, and I promise I will leave right after that," I pleaded.

"I'm sorry, but she doesn't want to talk to you. So get off my porch before I call the cops."

"Who are you talking to, honey?" I heard Mrs. Bryant yelling from another part of the house.

"I'm talking to this loser son-in-law of yours," he yelled back.

"Mr. Bryant, everything you're saying about me is true.

But all I wanna do is tell Dawn something really quick and I promise I will leave," I begged him.

"You think you can come to my house and make a deal with me? I don't make deals with my family. We're honest, good folk in this household. So, for the last time, take your ass off my porch, or else."

"What's going on?" Mrs. Bryant asked as she approached the front door.

"Mrs. Bryant, I just need two seconds to talk to Dawn. Will you please tell her that I'm out here?"

"My wife isn't doing shit for you, you freaking scumbag. You've wasted so many years of my daughter's life. She could've been happily married with a houseful of kids if she wasn't with you," Mr. Bryant barked.

"Who's Dad fussing with?" I heard Dawn say. I could tell that she was in another part of the house.

"It's your husband," Mrs. Bryant yelled back at Dawn.

I yelled over Mr. and Mrs. Bryant's heads, "Baby, it's me, Reese. Please come to the door. I just got one thing to tell you and then I will leave."

"Get off my damn porch right now!" Mr. Bryant roared. And when he saw that I wasn't budging he looked back at his wife and said, "Bonnie, call the cops and tell them we have someone trespassing on our property. And if they don't come, then I'll be forced to shoot him with my shotgun," he continued.

Thankfully, Dawn came to the front door after she heard all the commotion and when I saw her face I almost broke down in tears. "Baby, I need to talk to you. It's very important," I said, talking over Mr. Bryant, who was screaming his ass off at me for not taking heed to his threats.

"Reese, my dad doesn't want you here, so please leave," Dawn told me. Hearing her words cut me deep in the heart. It felt like I was losing her to this meddling fucking family.

"Dawn, I know you want to divorce me and that's fine.

But I just left Todd and he told me that we're in danger. He said that we need to leave town for a little while."

"My daughter isn't in any danger. You're the only fool that's in danger," Mr. Bryant barked at me.

"She is, Mr. Bryant," I said, looking directly into Dawn's father's face. And then I turned my attention back toward Dawn. "The car that's been parked outside our house was someone working for the Chinese boss behind the human trafficking case. Brian and Ed are already dead because we screwed up the job. And Todd said that if we don't leave town, we could be killed next."

"I knew it," Dawn's father yelled. "Bonnie, didn't I tell you that this son-of-a-bitch was involved with that case?"

"Oh my God!" Mrs. Bryant said as she placed her hand over her mouth. "How can you look at yourself in the mirror knowing that you had something to do with those people in those containers?"

"It wasn't my fault. Those people died because of the harsh conditions in that metal container."

"You're gonna stand in my face and not take responsibility for your actions? Are you freaking kidding me right now?" Mr. Bryant roared, taking two steps toward me. Luckily, Dawn's mother grabbed him and pulled him backwards, because if that man would've put his hands on me, I know I would've hurt him.

"Mr. Bryant, I didn't do anything to those people. All I did was move the containers from the ship to the railroad cars. That's it. Now, I'm here to warn my wife that the millionaire dude Que Ming is now trying to eliminate everyone that worked that night. So, please let me take my wife away from here and take her to a safer place until all of this blows over," I said, looking at everyone standing at the front door.

"I'm not letting you take my daughter anywhere, you freaking criminal. Now get off my property right now!" he screamed.

"Calm down, honey, he's gonna leave," Mrs. Bryant said.

"Dawn, are you coming with me?" I looked over her parents' shoulders, with the sincerest facial expression I could muster up. I did this hoping she'd stand up to her parents and tell them to move out of the way so she could come outside and talk to me.

Surprisingly, that didn't work. She wouldn't move an inch. "Reese, please leave," she said, as she stood a few feet back from the door and her father cursed me out.

"You heard what she said, she's not going away with you. You think that if you leave town those people aren't gonna find you? Well, guess what? They will. And my daughter isn't going to be with you when they do find you. So, get to stepping, you fucking loser!"

Allowing Dawn's father to continue to disrespect me was getting real old. I mean, how much could I take? Got this old-ass nigga in my face like he can kick my ass. The only reason why I haven't hit his ass yet is because of the love I have for Dawn. But if this nigga don't get out of my face, I'm gonna lay him on his back. "Look, old man, you don't know what you're talking about! And instead of worrying about my relationship with my wife, worry about the women you be sleeping with that work down at the terminal. Yeah, the same time you were doing a background check on me, I dug up some dirt on your cheating ass too," I spat. I was sick of this nigga once and for all.

"That's not cool, Reese," Dawn said, but she still kept her distance from me.

"What is he talking about, Joe?" Dawn's mother asked him.

"Tell your wife about Lisa and Trina and the other tricks you been fucking around with for the last couple of years," I continued. Just like he wanted to air my dirty laundry, I will also air his.

"You don't know what the hell you're talking about!" Mr. Bryant said, gritting his teeth. He was getting angrier by the second, and I was loving it.

"Joe, who are Lisa and Trina?"

"Tell her, Joe! Tell her that Lisa works as a timekeeper down at the terminal while Trina works as an officer for the union," I pointed out.

"Get the fuck off my porch now!" Mr. Bryant yelled, and then he lunged toward me. But his timing was off. When he came at me I stepped to my right and he stumbled a bit and fell onto his knees. Mrs. Bryant rushed out on the porch to help him get up. Dawn rushed toward him too. And when she got within arm's reach of me, I grabbed her by the arm and pulled her off the porch.

"Baby, you were right. It was somebody sitting in that car watching our house. And I'm sorry I brought you in the middle of this, but please let me make it up to you by taking you away from here. Take you somewhere safe and away from all of this shit surrounding us," I begged.

"Get away from her!" I heard her father yelling while his wife was trying to help him stand back up on his feet.

"Let you take me where? And with what? Reese, you cleaned us out. We don't have any more money. You gambled it all up. So, tell me, what will we do for money? Drive to another city on fumes? The whole idea is stupid," she told me. "Look, just leave before my dad calls the cops, okay?" She turned around and walked back toward the house.

"I'm not leaving here without you. I can't live without you, Dawn. Can't you understand that?" I yelled, as she walked onto the front porch.

"Reese, get off our property now," Mrs. Bryant said while she was escorting her husband back into the house.

"Dawn, will you at least think about it?" I yelled once more before they closed the front door. But it was too late— Dawn had disappeared into the house.

I stood there like a lost and defeated puppy. Seeing Dawn walk away from me felt like a ton of bricks had slammed into my gut. She literally turned her back on me and she put her family before me as well. So, what am I going to do? Just lie down and die?

44

DAWN

I cannot believe that Reese had the gumption to show up to my parents' house and ask my dad if he could talk to me. Was he out of his fucking mind? I swear, this guy gets bolder and bolder by the day. I'm just glad that Reese didn't put his hands on my dad, even after my dad lunged at him.

By the time my mother had closed the front door and locked it, I was back in the den watching TV. I wanted to forget about what had just occurred, but the images of Reese's face while he stood facing my father wouldn't disappear for nothing in the world. And then to hear that he and I need to leave town for a while because we're in danger? What kind of shit is that? Did Reese really believe that my family would allow him to take me away and put me in harm's way? Was he that fucking stupid?

All I know is that everything Reese said tonight spooked me. And to look back at those times when I saw that car with the tinted windows stalk my house made my skin crawl. Does Reese realize that that person in the car could've killed me if they wanted to? Whoever was in that car had a handful of opportunities to cause me harm, and that's scary. Not to mention that this notorious millionaire has targets on Reese's friends' backs. And me too, for that matter. But why me? I haven't done anything wrong. I tried to talk him out of doing this job, but he didn't listen and now the heat is on. I can't let myself get involved—well, that is if I'm not already involved. I just hope Reese was wrong when he said that my life is in danger too.

Back in the den of my parents' house, my father and mother came in with a bunch of questions. My father started the conversation. "I can't believe that bum brought his butt over to my house. Dawn, is he on drugs or what?"

"No, Dad, he's not on drugs."

"Well, he's got to be on something," he continued as he took a seat in his favorite chair.

"What happened? Did I miss something?" Alexia asked as soon as she entered the den wearing her pajamas. She had just gotten out of the shower.

"Your sister's husband came over here and knocked on my door."

"Are you serious?" Alexia replied as if she was shocked.

"Serious as a heart attack. But I straightened him out. Opened the front door and gave him a taste of his own medicine."

"What did he want?" Alexia asked.

"He said he came here to take Dawn away with him because their lives are in danger. But I told him he's not taking her anywhere and for him to get the hell off my porch. Oh, and he finally confessed that he and his criminal friends had something to do with those Asian people that were found in those containers."

"Did he leave after you said that?" My sister's questions continued.

"No, he didn't budge until Dawn told him to."

"That's right, sis, shut his butt down!" Alexia said with excitement.

"I couldn't believe my ears when I heard her say it," my mother interjected, and then she looked at me.

"Proud of you, sis," Alexia said to me and then she looked back at my dad. "What's wrong with your knee, Dad?"

"He fell on the ground when he tried to hit Reese," I said, thinking back to exactly how it happened.

"Dad, what's gotten into you? You can't go around hitting people," Alexia said, like she was poking fun at him.

"I almost had 'im. If he hadn't moved to the left so fast, I know I could've gotten him."

"So, I take it Reese is gone now?" Alexia continued.

"After Dad fell down and hurt himself, I told Reese to leave," I chimed in.

"He's one lucky guy because I swear, if he would've caught one of these right and left hooks I got, I would've hurt him pretty bad," my dad said proudly. And he was dead serious too. Too bad he's a senior citizen now, because to hear my father tell it, if he was still in his prime he would've beat Reese's ass.

The part where Reese called my father out on his infidelity issues was hitting below the belt. I mean, come on, my dad wasn't on trial here. Reese was. So why throw my dad under a moving bus? But then again, when I looked back, the shit my dad was saying to Reese was out of pocket and disrespectful as well, so I can see why Reese came back at him like that. And now I think about it, I wonder if my mother was hurting right now. I saw her massaging my dad's feet and listening to him and Alexia talking. She seemed like she was okay. But then again, my mother was really good at hiding things too. I just hoped that Reese hadn't opened up a can of worms for my mother. If he did, then I'm gonna forever hate him for it because my mother didn't deserve to hear that. She's an innocent person in this situation. That wasn't cool and I would let him know it the next time I talked to him.

My family talked about the incident with Reese for another five minutes. Alexia was loving every minute of it, but I wasn't, so I said, "Can we leave this alone for right now? I swear, I am over it."

"We're just having a conversation, Dawn," my mother pointed out.

"Yeah, we are. It's not like we haven't done this before," my sister chimed in.

"But see, that's the thing. You guys are always talking about Reese. We already know that he's a loser and we also know that he doesn't have my best interests in mind. So why keep talking about him?"

"You know what, guys? She's right, let's drop it," my mother interjected.

"Wait a minute, are you taking up for him?" my dad hissed. He looked really irritated.

"No, I'm not. I'm just trying to move forward. But you guys are making it impossible because you're always bringing up his name."

"I detect an attitude coming on," Alexia commented sarcastically.

"I don't have an attitude. I'm just over this whole thing. And to tell you the truth, I'm so over it that I'm thinking about going home. I figure that it'll be more peaceful over there than here."

"Baby, you know you don't need to go home. Reese said that there are bad people out there looking for him. And it will just kill me and your dad if something happened to you," my mother said.

"No, Mommy! Let her go. She's just trying to come up with an excuse so she can leave here and go see her husband," Alexia chimed in.

"You obviously don't know me, if you think I've gotta make up excuses so I can leave here. Are you out of your damn mind?"

"No, I'm far from it. But you, on the other hand, gotta be, after being married to that man you got."

I paused for a second and then I said, "Yes, let's talk about my man."

"Come on, girls, let's not do this. We're family," my dad interjected.

Alexia wasn't backing down. "Nah, Daddy, let her talk. I can't wait to hear what she gotta say."

"Okay, since you want me to talk, let's talk about the fact that you've always been salty about Reese and I being together because you wanted him yourself."

"That's a damn lie! I never wanted him. He wanted me," Alexia spat.

"Now, that's enough, girls. We will not let that asshole come between us. We're a family." My dad tried to stand on his feet but his knee was still hurting him.

"Well, tell me what happened in the nightclub a few years ago when you and he met. Tell Mommy and Daddy how you wanted to give him some ass that same night, but you had your thotty girlfriends with you."

Alexia chuckled. "He told you that?" She smiled.

"Don't worry, he told me a lot of things. But for the sake of our parents, I'm gonna keep those little secrets close to the heart."

"Yeah, whatever!"

"Whatever is right!" I hissed, and then I stood up from the sofa and proceeded to leave the den.

"Baby, where are you going?" my mother wanted to know.

"I'm going in the guest room," I told her.

"Okay, if you need anything, let me know."

"I will, Mommy, thanks," I said and exited the room.

Back in the guest room, all I could think about was how Reese and my dad had acted outside. I had thought I was getting away from the arguments when I came back in the house, but then I got bombarded with a lot of fucking questions concerning Reese. To add insult to injury, getting into an argument with my sister was enough to send me over the edge. All everyone in the den had to do was leave well enough alone. Why do we always have to talk about Reese? Let's discuss something else, like what the weather's going to be today, or talk about how good God is to us. It's that simple. Hopefully one day they will get hip to it. If they don't, then too damn bad!

45

REESE

The ride back to my grandmother's house nearly killed me. My heart was so wounded after getting rejected by Dawn, it did some damage to me. My eyes teared up, but a tear wouldn't fall down my cheeks, and I wondered why. I also wondered why Dawn allowed her father to dictate to her how she should live her life. I'm her fucking husband! Not him!

What will it take to get my life back the way it was before I started gambling and messing up our finances? And let's just say that I find a way to do it, will Dawn give our marriage another chance?

After that meeting with Todd, I was more afraid and paranoid than I was when I found out that US Customs agents were going to investigate me and the boys. But now that I knew that the Asian millionaire Que Ming had a target on our backs, I knew that I had to be careful everywhere I went, and I couldn't be bringing that heat to my grandmother's house. It would kill me inside if one of them Asian motherfuckers put their hands on my grandmother. I would lose my mind really quick. So, as far as I could see, I was gonna have to look over my shoulder everywhere I went until I got out of town.

*   *   *

The drive back to my grandmother's house took me longer than usual. I purposely drove out of the way so no one would be able to follow me. I even rode by my street to see if an unfamiliar car was parked out in front of it, but there wasn't, so I kept moving along.

By the time I had made it back to my grandmother's house, I was more certain than ever that it would be best that I leave town. But then when I thought about how Dawn shot down the idea because she said we didn't have any money left, I realized that she was right. How could we leave this place and drive on fumes? Or be able to eat and find shelter? Things would be disastrous. I needed to figure a few things out before I made my first move.

"Reese, is that you?" my grandmother yelled from her bedroom after I opened the front door of her house.

"Yes, Grandma, it's me," I yelled back.

"Make sure you lock that front door," she instructed me.

"Yes, ma'am, I'm doing it now. Need anything before I go in the bedroom?"

"No, baby, I'm fine. I just sat back down from using the bathroom and pouring myself a cup of hot tea."

"Okay," I said, and then I went in my bedroom and closed the door.

I tried lying down on the bed, but I kept getting back up every time I heard a car ride by. After being in the room for five minutes, I think I got up at least twenty times to look out the window.

While I lay back on the bed, my cell phone started ringing. When I picked it up and looked at the caller ID I thought I was seeing things. I answered, "Dawn, baby, is this you?"

"Yes, Reese, it is," she whispered.

"Oh, baby, I swear you have just made me the happiest man on earth right now." I couldn't believe how a phone call could make me this happy.

"Is it true?" she said.

"Is what true?"

"Are our lives in danger?" she continued, her voice still low, like she wanted to prevent anyone from hearing her talk.

"Yes, we are in danger, Dawn. That's why I came by your parents' house to get you. It would kill me if something were to ever happen to you."

"What are you going to do?"

"I wanna pack up some of our things and leave this place for a while. At least until the dust settles. But I can't do it without you."

"But what if you're wrong? What if that Asian man doesn't want to kill us? We'd be leaving town for nothing."

"Baby, listen to me and listen good. Edward told Todd that as soon as we accepted the five-thousand-dollar advance for the job and didn't complete it, Que Ming put targets on our backs. Do you know how much money that man lost on this last job when those six people were found dead and the rest of them got detained? Human trafficking is a multimillion-dollar business. So, do you think that man is going to let us walk around here like we didn't cost him a lot of money? Hell, nah! So, that's why we gotta get out of here. I don't want us ending up like Edward and Brian."

"Do you love me?" she asked.

"You fucking right I love you. You're the best thing that has ever happened to me, Dawn, that's why I refuse to leave town without you. I need you by my side, baby."

"What will we do for money?"

"I talked to my grandmother when got back here and she said she'll lend the money to me," I lied. I felt like I had to say whatever I could to make our escape look easy.

"Come on, Reese, you know that whatever your grandmother gives you isn't going to be enough."

"Yes, it will," I insisted.

"Okay, so what do you want me to do now?"

"Will you be willing to meet back at our house in two hours? That way we can get a few more things to take with us."

"You promise you'll be there in two hours? You know I don't wanna be at that house by myself."

"Don't worry, baby. I will be there," I assured her.

It felt good when Dawn picked up her cell phone and called me. And to know that she finally agreed to leave town with me was like icing on the cake. I swear, she made me so happy. Now all I had to do was get enough money so we could get by as we made our way to safety.

My grandmother always went to bed early, so I figured I was going to grab one of her credit cards from her wallet and write myself a check for at least a couple of grand. I know this amount would definitely help Dawn and me live comfortably until all of this blew over.

Instead of waiting in my bedroom for my grandmother to go to sleep, I decided to go into her room and watch her fall asleep while I pretended to watch television with her. She seemed really happy when I told her I was gonna chill with her for a little while.

"You're gonna really sit in here and watch TV with me?" she asked. By this time she was lying in her bed, so I took a seat in her comfortable lounge chair.

"Yes, I am, Grandma. But what are you watching?"

"I'm watching the reruns of my favorite show, *Desperate Housewives*."

"I think I've heard of this show before."

"You should've, it's a very popular show."

"Is this what you do all day long, Grandma?"

"Do what, baby?"

"Sit in the house and watch TV all day?"

"Yeah, pretty much."

"Do you ever wish that you had a husband? I mean, I know it gets lonely sometimes."

"Well, of course, I wish sometimes I had a husband here with me. And yes, I do get lonely sometimes. But when you have a relationship with God, He will fill up those voids in your life."

"Easy for you to say."

"Yes, it is. But talk to God. He will make a way out of no way."

"If you say so, Grandma," I said, and then I turned my attention to her favorite show.

As soon as the episode ended, my grandmother warned me that she was ready to go to sleep, so she wouldn't be good company for the rest of the night.

"Do you mind if I sit in here to watch another episode?" I asked.

"Sure, honey. The television is all yours," she said, and then she turned over on her side and closed her eyes.

I waited for at least thirty minutes before I put my plan into motion. I had to make sure my grandmother was fully asleep. So when I heard her snoring a little I knew it was time to go in for the kill.

Growing up under her roof, I noticed that she was a creature of habit. She drank the same coffee. She ate her eggs a certain way. She still had the same dishes and cookware that she'd had for over fifteen years now. As far as where she kept her money, she has always hidden it in her chest in the back of her closet. "Grandma, can you hear me?" I whispered. And when she didn't answer, I knew now was the time to grab what I could get and get out of there.

Okay, now the whole time I was tiptoeing in her bedroom, I couldn't help looking back at her, just to make sure she wasn't looking at me. I swear, it would be so embarrassing if she caught me going into her things. I wouldn't know what to say if she woke up and asked me what I was doing. I knew I would freeze right there.

The room was dark, so I had to use the light coming

from the TV and the light from my cell phone. Once I got into the closet, I turned on the flashlight from my cell phone. "Come on, now, please let me find enough cash so I can get me and my wife out of town," I thought to myself after my eyes landed on the black trunk.

Very quietly, I got down on my knees, put the end of the cell phone into my mouth for the light, and then I very carefully opened the chest. I couldn't believe my eyes. The entire chest was fucking empty of anything that looked like currency. The only thing she had in there that was of value was an antique Bible and some old baby pictures of my mother. That's it. "Fuck!" I hissed, as I made my way back out of the closet. And as soon as I stood back up, I scanned the bedroom for her purse. It took me a couple of seconds, but I found it, sitting next to her lamp on the nightstand next to her bed. I tiptoed over, grabbed her purse, and then I exited her bedroom. I went straight to the kitchen where there was plenty of light and dumped all the contents onto the countertop. The first thing that fell out was her wallet, which was the most important thing. The second thing that fell out was her checkbook. I can't lie, I saw dollar signs instantly. First, I needed to find out how much cash I could take without her noticing that it was gone. But once again, I struck out because she only had a ten-dollar bill in the whole entire wallet. "Where the hell is your money, Grandma? You used to have money lying around all the time," I said softly.

Next up was the checkbook. I went directly to the last page of the booklet and searched her ledger. My grandmother was old-school, so she didn't go online to keep an account of the amount of money she had. When I looked at the bottom row, I saw that she had $21,784.19. My heart damn near jumped out of my chest. Without further hesitation, I went to the last two checks in her checkbook and wrote myself two checks. The first one was for $3,500 and the second one was for $4,500. I figured writing two checks for those amounts would be enough money for my getaway, and they wouldn't send out alerts to the bank since they were under $5,000 each.

After I put the amount on the line and in the box in the right corner, I wrote my name and then I put the words *renovation work* on the memo line. Writing the checks in this manner was genius on my part. But some people called it forgery. "You and Dawn are going to be good now," I whispered to myself, smiling from ear to ear.

I put my grandmother's checkbook back into her purse. But when I picked it up to take it back to her bedroom, I remembered that I hadn't taken one of her credit cards as a safety net, so I pulled her wallet back out and held the billfold open so I could decide which credit card to take. She had three of them in her purse. But the one that I knew she rarely used was the Capital One card, so that's the one I took. I wasn't sure what the credit limit was, but at that point it didn't matter. I needed to get out of town ASAP. And that's what I was going to do.

Thankfully she was still asleep when I returned her purse to her nightstand. And while I was exiting her bedroom, I powered off the TV.

Happy as hell because I got some money for me and my lady, I rushed back in my bedroom and packed my clothes. I was ready to leave this godforsaken town. With most of the guys I worked with at NIT dead, I felt now was my time to go. And who knows, maybe things would calm down and I could return. If not, then so be it.

46

DAWN

Instead of waiting around for two hours, I left my parents' house immediately after I got off the phone with Reese. I got some flak from my mother and father when I initially tried to leave, but I told them that I was leaving so I could clear my head of all the stuff that was going on. My mother tried to block the front door, but I pushed her out of the way. "Knock her down on the floor the next time, will you!" my sister said.

"Dawn, you can't seriously be trying to go out this time of the night," my father chimed in.

"Why don't you guys just leave me alone? I am a grown woman. If I want to leave your house, I have the right to do so," I spat.

"But what if something happens to you? It's not safe outside, honey," my mother said.

"I am a big girl. I can handle myself."

"Yes, she's right. She handled herself so well after that car pulled away from her house that she ran back into her house and packed an overnight bag quicker than I could blink my eyes," Alexia commented sarcastically.

"Please don't tell us you're going to be with Reese," my

mother said while she, my father, and my sister huddled around me.

"I'm not gonna tell y'all anything. Now if you guys don't leave me alone, I will leave out of here and I won't come back," I threatened.

One by one, they moved out of my way and allowed me to leave the house. My sister stuck her head out the front door and said, "I know you're going back home to be with Reese. So, be careful. Don't wanna get a phone call from the cops saying that you were killed."

I was going to hit Alexia below the belt with a nasty-ass comment, but I decided against it. I had better things to do and she wasn't one of them.

It felt good to be going home to meet Reese. I knew he'd done some ridiculous things, but the fact that he came to get me from my parents' house so he could get me out of harm's way said not only that this man loved me, it also said that he wanted to protect my life at all costs. So, why not leave town with him? I knew that if he changed his ways, there was a strong possibility that I wouldn't file for divorce.

Immediately after I got into my car, I called Reese. He answered my call on the second ring. "I just left my parents' house," I told him.

"Okay, well, be careful. And take the long way home just to make sure nobody is following you, because I've got to make one quick stop at the terminal and then I'll be home after that," he told me.

"I will. Don't worry," I assured him.

The drive to my house was a very long one considering the route I had to take. A couple of times I spotted a car going in the same direction as me, but when I switched things up and took exits and streets that weren't on my route, I felt a sense of relief when I lost them.

I finally arrived in my neighborhood forty minutes later. But before I was comfortable enough to get out of my car, I drove by my street to make sure the coast was clear. After circling the block twice, I drove up to my house, parked my car in our garage, and lowered the garage door to make people think that no one was at home.

Once inside, I went into my kitchen to get a bottle of water and then I went into my bedroom to see if there was anything out of place. And when I realized that everything was still intact, I took off my clothes and lay down on my bed to watch a little bit of TV. I figured watching a few episodes of *Black Ink Crew: New York* would suffice until Reese made it home. Watching reality shows always kept my mind occupied. So, I guess tonight wouldn't be any different.

I couldn't believe that I dozed off waiting for Reese to come to the house so we could talk about where we were going when we left town. When I looked at the clock I noticed that I'd been sleeping for a couple of hours. And what's crazy is, something told me to wake up. When I talked to Reese, he told me he was leaving his grandmother's house and gonna make a quick stop to NIT and then he was coming straight here. So where the fuck was he?

Before I could grab my cell phone and dial his number, my phone started ringing. I picked it up from the nightstand next to my bed and looked down at the caller ID. I let out a sigh of relief when I saw that it was Reese calling me.

"Hello," I said.

"Did I wake you up?" he asked. He sounded kind of weird.

"Reese, where are you?" I asked him, totally ignoring his question.

"I'm about to pull up to the house, so put on something and meet me outside."

"Meet you outside for what? *Do you know what time it*

is?" I screeched. He was making me angrier by the second because he was displaying some very odd behavior.

"Please don't ask me any questions. Just do what I say," he replied calmly.

"Bye," I said, and then I disconnected our call.

I was furious at the thought that I had to get out of my bed and put on clothes to meet him outside. What kind of fucking game was he trying to play? I grabbed a sweatshirt and a pair of sweatpants from my dresser drawer and a pair of sneakers from my closet and got dressed. I grabbed a jacket from the hall closet and headed toward the front door. My adrenaline was pumping. I was already thinking of what I was going to say to him if he was making me come outside for nothing. He was going to feel my wrath once and for all.

Blinded by the headlights of Reese's car parked in our driveway, I blinked my eyes a few times and then I held up my left arm to shield my eyes. I saw Reese's silhouette in the driver's seat, so I closed the front door behind me and walked over to his car. I was heading toward the driver side, until he rolled his window down halfway and told me to get into the car from the passenger side.

I obeyed his instructions and got into the car with him. As soon as I closed the door, I turned around and looked at him. "What the fuck is so important that I had to come outside and get into the car?" I asked him.

Reese wouldn't open his mouth to respond.

"What's wrong with you?" I questioned him.

A voice from behind me said, "He's dead!"

I turned my face slightly to the left and saw an Asian man with a gun and a silencer pointed directly at me. My heart dropped in the pit of my stomach. Anxiety and fear crippled me as I slowly moved my eyes away from the Asian man, back to my husband's face. At that moment, I realized that blood was seeping from a bullet hole in his head. I instantly froze. I knew then that this man was about to take my life too. "Where is my money?" He said softly.

"I don't know," I replied, heart beating uncontrollably. I couldn't think clearly with Reese's body starting to slump over in front of me.

"Look, bitch, I'm only gonna ask you one more time," he warned me as he gritted his teeth.

"I swear, I don't know." I began to cry. I sat in the front seat of Reese's car completely alone, in sheer terror. I had no one around to help me. What was I to do? How was I going to walk away from this situation alive?

"It's in the house," I lied.

"Get out of the car slowly," he instructed me as he continued to point the gun in my face.

"Okay," I said and grabbed ahold of the door handle. "I'm getting ready to open the door now, so please don't shoot," I begged him, hoping he understood what I was saying.

"Slow," he replied, keeping the gun aimed at me.

I slowly opened the door and backed out of the car, never turning my head once. "I'm getting out now," I explained while I watched the barrel of the gun. I knew that if I made the slightest move in the wrong way, he was going to blow my fucking head off my shoulders. And I didn't want that. I wanted to live. I wanted to have a baby and love that child before I left this earth. But I wasn't sure if that was going to happen. I see now why my father and everyone who loved me warned me about Reese. Reese was a ticking time bomb and he finally exploded. And from the way things looked, he was taking me down the same road too. I never deserved to reap all the bullshit he sowed. So why was I being punished for his misdeeds?

After carefully backing out of Reese's car, I stood straight up and watched the Asian guy try to do the same. But when he moved to stand up, I pushed the back door against him like three times, making him collapse on the ground and drop his gun. I heard the gun hitting the pavement and then I heard it slide. He started cursing in his native language and I made a run for it.

I put one foot in front of the other one and ran toward my front door. I figured all I needed to do was get inside my house, lock my door, and call the cops and everything would be all right. Boy, was I wrong.

When I reached my front door and grabbed ahold of the doorknob and turned it, the fucking door wouldn't open. "Shit! No! No! Please don't tell me I locked myself out!" I began to cry, periodically looking back at the Asian guy as he searched for the gun. After making five attempts to open the front door, I decided to make a run for my next-door neighbor's house. "Mrs. Mildred, Mr. Tom, please help me!" I screamed at the top of my voice as I ran toward their front door. I leaped across their lawn and made it to their front porch in less than three seconds. I immediately started banging on their front door. "Mrs. Mildred! Tom! Please open the door. Someone is trying to kill me!" I yelled.

Thankfully, Mr. Tom heard my cry and turned on the living room lights. "Who is it?" I heard him yell from the other side of the door. "It's me, Dawn. Your next-door neighbor. Somebody is trying to kill me!" I continued to cry out. But then the front door opened and the light in the living room of his home shined brightly. A sense of relief fell upon me. And boy, was I happy to see this man's face. He took a step toward me and said, "Who's trying to kill you?" Before I could answer him, I felt a whoosh of air brush by my ear and a big hole opened in the middle of Mr. Tom's forehead. Seconds later blood started leaking from it and then Mr. Tom collapsed down on the floor. I screamed and tried to make a run for it, but as soon as I stepped foot over Mr. Tom's body, I felt heat in the back of my leg. I knew then that I was shot, and collapsed on the floor by Mr. Tom's head. I turned around slowly to get another look at my killer. He was a short Asian guy. He looked like he was a young man, mid- to late twenties. He also had a look of death plastered on his face. That alone let me know that he was going to kill me. No matter what I did or said. Reese owed him money and I saw his face. That was the recipe for murder.

The Asian guy brought me back to reality when he said, "You Americans no good."

"Fuck you!" I said. And for the life of me I couldn't tell you why I said it. I guess I wasn't afraid to die. Maybe Reese's lifestyle had rubbed off on me, like my family said.

"You trash," he said, and then I heard, "You killed my husband!" I opened my eyes and saw Mrs. Mildred open fire at that fucking Asian guy. *Boom! Boom! Boom! Boom!* She had a shotgun aimed at him and let him have four consecutive rounds. He fell backwards against the wall by her front door with four bullet holes carved through his little-ass chest.

"You fucking killer!" I yelled at him. "How you feel now? You can't come around here and not think we're gonna fight back, you fucking piece of shit!" I roared. I cursed at the dead guy for at least another fifteen seconds while Mrs. Mildred called 911 and held Mr. Tom in her arms the whole time.

I felt bad looking at her hold his lifeless body in her arms. If I hadn't come over here, he wouldn't be dead. Damn! I knew I was gonna feel fucked up about this for the rest of my life.

I just hoped that Mrs. Mildred didn't hold any ill will toward me. I didn't mean for her husband to get killed. Maybe one day she'd see that.

EPILOGUE

The paramedics decided to take me to the hospital even though I hadn't suffered any major wounds. I was pretty beaten up by the images of Reese's face after the Asian guy shot him. I didn't know if I could ever erase that image from my head, but I did know that my husband died to protect me, and I owed him the world because of it.

While I was lying in the hospital bed, my mother, father, and sister showed up. Everyone looked happy to see me when they pulled the curtain back. "Baby, are you okay?" my mother was the first to say as she hugged me.

"Yes, how are you?" my dad wanted to know.

"I am beaten up a little bit, but I'm okay," I told them.

Then Alexia walked over and stood next to me. A few seconds later, she smiled and hugged me. "You know I love you, right?"

"Yes, I know you love me," I assured her as I kissed her on her cheek.

"How are you really feeling?" my mother asked.

"Mom, I am so torn up on the inside. Whether you guys liked him or not, I loved him with all his flaws. He will be truly missed."

"Has someone contacted his grandmother?" my dad chimed in.

"I'm not sure. I'm hoping they'll wait until morning; that way she won't come out of the house this time of the night," I said.

"Yes, I agree with you one hundred percent," my mother commented.

"What kind of drugs have they given you?" Alexia asked me. And I knew exactly where she was going with this conversation.

"I'm not telling you," I told her, and then I turned my attention to my dad because he walked closer to me. "What's up, Dad?" He looked like he had something important on his mind.

"I know that I was a jackass when it came to Reese. So, right now I wanna say I'm sorry for how I treated him. And that I hope he's going to a better place," my dad said, as a tear appeared in his left eye.

I placed my hand over my dad's cheek so I could catch the tear when it fell. I even used my other arm to embrace him. "I really appreciate you saying that, Daddy."

Everyone stood around my bed until the doctor walked into the room. He introduced himself and then he used a few medical terms to sum up the diagnosis. After that, he expressed his sympathy because I lost Reese. I thought that was kind of him to say, especially since he didn't know my husband. And before he left my room, he gave me specific instructions on how to treat my wounds. I thanked him and allowed my dad to push me out of the hospital in a huge wheelchair.

The wheelchair ride down the elevator to the front sliding doors of the hospital was one bumpy ride. "Stay right here, I'm gonna go and get my car," my dad said, and then he raced off into the parking lot.

The night air was cool and breezy and the stars were

out, shining on us. The light hit my face softly while I tried to look at the bright side of things because I was still alive, and my God in heaven and my neighbor made sure of that. But at the same time, it was bittersweet because I knew I wouldn't see Reese ever again. I tried to come to grips with the fact that after I got in my dad's car and left this hospital, my life would forever be different.

While I stared at the sky, in my peripheral vision I saw my father's car coming toward us. "Are you ready, baby?" my mother asked me.

"Yeah, I guess," I told her, looking up at her where she stood on my right. And when I turned my attention back toward the pickup area, a car pulled up in front of us with the passenger-side window rolled down. I gasped when I looked into the car and saw an Asian guy with a gun in his hand, pointed directly at me. My heart dropped into the pit of my stomach when I realized that this was the same car that had been parked outside my house all those times. "That is the car! He's gonna kill—" I screamed but it was too late, the Asian guy had already pulled the trigger.

Boom! Boom!

1

MISTY

I'd been in this world too long to just now be finding my way. But here I was, feeling grateful and shit about being healthy and having a roof over my head, thanks to the steady pay from my latest employer.

For the last five and a half months, I'd been collecting a check working as a pharmacy tech. The job was easy and my boss, Dr. Sanjay Malik, was a dream to work with. Not only was he a nice guy, he was very generous with the monthly bonuses he paid me, and he would occasionally let me get off work early. The bonuses were for the extra work I did delivering prescriptions to senior citizens who weren't mobile or couldn't pick up their medication. Sanjay would have me deliver their meds to them, and after I completed the deliveries, he usually told me to take off work for the rest of the day, which I found awesome.

But three weeks ago, I noticed that Sanjay had me delivering meds to dark and questionable neighborhoods. I never said anything to him about it because who was I? And what was I going to get out of questioning him? He owned this place, which meant that he could fire my ass on the spot. So I left well enough alone and minded my own damn business.

Sanjay wasn't aware of this, but I'd taken a few pills here and there for my cousin Jillian. Jillian got into a bad car accident over a year ago and hadn't fully recovered from it. Her doctor cut off her prescription meds six months ago, so I stepped in and threw a few pills at her when I was able to get my hands on some.

The first time, I stole two Percocet pills and two Vicodin pills. Each time I stole from the pharmacy, I took a few more pills. My nerves used to be on edge for about a day after each time I pocketed those pills, but since cops never showed up to cuff me, I knew Sanjay hadn't figured out I'd been stealing from him. I hoped he never would.

As soon as I walked into the pharmacy, I noticed that there were only three customers waiting for their prescriptions. I said good morning to everyone waiting as I walked behind the counter, clocked in, and went to work.

It didn't take long for Sanjay and I to ready those customers' prescriptions and get them on their way. After ringing up the last customer, I turned to Sanjay. "We got any deliveries?" I asked him while I searched through our online refill requests.

"I think we have six or maybe seven," he replied, before turning to answer the phone.

Sanjay was a handsome man. He resembled Janet Jackson's billionaire ex-husband. But unlike Janet Jackson's ex, Sanjay wasn't wealthy, at least to my knowledge. He owned this little pharmacy on the city limits of Virginia Beach, near Pembroke Mall. There was nothing fancy about the place, just your basic small business. But I often wondered why this doctor, who was doing well enough to own this place and have employees like me, wasn't married? From time to time I'd jokingly tell him that I was going to set him up with one of my friends. And his response would always be, "Oh, no. Believe me, I am fine. Women require too much."

Not too long after I started working here, he told me that his family was from Cairo, Egypt. From the way he talked about their homes and travel, I knew they were doing well for themselves. He also told me that education was a big deal in his country. And arranged marriages too.

"Think I could get me a man over in Cairo?" I'd teased. But his answer had no humor in it.

"You wouldn't want a husband from my country, because the men are very strict and the women they marry are disciplined. The things you say and do here in the US wouldn't be tolerated where I'm from."

Damn! "Yeah, whatever, Sanjay!" I'd chuckled.

Working at Sanjay's pharmacy was fairly easy. Time would go by fast. The first half of the day, it would be somewhat busy, and after two p.m. the traffic would die down. This was when I'd take my lunch break. If I didn't bring in my lunch from home, I'd leave the pharmacy and walk over to the food court in Pembroke Mall. This day was one of those days.

"I'm going to lunch, Sanjay. Want anything from Pembroke Mall?" I asked him.

"No, I'm fine. But thank you," he replied.

I walked over to the computer, clocked out, and then I left the building. On my way out, I ran into Sanjay's brother, Amir. As usual, he said nothing to me.

I'd always found it odd that Amir would stop by to see Sanjay during my lunch break. And if I was there when Amir walked into the pharmacy, Sanjay would send me on my lunch break or even send me home for the rest of the day. Now, I wasn't complaining because I loved when he let me leave work early, but at the same time, there aren't any coincidences. Something wasn't right with that guy and I knew it.

Sanjay had spoken to me about his brother, but I didn't

know much. He lived close by and was married with three children. And just like Sanjay, Amir was also very handsome. But Amir never said a word to me. If I hadn't heard Amir greet Sanjay, I'd wonder if he could speak at all. He'd wave at me when he'd come and go, but that was it. I never asked Sanjay how old his brother was because you could clearly see that Amir was younger. He was never flashy. He always wore a pair of casual pants and a regular button-down shirt. He had the look of a car salesman.

I grabbed some Chinese food from the food court in the mall and then I took a seat at one of the tables near one of the mall's exits. While I was eating, I got a call from my cousin Jillian. Her father and my mother are siblings. My uncle committed suicide when we were kids, so she lived with her mother until she turned eighteen. From there she'd been back and forth from having her own apartment to sleeping under our grandmother's roof. Jillian was a pretty, twenty-six-year-old, full-figured woman. She wasn't the brightest when it came to picking the men in her life, but she had a good heart and that's all that mattered to me.

She'd barely said hello before she asked, "Think you can bring me a couple of Percocets on your way home?"

"Jillian, not today," I griped.

"You're acting like I'm asking you to bring me a pill bottle of 'em," Jillian protested. "And besides, you know I don't ask you unless I really need them."

I let out a long sigh and said, "I'm gonna bring you only two. And that's it."

"Thank you," Jillian said with excitement.

"Yeah, whatever. You're such a spoiled brat," I told her.

"So. What are you doing?"

"Sitting in the food court of Pembroke Mall, eating some Chinese food."

"What time do you get off today?"

"I think I'm gonna leave at about seven since it's Saturday."

"Has it been busy today?"

"Kinda . . . sorta," I replied between each chew.

"So, what are you doing after work?"

"Terrell has been harassing me, talking about he wants to see me," I told her. Terrell was my on-and-off-again boyfriend.

"That sounds so boring."

"What do you want me to do, sit around all day like you and get high off prescription drugs?" I said sarcastically.

"Oh, Misty, that was a low blow. You know I don't do this shit for fun. If I don't take those drugs I'm going to be in serious pain."

"Look, I know you need 'em, so I'm going to get off your back. But from time to time, you do ask me for more than you should have."

"That's because I be trying to make a few dollars here and there. Oh, and speaking of which, I got a business proposition for you."

"What is it now?"

"I got a homeboy that will pay top dollar for twenty to twenty-five Vicodin pills."

"Jillian, are you freaking crazy?! There's no way in hell that I'm going to be able to get that many pills at one time."

"He's paying four hundred dollars. But I'm gonna have to get my cut off the top, which would be a hundred."

I sighed. "Jillian, I'm not doing it."

"Come on, Misty, stop being paranoid. You can do it," Jillian whined.

"Do you want me to lose my job?"

"Of course not. But you're acting like you've never taken drugs from your job before."

"Look, I'm not doing it. Case closed."

"Just think about it." Jillian pressed the issue, but I ignored her.

I changed the subject. "Is Grandma home?"

"She's in the laundry room folding clothes."

"Did she say she was cooking dinner?"

"Yeah, she's got a pot roast in the oven."

"Save some for me," I told Jillian.

"You know I will."

I changed the subject again. "You still talking to Edmund?"

"I just got off the phone with his frugal ass!"

I chuckled. "What has he refused to pay for now?"

"I asked him to order me a pizza online and he told me that he ain't have any money."

"Doesn't he own and operate a janitorial business?"

"Yep."

"Then he shouldn't be broke," I said. "Look, just leave that fool alone. You give him too much pussy for him to not feed you."

"I know, right!" she agreed. But I read her like a book because as soon as we got off the phone with one another, I knew she'd call that selfish-ass nigga and act like her stomach wasn't growling.

She and I talked for another ten minutes or so about her finding another job instead of sitting on her ass all day, crying about how much pain she's in. It seemed like my grandmother let her ride with that lame-ass excuse, but I knew better. My grandmother knew exactly what was going on, but looked the other way because she enjoyed Jillian's company and she didn't want to be alone in that big house. Jillian had a free ride any way you looked at it.

"Don't forget to put some of that pot roast aside," I reminded her.

"I won't," she said, and right before I hung up, I heard her add, "Don't forget my meds either."

My only response to that was a head shake.

1

A year ago today, Mallory Knight's world had changed. She found her best friend dead, sprawled on top of a comforter. The one Leigh had excitedly shown Mallory just days before, another extravagant gift from her friend's secret, obviously rich lover, the cost of which, Mallory had pointed out, could have housed a thousand homeless for a week. Or fed them for two. Leigh had shrugged, laughed, lain back against the ultra-soft fabric. Her deep cocoa skin beautifully contrasted against golden raw silk.

That day, when the earth shifted on its axis, Leigh had lain there again. Putrid. Naked. Grotesquely displayed. Left uncovered to not disturb potential evidence, investigators told her. Contaminate the scene. *With what, decency?* She had ignored them, had wrenched a towel from the en suite bath and placed it over her friend and colleague's private parts. Her glare at the four men in the room was an unspoken dare for them to remove it. That would happen only over her dead body.

She'd steeled herself. She looked again, at the bed and around the room. Whoever had killed Leigh had wanted her shamed. The way the body was positioned left no doubt about that. For Mallory, the cause of death wasn't in doubt, either. Murder. Not suicide, as the coroner claimed. But his findings matched what the detectives believed, what the scant evidence showed so . . . case closed. Even though the half-empty bottle of high-dose opioids found on Leigh's nightstand weren't hers. Even though forensics found a second set of prints on one of two wineglasses next to the pills. Even though Mallory told investigators her friend preferred white wine to red and abhorred drugs of any kind. She suffered through headaches and saw an acupuncturist for menstrual cramps. Even though for Leigh Jackson image was everything. She'd never announce to the world she'd killed herself by leaving the pill bottle out on the table, get buck naked to do the deed, then drift into forever sleep with her legs gaping open. Details like those wouldn't have gotten past a female detective. They didn't get by Mallory, either. Beautiful women like Leigh tended to be self-conscious. What did Mallory see in that god-awful crime scene? Not even a porn star would have chosen that pose for her last close-up.

The adrenaline ran high that fateful morning, Mallory remembered. Early January. As bitterly cold as hell was hot. Back-to-back storms in the forecast. This time last year, New York had been in the grips of a record-breaking winter. Almost a foot of snow had been dumped on the city the night before. Mallory had bundled up in the usual multiple layers of cashmere and wool. She had pulled on knee-high, insulated riding boots and laughed out loud at the sound of Leigh's voice in her head, a replay of the conversation after showing Leigh what she'd bought.

"Those are by far the ugliest boots I've ever seen."

"Warm, though," Mallory had retorted. "I'm going for substance, not style."

"They'd be fine for Iceland. Or Antarctica. Or Alaska. Not Anchorage, though. Too many people. One of those outback places with more bears than humans. Reachable only by boat or plane."

Mallory had offered a side-eye. "So what you're saying is this was a great choice for a record cold winter."

"Absolutely . . . if you lived in an igloo. You live in an apartment in Brooklyn, next door to Manhattan. The fucking fashion capital of the world, hello?"

Mallory had laughed so hard she snorted, which caused Leigh's lips to tremble until she couldn't hold back and joined her friend in an all-out guffaw. Complete opposites, those ladies. One practicality and comfort, stretch jeans and tees. The other back-breaking stilettos and designer everything. They'd met at an IRE conference, an annual event for investigative reporters and editors, and bonded over the shared position of feeling like family outcasts who used work to fill the void. Leigh was the self-proclaimed heathen in a family of Jehovah's Witnesses while second marriages and much younger siblings had made Mallory feel like a third wheel in both parents' households. To Mallory, Leigh felt like the little sister she'd imagined having before her parents divorced.

That morning a year ago she'd stopped at the coffee shop for her usual extra-large with an espresso shot, two creams, and three sugars. She crossed the street and headed down into the subway to take the R from her roomy two-bed, two-bath walkup in Brooklyn to a cramped shared office in midtown Manhattan, a five-minute walk from Penn Station that felt more like fifteen in the foot of snow. She'd just grabbed a cab when her phone rang. An informant with a tip. Another single, successful, beautiful female found dead. One of many tips she'd received since beginning the series for which she'd just won a prestigious award. "Why They Disappear. Why They Die." Why did they? Mysteriously. Suspiciously. Most cases remained unsolved. Heart racing, Mallory had redirected the cabbie away from her office down to Water Street and a tony building across from the South Street Seaport. The building where Leigh lived. Where they'd joked and laughed just days before. She'd shut down her thoughts then. Refused to believe it could be her best friend. There were nine other residences in that building. She'd go to any of the condominiums, all of them, except number 10. But that very apartment is where she'd been directed. The apartment teeming with police, marked with crime tape.

"Knight."

Jolted back into the present, Mallory sucked in a breath, turned her eyes away from the memory, and looked at her boss. "Hey, Charlie."

"What are you doing here? It's Friday. I thought I told you to take the rest of the day off and start your weekend early."

"I am."

"Yeah, I see how off you are." He walked over to her corner of the office, moved a stack of books and papers off a chair, and plopped down. He shuffled an ever-present electronic cigarette from one side of his mouth to the other with his tongue. "That wasn't a suggestion. It was an order. Get out of here."

He sounded brusque, but Charlie's frown was worse than his fist. It had taken her almost three years to figure that out. When she started working at *New York News* just over four years ago he was intimidating, forceful, and Mallory didn't shrink easily. Six foot five with a shock of thick salt-and-pepper hair and a paunch that suggested too many hoagies, not enough salad, and no exercise, he'd pushed Mallory to her limit more than once. She'd pushed back. Worked harder. Won his respect.

"I know it's a hard day for you." His voice was softer, gentler now.

"Yep." One she didn't want to talk about. She powered down her laptop, reached for the bag.

"She'd have been proud of you for that."

"What?" He nodded toward her inbox. "Oh, that."

"'Oh, that,'" he mimicked. "That, Knight, is what investigative journalists work all of their lives for and hope to achieve. Helluva lot of work you put in to get the Prober's Pen. Great work. Exceptional work. Congrats again."

It was true. In this specialized circle of journalism, the Prober's Pen, most often called simply the Pen, was right up there with the Pulitzer for distinctive honor.

"Thanks, Charlie. A lot of work, but not enough. We still don't know who killed her." A lump, sudden and unexpected, clogged her throat. Eyes burned. Mallory yanked the power cord from the wall, stood and shoved it into the computer bag along with her laptop. She reached for her purse. No way would she cry around Charlie. Investigative reporters had no time for tears.

She was two seconds from a clean escape before his big paw clamped her shoulder and halted her gait. She looked back, not at him, in his direction, but not in his eyes. One look at those compassion-filled baby blues and she'd be toast.

"What, Callahan?" Terse. Impatient. A tone you could get away with in New York. Even with your boss. Especially one like Charlie.

"Your column helped solve several cases. You deserved that award. Appreciate it. Appreciate life . . . for Leigh."

"Yeah, yeah, yeah. Out of my way, softie." Mallory pushed past him the way she wished she could push past the pain.

"Got a new assignment when you come back, Knight!"

She waved without turning around.

Later that evening Mallory went for counseling. Her therapists? Friends and colleagues Ava and Sam. The prescription? Alcohol. Lots of it. And laughter. No tears. At first, she'd declined, but they insisted. Had they remembered the anniversary, too? One drink was all she'd promised them. Then home she'd go to mourn her friend and lament her failed attempts to get at the truth. After that she'd go to visit her bestie. Take flowers. Maybe even shed a tear or two. If she dared.

Mallory left her apartment, tightened her scarf against the late-January chill, and walked three short blocks to Newsroom, an aptly named bar and restaurant in Brooklyn, opened by the daughter of a famous national news anchor, frequented by journalists and other creative types. Stiff drinks. Good food. Reasonable prices. Not everyone made six figures like Mallory Knight. In America's priciest city, even a hundred thousand dollars was no guarantee of champagne wishes and caviar dreams.

Bowing her head against the wind, she hurried toward the restaurant door. One yank and a blast of heat greeted her, followed by the drone of conversation and the smell of grilled onions. Her mouth watered. An intestinal growl followed, a clear reminder she hadn't had lunch. She unwrapped the scarf from around her head and neck, tightened the band struggling to hold back a mop of unruly curls, and looked for her friends.

"In the back." The hostess smiled and pointed toward the dining room.

"Thanks."

"Heard you won the Pen. Way to go."

"Gosh, word gets around."

"It's one of the highest honors a reporter can receive, Mallory so, yeah, a few people know."

She turned into the dining room and was met by applause. Those knowing people the hostess had described were all standing and cheering. After picking her jaw off the floor, Mallory's narrowed eyes searched the room for her partners in crime. A shock of red hair ducked behind . . . Gary? Special correspondent for NBC? Indeed. And other familiar faces, too. The *Post*, *Times*, *Daily News*, the *Brooklyn Eagle*, *Amsterdam News*, and other local and national news outlets were represented. Highly embarrassed and deeply moved, Mallory made her way across the room, through good-natured barbs, hugs, and high fives, over to Gary, who gave her a hug, inches from the dynamic duo who'd undoubtedly planned the surprise.

"You two." Mallory jabbed an accusatory finger into a still shrinking Sam's shoulder while eyeing Ava, who smiled broadly. "When did you guys have time to do all this?"

"Calm down, girl." Ava shooed the question away. "Group text. Took five seconds."

Ava. Her girl. Keep-it-real Holyfield. "Thanks for making me feel special."

"You're welcome." Ava munched on a fry. "Always happy to help."

Just when Mallory thought she couldn't be shocked further, a voice caused her to whip her head clean around.

"Can I have everyone's attention, please?"

There stood Charlie, red-faced and grinning, holding up a shot glass as two tray-carrying waiters gave a glass to everyone in the room. Her boss was in on it, too? All that insistence that she get out of the office? Damn, he was trying hard to make her cry.

"She doesn't like the spotlight, so I'll pay for this next week. But I was thrilled to learn that a celebration was being planned for one of the best reporters I've ever had the pleasure of working with, Mallory Knight." He paused for claps and cheers. "Most of you know this, though some may not. The hard work done on the Why series has resulted in three women being found and reunited with their families and two arrests, one of which was a cold case that had remained unsolved for fifteen years. Good job, kiddo."

Mallory accepted his hug. "Thanks, Charlie."

"Speech! Speech!" echoed around the room.

"As most of you know, I'm a much better writer than I

am a speaker. At least not without a lot more of these, so . . ." Mallory held up a shot glass holding pricey vodka. "Hear, hear."

She downed the drink, swallowed the liquid along with the burn that accompanied its journey down the hatch. Holding up a hand quieted the crowd.

"Okay, I . . . um . . . thank you guys for coming. The Pen means a lot. But your support means a lot more. Um . . . that first toast was for me. Let's do one more for another IR, Leigh Jackson. Everybody here who knew her knew she was . . . pretty amazing."

Mallory blinked back tears. "She was the inspiration behind the series and why I have this award." She held up a second shot glass. "To Leigh!"

For the next half hour Mallory accepted congrats and well wishes from her colleagues, along with a medium-rare steak dinner and more vodka. The crowd thinned. Mallory grew quieter.

Sam squeezed her shoulder. "You okay?"

Seconds passed as she pondered the question. A slow nod followed. "As of a few seconds ago, I feel a lot better."

"Why?" Ava asked.

"I just made a decision." Mallory looked from Ava to Sam. "I know I said I'd let it go. But I can't. Whoever killed Leigh is not going to get away with it. I'm going to find out who did it, and make sure they pay for her murder."

Sam's expression morphed into one of true concern. "Oh, no, Mal. Not that again."

"You think a cold-blooded murderer should walk around free?"

"You know what she means." Ava's response was unbowed by Mallory's clear displeasure. "Or have you forgotten those first couple months after she died, when you were so bent on proving Leigh's suicide was murder that you almost worked yourself into the grave?"

"But I didn't die, did I? Instead, I got the Pen." Mallory's voice calmed as she slumped against her chair. "I'd much rather get Leigh's killer."

"I know you loved Leigh," Ava said, her voice now as soft as the look in her eyes. "And while Sam and I didn't know her as well as you did, we both liked her a lot and respected the hell out of her work as a journalist. You did everything you could right after it happened. Let the police continue to handle it from here on out."

"That's just it. They think it's already handled. The death was ruled a suicide. Case closed."

There wasn't a comeback for that harsh truth. Mallory held up a finger for another shot. Ava's brow arched in amazement.

"How many of those can you hold, Mal? You're taller than me, but I've got you by at least thirty pounds."

Mallory looked up to see Charlie wave and head to the door. Ignoring Ava, she called out to him. "Charlie!"

He waited by the hostess stand, the area now cold and crowded from the rush of dinner guests and a constantly opening door.

"What is it, kiddo?"

"Can't believe you knew about this and didn't tell me."

"Had you known, you wouldn't have shown up."

"That's probably true. I appreciate what you said up there. Thanks."

"Think nothing of it." He looked at his watch. "I gotta run. See you next week."

"One more thing. The new assignment you mentioned earlier. What's it about?"

Charlie hesitated.

Mallory's eyes narrowed. "Charlie . . ."

"Change of pace. You're going to love it."

"What's the topic?"

"Basketball."

"You want me to cover sports?" Incredulity raised Mallory's voice an octave.

"Told you that you'd love it," Charlie threw over his shoulder as he caught the door a customer just opened and hurried out.

"Charlie!"

Mallory frowned as she watched her boss's hurried steps, his head bowed against the wind and swirling snow. His answer to her question only raised several more. *Why would Charlie want an investigative reporter on a sports story? Why wasn't the sports editor handling it? Freelance writers clamored for free tickets to sports events. Why couldn't he give the assignment to one of them?* She wanted to continue doing stories that mattered, like those on missing women and unsolved murders that had won her the Pen. And Charlie wanted her to write about grown men playing games? Her mood darkened, and shivering at the blast of cold wind accompanying the next customer through the front door, Mallory went back to the table, hugged her friends goodbye, and began the short walk home. She lived less than ten minutes from the restaurant, and although the temperature had dropped and snow was falling, she barely noticed. Mallory's thoughts were on her dead best friend, the botched closed case, and how to regenerate interest in catching a killer. Because whether officially or not, for work or not, Mallory would never stop trying to find out who killed Leigh Jackson. Never. Ever. No fucking way.

CHAPTER 1

The black Tahoe crept onto the rooftop of the parking garage overlooking downtown Fayetteville and stopped. The driver lumbered his hefty frame out of the truck and stood to his full six-foot-seven-inch height. He flipped the collar up on his heavy mink coat, readjusted the sawed-off shotgun tucked beneath his arm, and scanned his surroundings for danger. Satisfied that the area was clear, he tapped on the passenger window of the truck. The tinted window eased down halfway, and a cloud of smoke was released into the air.

"It's clear," the giant reported.

"Good. Now go post up over there so you can see the street, make sure no funny biz popping off," the man in the truck instructed.

The giant hesitated a moment. "You sure about this? I mean, I don't trust these dudes like that," he said.

The man smiled. "You worry too much, Samson. Nobody would dare violate this thing of ours again. Look around you, it's just us and them. This is crew business, and this shit has gone on long enough. Tonight, it ends, one way or another."

The window glided up, and the giant assumed his position near the edge of the parking garage.

Behind the dark glass of the Tahoe, two men sat in the back seat sharing a blunt while a brooding hip-hop track thumped through the speakers. The men casually passed the blunt and enjoyed the music as if they were at a party, and not on the precipice of a drug war for control of the city's lucrative narcotics trade. Although partners, each of the men was a boss in his own right. Their leadership styles were different—one was fire, the other was ice—but it was the balance that made their team so strong.

In the back seat of the Tahoe sat Qwess and Reece, leaders of the notorious Crescent Crew.

"Yo, that beat is bananas, son!" Reece remarked to Qwess. "You did that?"

Qwess nodded. "You knowww it," he sang.

"Word. You already wrote to it?"

"I'm writing to it right now," he replied. He pointed to his temple. "Right here."

"I hear ya, Jay-Z," Reece joked. "So, anyway, how you want to handle this when these niggas get here?"

Qwess nodded. "Let me talk some sense into them, let them know they violated."

"Son, they know they violated."

"Still, let me handle it, because you know how you can be."

Reece scowled. "How I can be? Fuck is that supposed to mean?"

"You know how you can be," Qwess insisted.

"What? Efficient?"

"If you want to call it that."

Headlights bent around the corner and a dark gray H2 Hummer came into view. The Hummer drove to the edge of the garage and stopped inches in front of Samson. He spun around to face the truck. The giant, clad in a full-length mink, resembled King Kong in the glow of the xenon headlamps.

Inside the truck, Qwess craned his head over the seat to confirm their guests. "That's them," he noted as he passed Reece the blunt. He climbed from the back of the truck and tossed his partner a smirk. "Stay here, I got it."

Qwess joined Samson while men poured out of the Hummer. When the men stood before Qwess, someone very important was absent.

Qwess raised his palm. "Whoa, whoa, someone's missing from this little shindig," he observed, scanning the faces. "Where is Black Vic?"

One of the minions stepped forward. He wore a bald head and a scowl. "Black Vic couldn't be here tonight. He sends his regards." The man thumbed his chest with authority. "He sent me in his place."

Qwess frowned. "He sent you in his place? Are you kidding me? We asked for a meeting with the boss of your crew, and he sends you?"

The man nodded. "Yep."

Qwess shook his head. "Yo, get Black Vic on the phone and tell him to get his ass down here now."

The minion chuckled. "I see you got things confused, dawg. You run shit over there, not over here. Now are we talking or what?"

Samson took a step forward. The other three men took two steps back. Qwess gently placed a hand on Samson's arm. The giant stood down.

"I need to talk to the man in charge," Qwess insisted. "Because we only going to have this conversation one time."

"Word?"

"Word!"

Suddenly, the back door to the Tahoe was flung open, and all eyes shifted in that direction. Reece stepped out into the night and flung his dreads wildly. Time seemed to slow down as he diddy-bopped over to them, his Cuban link and heavy medallion swinging around his neck. He pulled back the lapels on his jacket and placed his hands on his waist, revealing his Gucci belt and his two .45s.

"Yo, where Victor at?" Reece asked.

Qwess scoffed. "He ain't here. He sent *these* niggas."

Reece looked at each man, slowly nodding his head. "So Victor doesn't respect us enough to show his face and address his violation? He took two kis from my little man, beat him down. My li'l homie from Skibo hit him with consignment, and he decided to keep shit. Now, we trying to resolve this shit 'cause war is bad for business—for everybody, and he wanna say, 'fuck us'?"

"Black Vic said that you said 'fuck us' when you would-n't show us no flex on the prices," the minion countered.

"Oh, yeah? That what he said?" Reece asked. He shook his head and mocked, "*He said, she said, we said* . . . See, that's that bitch shit. That's why Victor should've came himself. But he sent you to speak for him, right?"

The bald-headed minion puffed out his bird chest. "That's right."

"Okay." Reece nodded his head and looked around the rooftop of the garage. "Well, tell Victor this!"

SMACK!

Without warning, Reece lit the minion's jaws up with an open palm slap. Samson lunged forward and wrapped his huge mittens around the neck of one of the other minions, who wore a skully pulled low over his eyes. Qwess drew his pistol and aimed it at the other minion in a hoodie, while the soldier in the passenger seat of the Tahoe popped out of the roof holding an AK-47.

"Y'all thought it was sweet?" Reece taunted. He smacked the bald-headed minion again, and he crumpled to the floor semiconscious. "I got a message for Victor's ass, though."

Reece dragged the man over to the Hummer and pitched his body to the ground in front of the pulley at-tached to the front of the truck. He reached inside the

Hummer to release the lever for the pulley, then returned to the front of the Hummer. While the spectators watched in horror, Reece pulled lengths of metal cable from the pulley and wrapped it around the man's neck. Qwess came over to help, and when they were done, the two of them hoisted the man up onto the railing.

"Wait, man! Please don't do this!" the minion pleaded. He was fully conscious now, and scrapping for his life. Qwess cracked him in the jaw and knocked the fight right out of him.

Reece fixed him with a cold gaze. "*We* not doing this to you, homie. Your man Victor is," he explained. "His ass should've showed up. Now, of course, this means war."

Reece and Qwess flipped the man over the railing. His body sailed through the air, and the pulley whirred to life, guiding his descent. His banshee-like wail echoed through the quiet night as he desperately tugged at the rope around his neck. Then suddenly, the pulley ran out of rope and caught, snapping his neck like a chicken. Both Qwess and Reece spared a look over the edge and saw his lifeless body dangling against the side of the building.

Reece turned to face the others. Slowly, he slid his thumb across his naked throat, and the AK-47 sparked three times. All head shots.

This was crew business.

Connect with

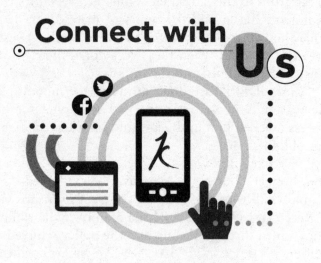

Us

Visit us online at
KensingtonBooks.com
to read more from your favorite authors, see books
by series, view reading group guides, and more.

Join us on social media
for sneak peeks, chances to win books and prize packs,
and to share your thoughts with other readers.

facebook.com/kensingtonpublishing
twitter.com/kensingtonbooks

Tell us what you think!

To share your thoughts, submit a review,
or sign up for our eNewsletters, please visit:
KensingtonBooks.com/TellUs.